"Will you marry me?"

Susanna still held Quinton's hand. Perhaps she was holding it too closely, and it was large. Rougher than she'd expected, but somehow gentle.

"Neither you nor I believe ourselves in that sad emotional state of love, and in fact, I don't believe in that feeling itself. And you would be an excellent countess."

"Countess?" She gulped as if he'd proposed something entirely the opposite, and then collected her equilibrium. "But there's that marriage situation involved. And that concerns me."

"I would think of it as a private partnership between two parties. A marriage deal, you could say."

"Between us?" She indicated him, and then touched her own chest. "You and I?"

"Yes. We'd appear in public together on a regular basis. Convince everyone we're well and truly married. That it is a match of the heart."

"That could backfire." Eyes tensed. "We may convince everyone we're married and end up believing it ourselves."

LIZ
TYNER

Marriage Deal
with the Earl

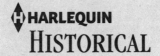
HARLEQUIN
HISTORICAL

Recycling programs
for this product may
not exist in your area.

ISBN-13: 978-1-335-72367-3

Marriage Deal with the Earl

Copyright © 2023 by Elizabeth Tyner

For questions and comments about the quality of this book, please contact us at CustomerService@Harlequin.com.

Harlequin Enterprises ULC
22 Adelaide St. West, 41st Floor
Toronto, Ontario M5H 4E3, Canada
www.Harlequin.com

Printed in U.S.A.

Liz Tyner lives with her husband on an Oklahoma acreage she imagines is similar to the ones in the children's book *Where the Wild Things Are*. Her lifestyle is a blend of old and new, and is sometimes comparable to the way people lived long ago. Liz is a member of various writing groups and has been writing since childhood. For more about her, visit liztyner.com.

Books by Liz Tyner

Harlequin Historical

The Wallflower Duchess
Redeeming the Roguish Rake
Saying I Do to the Scoundrel
To Win a Wallflower
It's Marriage or Ruin
Compromised into Marriage
A Cinderella for the Viscount
Tempting a Reformed Rake
A Marquess Too Rakish to Wed

English Rogues and Grecian Goddesses

Safe in the Earl's Arms
A Captain and a Rogue
Forbidden to the Duke

Visit the Author Profile page
at Harlequin.com.

Chapter One

'Lord Amesbury,' the carriage driver called to him. 'My apologies for getting misdirected. The instructions were confusing. I have the proper way to Mr Adair's new location now.'

Unfamiliar with the new title, Quinton caught himself just before he looked around for his uncle.

Lord Amesbury. He wasn't only Quinton Langford, the physician. He was now the Earl of Amesbury, a man he'd never truly expected to be.

He waited while the driver walked to the front of the vehicle. Moments later, the carriage jolted forward, stirring the rain-scented air.

Susanna. He wondered if widowhood had devastated her. When he'd been curious and asked about her, it was almost as if she'd disappeared.

Odd how the memory of her kept resurfacing in his mind, but he'd always had a grand time when they'd seen each other—until the day he'd told her he was leaving for university.

His carriage stopped again, and he saw the stone home, noting the sagging pediment surround in front. Little better than the decrepit home he'd been raised in—only bigger. Apparently, the tales were true.

He wanted to help her.

'This be it,' the driver said, voice proud, opening the door. 'Two top windows bricked over from the inside just like the man said.'

Quinton stared up at the three-storey home and saw the windows, and that one of the lower panes also didn't reflect as it should. A dark drapery concealed the interior.

Moving forward, he rapped on the scarred wooden door, hoping the house didn't fall down from the added stress of his knock.

Finally, a butler answered, shoulders stooped and eyebrows thicker than the hair on his head. He remembered the man from the other home and saw recognition behind the unimpressed eyes.

'Is Mr Adair in?'

The butler took his card, held it a distance from his sight and, after a squint, he nodded, taking his time. 'The master is out, but—'

His demeanour changed, and he gave Quinton a decidedly not subservient glance. 'Follow me,' the servant instructed.

Quinton stared at the butler, surprised at the command in the frail man's voice.

The older man didn't stop on his journey up the stairway.

They moved upstairs into the dim hall, shadows obscuring the pictures on the wall, and the butler showed Quinton to the sitting room, an area overstuffed with a sofa, several chairs and a table snug against them. A piano hardly had room for the bench.

'I will send Miss Susanna your way.' The man's words

were commanding, but Quinton didn't mind. Truly, his memories of Susanna had brought him here.

A short while later, light footsteps danced down the stairs. Then Quinton saw her in the doorway. He remembered her as if only yesterday he'd heard her laughter. He stilled, taking in the moment. Her dress had no lace or anything to make it stand out from a shopkeeper's wife's clothing, but still, she had a regal air and a genuine smile. She could have been the child of a royal.

'The Earl of Amesbury.' Susanna paused, studying him. She held what appeared to be a ragged ball in one hand and his card in the other. She walked closer and put the ball on a table, then propped the card against a vase and studied it a moment. 'The title suits you.' She nodded, her gaze still studious as she met his eyes. 'It makes you look even taller.'

'If I'd inherited a ducal title perhaps…'

'Oh, no. I'm sure you've increased in height.' She studied the top of his head. 'Yes. You're taller than when I saw you last, and you will just have to take my word on that.'

'Then we must thank my boot maker.'

'Amesbury. You have not changed—except for the height,' she continued, voice rich, surrounding him with a music that erased every concern in his world. 'And such a help to my father when he was ill. I did appreciate your reassurances.'

She still had on the lavender of half mourning, but it had been well over a year since her husband had died. She must have cared deeply for the wastrel.

'And now you are Lord Amesbury. Do you remember that day we met?'

'I do.'

'At the picnic. You chased down the dog, and retrieved my doll.' She took another step, laughter embellishing her

voice even more. 'And you brushed off Carolina's dirty face, tried to remove the dog bite marks from her dress and presented her to me. You were my knight. And the other boy made fun of me. Yet you crossed your eyes and made him appear the foolish one.'

He'd forgotten how her face could sparkle.

'It's been so long since I've seen you,' she said. 'What brings you in this direction?'

'I'd heard your father has had some difficulties.' He stepped forward. 'And I thought I might check on his health.'

'He did have a sniffle recently, but it only scared us because he'd been so sick that one time. We believe he's completely recovered. Now, he's out searching for a man to assist with the work on the house. I don't believe he is expected home until much later. He only left a short while before you arrived.'

He remained. Unmoving. 'Since I'm not needed here, then I suppose I should be on my way.' Neither spoke for a long moment. 'If you're completely certain your father is well.'

'I am, but it is a delight to see you again. It would be wonderful to catch up, if you have time,' she said. Her lips turned up, and he felt someone had dusted him with sunshine on a winter's day.

'But please give me a moment.' She moved to the window facing away from the street. Slender arms extended, she tried to open it, but the wood didn't move.

'Let me,' he said, stepping close enough to smell the freshness of soap and feel a fluttering brush of fabric against his arm.

With one heave he lifted the window, then heard the rasp. The scent of springtime lilacs drifted in through the opening.

He saw a little boy beneath look up. He'd forgotten she'd had a child.

She leaned out so far it was all he could do not to pull her back. He stood ready in case she lost her balance.

Picking up the ball once more, and tossing it to the child, she called out. 'Play alone for a few moments, Christopher. I will ask Cook to fix apricot tarts for us soon.'

Then she waved Quinton aside, bit her bottom lip, gathered her strength and pulled the window closed with a thump. He wasn't certain, but he thought a fleck of the ceiling's plaster floated down to land on her shoulder.

He wanted to brush it away but felt it presumptuous.

'It's still a little too cool for me to leave the window open, but he appears to have already discarded his coat.' She clasped her hands in front of her, then took a chair and indicated for him to be seated.

'I never did offer condolences on the loss of your husband,' he said.

She waved away his words, her voice losing its *joie de vivre*. 'Our marriage was not always smooth, and I do think of him as a great loss. A terrible loss. An unforgettable loss.' She tilted her head. 'A loss, mainly.'

'I am sorry.'

'I truly was full of emotion when my husband died,' she said. 'But we had not lived together in years. I was deeply in love when we wed, of course. He was incredibly charming at times, but neither of us were truly happy together. It was sad. But it has made me…appreciate being a widow.'

'I didn't get on well with your husband.'

'You were not the only one, Quinton.' She looked at the fireplace briefly, then returned her gaze to him. 'My husband would have been impressed that you are visiting. But everything impressed him…at first.'

'I didn't.'

'Because you were a physician, Quinton Langford, then. Not the Earl.' She apologised with her eyes. 'But let's not talk about my husband. I try not to even think of him, although since we've moved here, it's almost as if his memory has become larger instead of fading.'

She brushed her shoulder, dislodging the fragment. 'I'm surprised you even knew where to find us. We've only recently relocated, and Father has plans to renovate this house.' Her voice faded on the last word. 'I think it is going to be more of an undertaking than he expected, but, of course, I could not say a word against it. He had a carpenter in yesterday to explain the repairs needed. He has more plans than I could imagine.'

'Someone told me you'd moved.' And he'd heard the family's finances were strained. It was obviously true. 'Living here will take you longer to travel to soirées.'

She shook her head, cheeks tightening. 'I enjoyed them once, but not so much after I married. I like being at home.'

'It suits you.' He considered the top of her head. 'You're taller than I remembered, too.'

She lifted a folded handkerchief from the table beside him and acted as if she might throw the cloth at him. 'Quinton Langford, I told the truth about you.'

'So did I, Susanna Walton.'

She shuddered, dropping the handkerchief aside. 'Please don't call me that name.'

'I won't if it disturbs you.'

'I tried not to let anyone know but I never adjusted to it. And when I moved back in with my parents, I pretended it was just a visit. They knew, though. Because I was so determined not to see him more than occasionally.'

'I suspected.'

'Well, you were always insightful. And you gave me my first kiss.'

'I did not.' His eyes widened. 'That could hardly count, and actually you kissed me.'

'I specifically remember. You were leaving to go to university and you visited me to say goodbye. And you gave me the sweetest kiss.'

'It is kind of you to remember it that way, but you gave me the chastest kiss, half missing my mouth. A definite goodbye.'

She gave a cross between a squeak and a hum, and she had a regal upturn of her chin. 'Remember it how you will. I doubt I can convince you otherwise.'

'I doubt you can.' He smiled. 'Because I was there.' He still remembered the sight of her running back inside, and the feeling that they would never again have the friendship he had so valued.

The blasted innocence. She'd been almost like the dolls he'd remembered her having—too unaware of the world to really know much. Needing to be protected. But it was not his place, and he was little more than a poor orphan at the time, though he'd had a wealthy uncle who'd been determined to push him ahead…not that he'd minded being given an opportunity. And she had been so far above him.

She looked at her handkerchief again, and then she folded it.

He suspected a sigh escaped her lips.

Susanna kept her smile firmly in place, busying her hands with the precise turns of the fabric, trying to make the cloth appear fresh from the iron.

It truly was wonderful to see Quinton again. He'd

matured into such a stalwart man—but even as a youth, she'd been so impressed by the strength he possessed.

After he'd left for university, it was as if he'd forgotten she existed. She'd been hurt at the time that he'd only occasionally visited her family afterwards, and never seemed interested in contacting her. But she'd moved on. There were too many events to distract her, and he rarely appeared at any of them.

Then Walton had moved into her life.

A disaster.

After the first few months of her marriage, she'd refused to attend any occasions except those with family. Once she'd wed, Walton had been too familiar with the other ladies, and had hardly noticed when she was with him, actually preferring for her to remain behind. She'd been more than hurt. She'd never understood how truly innocent she'd been until then.

Walton, the man who'd so readily accepted her flaws before they were married, had hissed them at her in public so loudly she'd been afraid others would hear.

Most of their invitations had stopped arriving, or she'd burned everything that appeared to be a request.

She gave her head a quick shake, trying to relegate those memories to the list of things from the past to be forgotten.

'I've not been to many events and plan to be attending more,' he said. 'But I don't believe anyone has seen you out in society recently.'

She again shook her head. It had been better to avoid people than see their pity.

'We did have a grand time as children that day we met at the picnic, though,' she said, changing the subject to happier times. 'And you were so kind to amuse me and keep me from getting bored.'

'I'm sure I enjoyed it more than you did,' he said.

'So gallant of you. But then, you always were.' Her gaze flicked away. 'Mostly.'

'Mostly…?' Quinton appeared as if a bug had fluttered into his vision.

She took in a breath. 'After you began studies at the Royal Physician's College, you never visited again until father was ill.'

'Before I left the first time, I visited you that day, and asked if you wished for me to write to you. And you said…no, before kissing me goodbye.'

Susanna stared at him. She would never have told anyone *no* with the emphasis he'd placed on the word.

'I told you I was not much for correspondence.' She shrugged. 'That was all. And you said you were not either.'

'I was overwhelmed with studies and learning and such, and I didn't write to anyone, but I would have written to *you*.' He studied her as if she'd been daft to think otherwise.

She said nothing.

'I would have written at least a few times,' he admitted.

'Only a few?' she asked, her happiness fading. 'That's what I meant. I sensed that in you. The distance. After we were older.'

'I was on my best manners—my best behaviour—when we spoke. I had had it drilled it into my head that I had better not misbehave and I had better treat all the women in society like angels.'

'You were treating me like an angel?' She laughed, softly. 'I guess I didn't grasp that. I just noticed you were dear, proper and sometimes extremely distant.'

'You were…you were—' He took in a deep breath. 'You could say you were changing from a child who enjoyed dolls and lightness and laughter to a young woman who didn't want me to correspond with her. I understood.'

'I said we could still be friends. And then someone kissed someone.'

His brows lifted. He lowered his chin. 'I assure you, that was a goodbye kiss. Not an...until later kiss.'

'So, you avoided me,' she said.

'Yes. That's what one does with the still-can-be-friends-but-don't-contact-me friends. And then one is given a kiss goodbye.'

'That isn't at all what I meant when I said that. And then you all but disappeared until father was ill.'

'I don't always understand the intricacies of society,' he said. 'But I am fairly certain I know how, um, personal predicaments end politely, or get nipped in the bud before even starting.'

'I remember.' She raised her voice. 'I said firmly, and emphasised, that we could still be friends.' Her tone softened. 'I just was not inclined to write.'

'Truly, I wasn't either.' He flexed his fingers. 'Sitting all day at a desk got old quickly. But I'm so grateful I had the opportunity for the education. It meant a lot.'

He waited, then added, 'And you were not telling me to take my leave?'

'We had enjoyed ourselves the times we saw each other.'

'You smiled easily. Except I didn't like it that one time.'

'You ran into a tree. At first, I thought you were making a jest.'

Quinton remembered the incident. Now it made him smile. He'd been running because his uncle had summoned him to leave—three times. He'd looked back to tell her goodbye, still running. Then he'd turned around just as he'd careened into a tree. The bruise on his cheek had been prominent. That had been one of the few times in his life he'd been embarrassed.

'Someone said it must have been a big man who'd hit me, and I said, "Tall as a tree, and just as solid."'

'I thought you were just pretending not to see the tree,' she said.

'The tree moved. I'm sure of it.'

'Yes. It did. A tremendous amount. Perhaps a leaf.'

'So we can agree on that?'

'We can agree on many things, I'm sure,' she said. 'We just don't always choose to.'

'Like the first time we met, and you kept testing me about your dolls. As if I could remember Lady Matilda Margaret Montague and Lady Louise Whatever-Whatever and those tales you wove about their pets who did not have simple names either.'

'Their pets were important,' she said.

'You were so insistent,' he recalled. 'And no doll needs so many imaginary pets, one of which is a lion, and another an elephant who has a talking bird.'

'Lady Matilda did.'

'You lined your toys up by order of rank. I swore you kept changing their peerages.'

He'd been astounded that one little girl could possess so many toys and be allowed to have them with her.

'I may have,' she admitted. 'To keep you on your toes.'

She glanced to the window. 'And later, I never thanked you for taking care of my father. I was so happy when I visited and saw you were watching over him.'

She stood, and he rose as well. 'I'm rambling on. And you're here to see my parents. I'll fetch my mother.'

'I was concerned about your father. But if he's not ill, then I don't need to wait for him.'

'I'm happy Father is well, but I'm sorry your trip was wasted.'

'Hardly wasted,' he said. 'Seeing you again… I hope you start attending events again.'

'Sometimes I miss it. But…'

'When I was at the last soirée, I saw someone from a distance and at first I thought it was you. Then I remembered how you were quite accomplished at dancing—at speaking with everyone.'

She laughed. 'I suppose I did well because I like dancing. But those days are over. I have a little boy now, and my days are taken up with more mundane events.'

'Such as tossing a ball out of a window?'

'Yes. Someone has to do it, I suppose.' Her complaint ended on a smile. 'The governess is visiting her family today.'

A silence followed, and he considered the past, the present and the future. Susanna was in financial difficulty. He'd heard rumours her father's finances had been suffering. It was obviously true.

'I must tell Mother you're here,' she said. 'She would be upset if she didn't get a chance to speak with you. I am so pleased you visited, Lord Amesbury. And please don't correct me. It sounds very impressive. I'm happy you're doing well. I will be back after I collect Mother.'

She was exiting so prettily, as if she hated to leave. In the doorway, she hesitated and looked back at him.

He wondered if he was again being told they could still be acquaintances, but only from a distance. He wasn't sure.

And in that instant, he understood why he remembered her so well.

Susanna had been the only woman he'd ever seen who

had such a regal air but could charm anyone from a peer to a servant to a dog who'd tried to abduct her doll.

'You truly did enjoy our friendship?' Although he still wasn't certain he'd misunderstood.

'Quinton, you toss that thought right out of your head if you think otherwise.' She spoke as if scolding him, and yet, it was pleasant.

She could still help him as she had when they were youngsters. Back then she'd told him how he was to interact with the peerage and schooled him on manners. True, his mother's sister had done the same, but it had sounded much better from Susanna.

Susanna was a woman with a child and reputable parents, and one who did not court adverse attentions. She could increase his status within society and give him an immediate air of respectability that would protect him as he moved among the people who were shunned by the most prosperous.

He'd not felt the stain of his past when he'd been at university. He'd been proud of the knowledge he had gained. But as an earl, he didn't want his past resurfacing—the childhood with a mother only one step from the brothel, and an aunt who'd allowed him to clean the rooms for the ladies who worked for her. Not only that, he'd had a society father who couldn't take care of himself.

He studied the room again and compared it to the estate he lived in now, and the home her father had lived in previously. Her finances had definitely taken a turn for the worse.

'Of course, I had a fondness for you.' She hesitated. 'But I don't correspond with anyone.' She stepped forward and took his right hand.

'What about your husband when you were courting?'

'No. Now that I look back, we didn't even stay in

contact long. I suppose marriage truly tests a companionship.'

'Well, if that's how you look at it, that's a test I've yet to take.' He lifted her fingertips slightly. 'But I'm willing to take the challenge.'

'I'm sure you would make an admirable husband.' Her words ended on a smile.

He saw acceptance in her gaze. Shared memories.

'If you truly believe I will make an admirable husband, then will you consider marriage?'

The words he'd spoken surprised him, but the thought didn't. Susanna always appeared so upstanding.

He remembered seeing her father and mother get into the carriage after Sunday services. Susanna and her two sisters had crowded in, almost sitting on each other's laps, and their carriage had left in a completely different direction than he'd travelled. His uncle hadn't even been willing to transport him to the door of his home, and had only taken Quinton part of the way.

She studied him.

'Will you?' he asked again. 'To me?'

Chapter Two

Susanna's heart fluttered. Suddenly she saw Quinton in a different light. He really was taller than she remembered, and his eyes were still distant, but when he'd opened the window for her, the sight of his muscles rippling beneath his coat had made her knees weak. She was always wool-gathering. Sunshine must affect hearing. 'Pardon? What did you say, Quinton?'

'Will you marry me?'

She realised she still held his hand. Perhaps she was holding it too closely, and it was large—rougher than she'd expected, but somehow gentle. She stared at their fingers. 'Was I perhaps inappropriate?' she asked, moving away, losing contact.

'No.'

She had not meant to give him the idea that she would be interested in marriage. That was not in her plans.

'Quinton, we have been friendly since childhood, although we lost touch. And while I consider you a dear acquaintance, I am not interested in being courted by anyone. That is perhaps another reason I have avoided events. I don't want to give anyone the impression I am interested in finding love.'

Ever again, she wanted to add emphatically.

But then he chuckled. 'We are in total agreement on that. But I would like you to consider marriage. I realise the proposal is abrupt, but I see no reason to linger over a good decision.'

'I did wed once. It was not what I expected. I would go so far as to say it was the opposite of what I had hoped for.'

'And he, of course, told you he loved you?'

She couldn't help looking skyward. 'Yes, and I thought I reciprocated those feelings, yet it was more of an indigestion of the brain, and it befuddled my thoughts, but led to my cherished son, and widowhood.'

'It seems to be agreeing with you.'

'Widowhood is a state I find welcome compared to marriage. Much more welcome.'

'But neither you nor I believe ourselves to be in that sad emotional state of love, and in fact, I don't believe in that feeling itself. Therefore, you would be an excellent countess.'

'Countess?' She gulped as if he'd proposed something entirely the opposite, and then collected her equilibrium. She extended a pointed finger to the side and waved it in a circular motion. 'But there's that marriage situation involved. And that concerns me.'

'I would think of it as a private partnership between two parties. A marriage deal, you could say.'

'Between us?' She indicated him, and then touched her own chest. 'You and I?'

'Yes. We'd appear in public together on a regular basis. I would want everyone to believe we're well and truly married. People could easily accept our connection because we were childhood friends. I want everyone to suppose that it is a match of the…heart. I have made certain promises to myself which would give you privacy at my home. You would host social events. Funds would not be a concern. And I could continue my work as a physician and treat people from the stews who have no other chance for care.'

'That could backfire on us.' Her eyes tensed. 'We may convince everyone we're married and end up believing it ourselves. That would be horrible.'

He even seemed to understand her reluctance, which was definitely different than her husband. Quinton studied her, but she didn't feel at a disadvantage.

Her son ran into the room, calling out, interrupting them in a twinkling. He held the ball, and she could see it was becoming even more unsewn. 'Look. It came apart. May I have another one?'

'We will talk about it later,' she said, biting her lip afterwards, knowing there was no money she dared take for something so frivolous. Her father needed every penny for the repairs on the home, and the governess, Celeste, had agreed to work without pay. Almost every servant had agreed to work without pay, yet the funds from the sale of the mansion would not last for ever—or even until her son grew up. Her mother had mentioned selling the piano and getting him a tutor. But it was highly unlikely they would find a new employee who would be so gracious as the ones under their roof—their leaking roof.

'Now, go and find your grandmother, Christopher, and I'll join you soon. I have a guest.' She patted her son's shoulder and sent him on his way.

'Yes, Mother.'

He gave her the worn ball, and she tried to jab its stuffing back into place while he ran out the door.

She feared what would happen when Christopher tried

to learn to read, and could only hope he hadn't inherited his skills from her. His governess, Celeste, couldn't teach him, but then she was French and didn't read English either.

Susanna grasped how much a marriage to Quinton could assist her family. If she wed him, and Christopher had received her inadequacy, then Quinton's funds and status could help Christopher survive in the world. In truth, her father couldn't truly afford to get her son a tutor. He was six years old, and they had already put off his education.

She couldn't confess her inability to read. If Quinton found out she was illiterate, he'd likely withdraw his proposal. Two different governesses had tried to teach her reading when she was younger, and she'd seen how quickly her two sisters had learned.

If she wed a second time, her husband might find out she couldn't read. Walton had taunted her for it, and she didn't plan to go through that again. She didn't want anyone ever to discover how senseless she was.

She'd been honest with Walton, thought he had accepted her, and when they'd had the slightest difference of opinion, he'd always discarded everything she said because, after all, she was a dullard. Her appearance was the only thing about her that could be valued, and he had complained that she was losing even that when she was going to have Christopher.

She looked into Quinton's eyes and wondered if she could trust him. He'd not always lived among the affluent. She remembered his tales about the streets, and recalled her amazement when she was trying to teach him about the peerage and introductions. She'd thought he would know the hierarchy better than she.

'After you started visiting your father's brother more—

when your father was ill and was living with him—you once asked me about the peerage,' she said.

'I asked if a viscount was addressed as Mr or Lord.'

'Forgive me for being a little know-it-all. I rattled off a whole list of rules.'

'You were gracious.'

Silence lingered in the air between them.

'And I hope I am again gracious, but I feel I must be completely direct.' She could not seem to get the stuffing back into the ball, and the threads became even more unsewn.

'I want you to be straightforward.'

'You would expect heirs…' A small shake of her head emphasised her words.

'The problem of an heir is not mine. I would not be here to concern myself with it,' he said.

'Will you walk with me to my carriage?' Quinton asked, knowing she was refusing him and wanting to spare her more difficulty. 'This time we will not lose contact.'

Although he knew they would. He already had more people to take up his time than he'd ever anticipated.

Truly, he'd never expected to inherit the earldom. He'd never even known any of his father's family until he was about ten and discovered his father, the younger son of an earl, was drinking himself into insensibility, along with Quinton's older cousin. They both believed that if one could still speak more drinks were called for.

The old earl, his grandfather, had refused to accept either Quinton or his younger brother Eldon as a grandson because he'd been upset with the marriage. Then the title had passed to the Earl's eldest son, Quinton's uncle, a sickly man who'd inherited most of the old earl's irritableness and had begun to detest his own son because he was intemperate, self-indulgent and living too dangerously with drink.

Quinton's father had hardly acknowledged him either, although he did recognise him as a son, but he'd sworn that Eldon could not possibly be his child. And Quinton's mother had hissed when questioned and told him that Eldon's father was whoever suited her most at the moment.

Quinton wanted to put all that behind him and a marriage to Susanna would help, but he could understand her refusal.

He gave a bow and took a step away.

'Don't leave—' She paused. 'I don't know.'

He flexed the fingers of his left hand, understanding what might be troubling her. 'I can have contracts drawn up for you to look over, if that is a worry for you. The funds. You would never have to concern yourself about money.'

'It is not so much the specifics of the financials that I am concerned with, but the specifics that are generally not put to paper. Would we cohabit?' Her cheeks brightened.

His control of his body was first and foremost in his mind. 'Your room would be yours. With a door, and it would not need to be locked because it would be closed. I would never enter without an invitation from you—written in the contract if you wish.'

'You must understand.' Her eyes did not waver. '*That* is not going to happen.'

'You should also understand,' he said. 'I have made promises to myself too. I don't believe in love. Intimacies are not to be a part of my marriage. Passions are to be contained. They destroy lives. People.'

'Intimacies weren't much a part of my marriage either.' She drew in a deep breath. 'I can see the advantage for me more than I can see the benefit to you.'

'I want a wife who could be the warden of the title, someone who oversees my home and increases my standing in society. I want few disruptions. No squabbling. No altercations. A peaceful, quiet home. Mutual respect.'

'That is a tall order.'

'I want to do well by the title, and I have made many friends from the lesser walks of life. They are true friends. I want them to feel as accepted as the richest peer in London. And I want the highest of society to also accept me, even with my physician background.'

'You should not be criticised for your wish to heal others.'

'Mixing society functions with the other duties I have is the problem,' he said. 'With the influx of visitors into my world, it has been impossible to continue giving medical care as I'd like. A wife would attend society events and give me the status that being a bachelor does not afford. A man visiting rough areas could be more easily seen to be doing so for his own gains, but if he has a wife at home—a family—his motives are more likely to be understood properly.'

'My husband had a wife at home. For a while.' She rolled her eyes, shaking her head. 'I misplaced my trust once, and I was most angry at myself. Not that I wasn't displeased at my husband, his family and well, even my parents… Only the butler escaped my wrath because he'd tried to warn me,' she admitted. 'I want a serene life for my son.'

'Understandable. And I can provide it.'

'But I am sure many women would consider you a fine person to wed.'

'I'm sure many women considered my father a fine

person to wed, and I've heard my mother was admired by many men. *Many* is not always a prerequisite for a peaceful existence. I want my house to be as quiet as my bachelor's lodgings. I have moved into a more affluent location and already been besieged by more well-wishers than I knew existed. And I must travel farther to visit my old friends.'

She crossed one arm over her stomach and rested her elbow on it, with her palm cupping her chin, one finger at the edge of her lips. 'I am not a fractious person, but it is nearly impossible, I would imagine, for two people to live under the same roof without some type of disagreement.'

'What of your parents?'

She didn't answer at first. 'You visited my parents often while Father was ill. You slept in the house and stayed at his bedside.'

'I did. It was the most silent place I'd ever heard.'

'Didn't my sisters visit?'

'Yes. It was, without a doubt, the quietest house I'd ever heard.' His lips turned up. 'Your sisters did have a concern over whether your father was warm enough, whether a draft might be the problem, and they did have different opinions regarding it.'

'You see what I mean,' she said. 'Families do bicker.'

He laughed, dipped his head a bit, and then raised it, eyes shining in a way that caused her to lean closer.

'That was a discussion,' he said. 'Not a fight.'

With her arm still across her stomach, she pursed her lips.

He didn't alter his stance. Waiting. Watching her. For the first time, she appeared as immovable as the tree.

'Some assistance may be needed to other members of my family… My parents'…finances…are not the best.'

'I can take care of that.'

'Could you be nice to my son? Could you promise to… treat him kindly? Not as a burden?'

He let out a long, slow breath. 'I wouldn't marry you if I planned to mistreat you, your child or your parents. But I don't see your child as being a part of my life.'

'Why would my son not be a part of your life?'

'You have a governess to care for him. And if he is well behaved, I don't see his path crossing with mine on a regular basis. You and I would live in different areas of the house.'

'Different storeys?' She considered. 'That could make a marriage less wearisome.'

'We are both in agreement that we don't want a troublesome life,' he said.

'Yes.'

'Then what is your decision on marriage?' he repeated.

She reached out, clasping his hands in both of hers, and he knew what she was going to say. He could see the genuine sorrow in her eyes.

'I simply can't,' she said. 'It is not that I don't think it a wonderful thought, but still, and I know you will understand, but I wed once. And I would not want to enter into a partnership—'

'With anyone you didn't love?' The word lodged on his tongue, but he forced it out, trying not to make it sound like an oath, but he could not put the hearts, flowers and posies around it. He could not.

In his youth, women had often told him they loved him, but he'd known they didn't.

His mother had told him repeatedly how much she loved her children—which had always signalled to him that she was up to something.

Only his mother's sister had never told such taradiddles, and she'd done right by him.

'I would not say the word *love* exactly. I don't know what I meant, just that a partnership takes more than emotions,' she said.

'They can be a bother.'

'You do understand?' she asked. She held his hands and he moved away, extricating himself.

'I do.'

He did. He had seen how love destroyed everything it touched. He hadn't ever thought of himself as ever being in such a sad state.

But he had also seen how the physical act of lovemaking could be treacherous, and it had taken all his strength to embrace celibacy and learn to live with it. And he could not go back to being controlled by his body. He had turned away from such an intemperate lifestyle and buried himself in work every time temptation appeared in his life. He had no idea what would happen if he unleashed those passions again, and he owed it to himself not to find out.

'It has been so nice to see you again, Quinton. You reminded me of happier times, and it was such a glorious day the day I met you. You were a knight to me. So kind to my doll when the other boy made fun of it.'

She was good at navigating herself to the door. She was already on the other side of it. He didn't think she'd even been aware of her actions.

'I'll get Mother,' she said. 'She'll be pleased to see you.'

'A knight? A mere knight?' he asked, jesting at his good fortune. He'd inherited an earldom.

Her mouth closed. 'You were thoughtful.' She didn't even seem to be aware of the poor joke he'd made.

'You should enquire about me for marriage references. I can tell you three people to speak with.'

She examined the list he gave her, unsure. 'Yes,' she admitted, staring at the words before raising soulful eyes to him. 'It is nothing personal, but simply that I swore never to wed again.'

'In truth, I wouldn't want you to think of yourself as a wife. And I do not want to think of myself as a husband. I am a physician and an earl. That fills my life to the brim—so full. But the housekeeper cannot dislodge guests in the way you could, and cannot travel with me to events as you would be able.'

'I cannot see myself as a person who would be rude to visitors.'

'I agree. You have been so considerate, and made me feel so welcome, and you were making your escape so graciously.'

She appeared puzzled for a second while she considered. 'I was only fetching Mother.'

'The kindness came so easily to you that you did not even notice it.'

She smiled.

He raised his chin. 'If I were to give you references that suited you, might you then consider a marriage?'

She gazed at him, unspeaking at first. 'I might.'

'One, your father. Two, your mother, and three, yourself.'

'Unfortunately, I'm not the best judge of who might make a good husband,' she said.

'Will you think about it again overnight? I will return tomorrow for your final answer.'

'I thought for months before my first marriage.'

'Susanna.' He took her hand and studied her fingers as he spoke. 'If you cannot come to a decision about wedding me more quickly than that, then I would have to agree with you that it is a bad idea.'

'Will you visit again tomorrow?' she asked.

'Of course.'

Chapter Three

Susanna watched Quinton's carriage leave. He didn't have to be a physician now, but he still wanted to treat people.

He was an earl who would not understand her inability to write an invitation or read one.

Yet he could help her son so much, and she knew she could easily attend society events. That had always been a joy for her.

Susanna rushed to her mother's room, navigating around a chair her mother had not really had space for, aware of the scent of the furniture polish which reminded her of a blacksmith's shop. Christopher was galloping around, pretending to be a horse.

'He is such a clever child, and I love him so.' Her mother gave him a quick hug when he ran by her.

He squirmed from her, beaming. 'I love Grandmother. She lets me jump on the bed. She's not mean like Celeste.'

Her mother frowned. 'You are forgetting our rule. If you can't say something nice about someone, you must say nothing at all. And your governess is good to you.'

'But she won't let me jump on the bed.'

'Christopher, you shouldn't jump on the bed or say

unkind things about Celeste. Now, go and find the maid and show her what happened to the ball,' Susanna said. 'Ask if she knows of another.'

Christopher trotted from the room, whinnying.

Her mother watched her grandson leave. 'Be sure to impress on Celeste that he is not to talk badly about people. People exaggerate so much and it's best he learn early not to be a talebearer.'

'Do you remember Quinton? The new Earl of Amesbury?'

'Oh, yes. The physician.'

'He visited today, but he's gone now.'

'Well, I hate that I didn't see him. True, he was a gangly youth, but he is a good physician, and now an earl as well.' She stood, fluffing her curls, arranging her fichu and straightening the line of her skirt.

'He wants me to wed him. But I don't know if I should.'

'Oh… How… That is—' Her mother jumped up, clapping her hands. 'My gracious. Wonderful beyond saying. Christopher—he will be able to live in a grand estate.'

'Mother.' Susanna heard the squeak in her voice. 'Quinton and I were friends as youngsters, but you did frown at us when we spoke for very long. Later, I know he spent a considerable amount of time visiting us while Father was recovering from his catarrh. And I grasped he helped with your shoulder pains. But until today, Quinton and I have not spoken privately since he became a physician. And there is, of course, no love between us.'

Susanna said words which her mother might grasp. She believed in love between a husband and wife. She'd grumbled many times about the lack of it in a union, a statement that hadn't been lost on Susanna.

'Woodle-dee-do.' Her mother's whole form shook when she answered, and she adjusted the scalloped edges of her fichu again. 'That man is an earl. And you loved that other wastrel and scoundrel, sneakier than a worm on a snail's underbelly—so-called human—whom you married, whom we let into our house, and our trust… Even a serpent would have been making a mistake to let him in close proximity, in my humble—but correct—opinion. The Earl could only be better.'

Her mother gave an encompassing wave. 'Plus, Quinton—I mean, Lord Amesbury—saved your father's life.' Then she chuckled. 'Don't hold that against him.'

'He said he didn't save Father's life. I remember hearing him talk with Father.'

'And he's humble, too. He doesn't take enough credit for his own skills.' Her mother sighed. 'I know personally that he is the best physician in London. Everyone says that, and a few hated to see him inherit the title because of that.'

She walked over and clasped Susanna's shoulders. 'Use your brain.'

Her brain? She was surprised her mother knew she had one. Her mother did not consider her the smartest of the three girls, but only the third because there wasn't a fourth.

Her mother sniffed loudly enough to shake the curtains. 'The house would be so forlorn without you and Christopher but still…' She held her head high. 'This would be an answer to my prayers. If you get an answer to your prayers, don't toss it out—even if it's not the answer you were hoping for.'

Her mother sighed. 'I'm so worried about your father with all the added concerns he's had lately. I know it's not your fault your father trusted your husband's family with all his financial decisions. And that wastrel gambled away everything we had. And anything left over, he gave to his father. He invested in a mine that caved in. And a ship that sank. If he'd invested in a desert, it would have flooded.'

'I know.'

'You do what you think is best, Susanna. It is your choice. The money from the sale of the house will keep us all going a few more years yet. And, we'll have enough to replace the roof. The sale of the piano will pay for Christopher's tutor. Your father and I understand why you don't really care to remarry.'

'I don't.'

'But you've avoided social events and you loved them so…' She took in a whoosh of a breath. 'And do reflect on what this could mean for Christopher.'

Susanna considered her future and her options. Quinton had always been a dear to her. It was said he was a bit rough. He'd told her that himself. But she'd only seen the endearing side of him.

'I'll think about it,' she said finally, leaving the room.

She scurried downstairs and found the butler. 'Graves, once, with great reluctance and respect, you told me that you wished I wouldn't marry Walton.'

'I did.' His eyes met hers.

'And you welcomed me back home.' He'd been the only one who'd passed no judgement on her for leaving her marriage.

'Of course.' Words without hesitation.

'What do you think of the man who just visited? The Earl of Amesbury?'

'Seems agreeable.' Tight words. 'Straightforward. Treats servants well. I know his parents were wayward, and people told tales of them, but people will say anything.'

She paused. She rarely listened to society gossip, preferring to dance and enjoy herself at an event. 'Well, I'm thinking about marriage again.'

'To him?' Spoken softer.

'Yes.'

'Well, I've often found myself on the wrong side of the coin, Miss Susanna.' His eyes shone. 'And a silk handkerchief feels better than a rough one when it wipes away tears. And life makes sure we all have tears.' He smiled at the end of his words. 'I'd say go for the silk. You can always return here if need be.'

She patted the worn sleeve on his coat and moved up the stairway.

She'd made her decision. She had chosen to marry Walton, and that had hurt her parents badly. So now she would make a decision which would change the lives of her family for the best.

If her marriage didn't turn out well, so be it. She could assist Quinton in society, and if she hated marriage again, no one would ever have to know. Not even Quinton. And her family would have a better life. She'd returned home once before. She could do it again. And if everyone called her a dullard... Well, it wouldn't be the first time she'd heard it.

Plus, she wouldn't be a burden to her parent's finances.

Her son would be able to have toys, and if he'd inherited her flaws, the funds Quinton provided would help them hide it.

The butler opened the door long before Quinton reached the entrance.

'Welcome, Your Lordship.' The butler bowed and spoke as if he announced a king. 'I will lead you to the sitting room and alert Miss Susanna, who is patiently awaiting you, as she is always ever so gracious.'

The butler led him back to the room and then asked, after giving another elaborate bow and backing out, 'Is there anything else Your Lordship requires of me? If not, I will fetch Miss Susanna.'

Quinton knew. He knew then.

In moments, Susanna strolled into the room, smiling pleasantly, arms at her side but one hand partially hidden behind the folds of her skirt.

'Mother and Father had a wager over whether you would return,' she said.

'Let's hope they both won.'

She sat, indicated he do the same with a wave of her arm and did all but consult a sheet of notepaper.

'A wife's societal duties could be varied. And you must know that I am not enamoured of spending long hours at a desk,' she said.

'Understood.'

'Would you need me to handle the penning of responses to the invitations you receive?'

'My housekeeper manages that well enough. And you could employ someone to assist if you desire it.'

She nodded. 'Agreed.'

She studied her fingernails and then raised her eyes. 'I would also want to bring the governess we already have for my son, and sometimes her English is not the best, but I could not leave her behind.'

'Agreed.'

'At some point soon, I expect my son to need a tutor, and I don't know… I don't know what his life might hold but I would hope you would help with Christopher's future.'

'When he is of age, I would see that he has opportunities for success.'

'In that case, I think it is a splendid idea that we wed,'

she said. Her smile enveloped him. Based on her appearance, he would have never guessed anything but joy answered his proposal.

'What date would you prefer?' he asked.

He saw the intake of breath. The slow exhale.

'Father has a friend who is a bishop and should be able to assist us with a special licence to wed tomorrow, if that meets with your approval.'

'So soon?' he asked, surprised by the suddenness.

'If it's the right thing to do, why wait? If you think it's the wrong thing to do, we should never wed at all.'

That was what he had wanted in a wife: a woman who considered things.

'Mother can assemble close family for a wedding breakfast in the morning, if all goes well with the ceremony plans, and she will send an announcement to the papers to alert everyone we're married.'

Her voice wavered over the word *married*, he noticed, but then it was one he'd never used in a sentence much himself and he understood the wobble.

'We must, you see, because it will help everyone be aware we...did such—since we're not having a large wedding breakfast.' She brushed the fingers of her left hand over her cheek. 'Mother will need your full title, just so she gets all the information correct, and any minor titles if you have them. And don't be surprised,' she said, 'if many well-wishers call at your estate over the next month, but the visitors should slow to a normal pace after that. I will certainly be available to receive them.'

She examined the knuckles of her closed hand. 'Have you thought of a ring?'

He shook his head. He'd not really even thought of the proposal.

She stepped forward and opened her palm. She held a

plain ring. 'This could work for our wedding,' she said. 'It has no true value, but will get us through the vows. It's the one—'

He waited tensely. He was not going to accept the ring from her first marriage.

'My father gave it as a jest to my mother once when she wanted jewellery, and secretly he'd hidden a ruby-and-sapphire ring to surprise her.'

She raised her gaze. 'It fits.'

'Not very impressively, I expect.' He took it and appraised it. 'You can select something different afterwards. Of course, you'd never have to worry about anyone stealing it,' he said, returning it.

She examined it. 'Or selling it. I've handkerchiefs worth more than this.'

'I would hope so.'

Then they stared at each other for a moment.

'I would like to discuss the marriage with your father,' he said. 'Then he can help me obtain an appointment with the bishop.'

'Oh, dear.' Her voice trembled.

'You can still change your mind on the bargain,' he said reassuringly. 'Until the moment of the vows. But I hope you don't.'

A strong gaze met his. 'A deal's a deal. We'll marry tomorrow.'

Chapter Four

She bit the inside of her lip and wished the vicar would get through the vows more quickly. After all, she'd heard them before and they'd not meant that much then either.

Then it was over, and the vicar said something else. Quinton answered. The men chuckled, and she wasn't even aware of what they'd mentioned, only that she had gotten married again. Well, it couldn't be worse than the first. She hoped.

Then Quinton took her elbow, and she jumped. The cleric's brow furrowed.

'That was lovely,' she said, thanking the man for the ceremony and hoping she didn't mar his vision with her smile.

Except the names, not one word of the vows was different from the ones of her first wedding, but she didn't think it would be a good time to comment on that.

They turned, and she walked from the church with her husband by her side, stepped into his carriage, and the wheels began to roll towards her new life.

She took her handkerchief from her reticule. She would go back to her parents' home, enjoy the wedding breakfast, and then go forward—or at least in a different direction than she'd been headed previously. She settled into the town coach, facing backwards, and hoped it was no indication of the future.

She could tell he noticed she'd sat across from him instead of at his side, but he settled comfortably, adjusting his coat.

'You just mopped your brow,' he said.

Surprised at her own actions, she put the handkerchief back into her bag.

'I suppose that's better than wiping your eyes.' His lips turned up at the end of his words.

'That ceremony never gets easier.'

'Well, Countess, let's hope you don't find that out again anytime soon.'

'No matter what happens, I give you my solemn vow this is my last marriage.'

'Good plan.' The carriage moved. 'For a moment earlier, you had me in suspense when the vicar asked you if you would—' he made a rolling motion with his hand '—take this man... However he said it. And you paused.'

'Were you not paying attention?' she asked.

'I assure you I was paying attention to you.'

She patted the base of her throat. 'My mouth dried. I couldn't speak.'

'I'm glad you didn't stop things to ask for a glass of communion wine.'

'The poor man would have been shocked. What of you?'

He laughed and clasped his fingertips together over his knee. 'I'm a physician. I would have fetched you a glass of wine, checked your throat and pronounced you well enough to continue.'

She noticed another carriage on the road, her sister inside, arriving for the breakfast.

'Do you think your brother will be able to make it?' she asked. 'Or any of your other relatives?'

'No. I haven't told my brother yet. I'll tell him next time I visit. I usually see him often, and I'll just tell him I've finally taken his advice on marriage, and more rapidly than he expected. Eldon has a small bakery and he has to be prised from it. That I'm wed will likely not surprise him.'

'What of your mother's family?'

Again, he smiled—or his lips did. 'They won't be here. My mother's sister, Auntie, is the only close person I have on her side of the family. And I remember telling her about you—that you had so many dolls.'

She laughed. 'I didn't know taking those dolls along would change the course of my life.'

'Perhaps. Perhaps not. I would have noticed you anyway. And we did always talk when my uncle had an event or insisted I attend Sunday services.'

When his uncle had realised his own son, Quinton's cousin, was not likely to live a long life, he'd considered the earldom and begun to drizzle some of his resources towards Quinton's education and future.

'I know. You were so angry one day because your younger brother was not invited.'

'Yes. I always felt my loyalty should be to him first. But I had to bite my tongue. My auntie insisted Eldon would appreciate it more in the long run. She was right.' Susanna had met many of the old earl's family as her parents had known him before he passed on. 'My mother has already sent a note to the dowager countess, on my behalf. She wanted it worded ever so correctly.'

It had irked her to ask her mother for help, but her mother had been thrilled to write to the dowager. And her mother was even more excited to host a wedding breakfast for Susanna.

The carriage rolled to a stop and Susanna was pleased that Quinton exited and waited for her.

He lifted her from the carriage when she stepped out, and gently lowered her to the ground. Her knees were shaky, and he held her a moment longer.

'You act as if no one ever helped you out of a carriage before,' he said.

'No one has but the carriage driver,' she said.

'They didn't know what they were missing, then.'

Susanna felt she should have been proud after the gentle way he'd helped her out of the carriage, and she was—but she walked into the entrance feeling more like a sacrificial lamb than a bride, and she remembered the sticky spider's web of a feeling that her first marriage had given her.

She'd only slept about an hour the night before, remembering the way Walton had treated her and reassuring herself she would not let Quinton know of her shortcomings. He had married her for her soirée strengths, and those would be all he would see.

Putting on her best smile, she emanated cheer, accepted her family's felicitations as she walked inside, and greeted the wedding breakfast arrivals.

No one seemed to notice that Quinton had no other relatives attending. Her family was absorbed with welcoming him, and she was immersed with getting through the morning.

Finally, Quinton asked her if she'd like to leave, and she gathered Christopher and moved to the carriage. At that moment, the new marriage exhausted her as much as the old one had.

In the carriage, Quinton positioned himself directly across from Susanna, noticing she again sat so he could face the front.

Christopher scooted closer to his mother, wide eyes taking Quinton in.

Shadows flickered over Susanna's face, her eyes on the window as the vehicle jolted ahead.

He sat in the town coach he'd once not even grasped that he could yearn for. It was polished and reflected glossily in the sunlight. The horses… Oh, he'd never dreamed to be able to afford such fine livestock. To own an old nag had been beyond his expectations.

He regarded Susanna. Yes, she would have been exactly the mate a man in this carriage would have expected.

Susanna had her hair piled high, and naturally carried herself aloof. She'd be elegance to stand beside at soirées. She knew all the pretty manners, and all the right bland, nonsensical comments to say about the weather, the delicious food and the beautiful music.

When he'd seen her during their childhood—even later on, when she was absorbed with Walton—he'd noticed her, a slender woman who managed to control her mother and father with a blink of her long lashes and a pout of her lower lip.

Susanna had been the spirited daughter, the one who commanded attention without even being aware of her own charm.

He kept his gaze impassive but could feel her eyes on him as the road's ruts jostled them along—his flawlessly groomed mate.

Her family was the most caring one he'd ever seen, and he'd continued to be amazed at them during the breakfast. Of course, he was an earl now, and most people befriended him, but her sisters had recalled him from the past and had accepted him in a sisterly fashion, claiming him a new brother. Only Susanna was distant, which suited him perfectly.

He'd understood he was not to have a true wife and was grateful. Life was busy enough without emotional upheaval.

'Are we going to live at your house?' Christopher interrupted Quinton's meanderings.

Quinton nodded.

Christopher kicked the seat. 'I want to go back to Grandmother's.'

'Be polite,' Susanna said firmly. 'Or your toy soldiers will go on manoeuvres without you again.'

The boy grumped out a breath of air and slumped, obeying. Susanna stilled, lost behind a façade.

Then she reached into her reticule, fumbled around and removed two toy soldiers, and gave them to him. He captured the men and bounced them around along the inside of the carriage, puffing out his cheeks and making soft popping noises as he played.

Nothing changed in Susanna's appearance as she watched out the window. She might as well have been in another vehicle.

Christopher put down his toys and looked at his mother, and Quinton could see planning in his gaze.

'Attack,' he said, and lunged into her arms.

She jumped, caught him, held him close for a moment without seeming to know she'd done it, and put him back in his seat. 'Soldier. No surprise attacks in the vehicle.'

'Yes, Mother.'

She and Christopher shared a glance, with him poking out his lip and her answering in kind, and Christopher relaxed back in his seat. When he sat silently, she absently gave him a pat of approval on his knee.

'Soldiers need to go to their tents after their training.'

She loosened the top of her reticule and held it open. He dropped the soldiers inside and she pulled the cords closed.

He snuggled against her.

Christopher's activity slowed, and his head nodded downwards. Susanna put her arm around him, and he dozed, and neither seemed surprised by the closeness.

The affection of a mother for her son jolted him.

He'd assumed Christopher was cared for by a governess and possibly his grandmother, and Susanna only did the minimal effort necessary.

The wheels creaked along, and Quinton tried to absorb the affection he'd witnessed.

Stunned, he averted his eyes, not wanting her aware of his unfamiliarity with the scene before him. When he turned back, he saw that she inclined her head towards her son.

If it weren't for the lightskirts treating him kindly when he was a child, he wouldn't have known affection existed. He'd certainly never seen such closeness between a mother and her child before.

Thankfully, his mother had rarely been in his life.

He remembered the sight of his little brother sitting beside the cart while Quinton tried to sell enough bread so they would have money to buy supplies to make more loaves and so they could eat as well. They'd been so fortunate their home had had a large bread oven. When he'd found out what it was, and how he could use it, he'd learned to bake.

Buying flour came before eating. And he had gone to sleep many nights hoping his brother would wake up happy and not fight him when he tried to clean him up. Without Eldon's little cherubic smile, the customers bought very little.

But the women would stop and admire him, and Quinton would sell them bread.

On the days Eldon cooperated, he'd taken him even farther from their home, and occasionally the servants in the fine houses would prefer Quinton's freshly baked bread for a different taste than the ones from their masters' stoves.

Sometimes he'd stopped the cart closer to the townhouse of the man whom his mother had followed after leaving his own father—probably the man who'd fathered Eldon.

The boor would pass them by without a smile, or even a glance or a pause to buy a loaf that would purchase more supplies. Quinton's insides had been ground down even finer than the flour. Sometimes he'd chosen that location as a deliberate challenge.

He would never let a child experience what he'd lived with, and Susanna had the respectability that would add to his standing. Not only that, marriage with a woman who'd already proven herself to be above falling to the level of a wastrel husband would give him the thing he craved: the morality, uprightness and decency he wanted foremost in his life.

He was an earl, but the reputable connections of Susanna and her family could help him. Their finances were strained, but he could make certain her father's home was refurbished as needed, and he would invite them to events at his estate and ensure they all appeared to be one well-entrenched family.

The carriage slowed—stopped, and she yawned, then moved Christopher, waking him. He jumped up, staring at the house.

The carriage swayed as the driver descended the perch,

but Quinton stepped out and helped his new family disembark.

She took in a breath, shaking herself, opening her eyes wide, but not seeing Quinton, and then moved to stare at the edifice.

By that time Christopher had run to inspect a rock, but she called him and he darted back, nearly colliding with Susanna.

Reflexively Quinton reached for Susanna's elbow, steadying her.

Immediately he slipped behind the impassive demeanour he'd adopted since birth. But the light clasp thundered the knowledge of her femininity into him. Damn.

Twice he'd touched her, and his awareness of her womanliness caused everything else to fade from his thoughts but her.

He'd been certain he'd killed that part of himself—buried it and thrown the shovel in for good measure. The momentary pleasure hadn't been worth the cost, even though he'd never paid a woman a penny for a tumble.

He forgot what he was going to say. Her skin made the air that had been stilled around him float through his clothes and drape around him like a caress. He could feel the glow in her, and at that moment he knew how plants grew into the sun, because she drew all of him to the light—the radiance that was Susanna. When she moved, the air around them changed and he breathed in the scent of vanilla and cinnamon and spice.

She continued along to the door, and it was as if she pulled him after her. His hand felt different—like it belonged to someone else—and his feet could do nothing but follow her.

They walked to the threshold as companionably as if they'd done it every day of their lives, but behind the shell of his skin, his body responded to her nearness with the heat of a thousand candles burning, pulsing alive.

He'd have to keep his distance. She could tempt him like no other woman, but a temptation was just that—it was not a fait accompli. It was just a thought to be shoved away. He was not an impulsive youth. And he had no desire to go to her rooms.

Chapter Five

Susanna stared at the house. Her new home.

The front entrance steps sprawled out, and four Doric columns, two offset, stood grandly holding the portico, with an arched window fanlight over the doorway. Bay windows on each side enhanced the exterior. She'd seen the house before—even visited it before—but it had just been another grand estate to her, and she'd not noticed it much.

She prayed he would not do something so foolish as carrying her over the threshold. Walton had, and then he'd pretended to drop her and it had all been downhill from there.

His steps were short on the way to the entrance, and she didn't believe he'd reduced them for her sake but to savour the moment. She couldn't blame him.

He paused, looking at her. 'The threshold? You would like to be carried inside?'

'Oh, no,' she said, shuddering. 'I did not find that act to bring me good fortune.'

She studied the house again. 'When I woke up two days ago, I could never have imagined myself standing here, married.'

'I hope you are content with the decision.'

She was. The adjustment would take time, and she didn't like moving, but his house had stood the test of time. And so far, the marriage had already gone so much better than her first one.

She smiled broadly, then sidestepped nearer, voice low. 'You rather look like you might need a physician.'

'I'm fine.'

With her gloved hand, she tapped the side of his lip. 'Is this broken? It seems to have fallen at the sides.'

He smiled broadly. 'Better?'

'Not much,' she said, but her spirit lightened.

He clasped her elbow and ushered them inside.

A woman met them at the door. The housekeeper. She'd expected a butler. Celeste had arrived earlier with a few trunks.

'This is Nettie,' Quinton said.

The servant lowered her eyes, cheeks rosy, the smell of lemon surrounding her, and greeted Susanna, welcoming her.

Other servants stood beside Nettie, introducing themselves, and she repeated their names when greeting them.

'Go on up.' He waved towards the upper storeys.

She paused.

'You will get used to the size of the house,' he said, after dismissing all the servants but the housekeeper.

'Nettie put your things away when they were sent over this morning. But the staff will happily move things around if you wish. I have the rooms on the first storey, and I hoped you would like the second, and Nettie will be happy to show it to you. You'll have more than enough room for Christopher, his governess and yourself—with plenty to spare.'

He turned his attention to the housekeeper. 'Nettie,

it appears Christopher would like to go on a tour of the house. Would you mind taking him?'

Nettie bobbed her head and took to the stairs. Christopher darted along, scurrying at her elbow.

After they left, Quinton addressed her.

'Susanna, it will be more as if we are neighbours than living in the same house, but let me show you the main sitting room on the first storey where we will receive visitors together when needed.'

'I've been here before…before I wed. Mother visited. The countess—dowager countess still lived here.'

'The extra servants who were in this house when I arrived have relocated to be with her, so don't expect as many staff members as there were. If you wish to add any employees, please discuss it with Nettie and she'll make sure you're accommodated.'

She followed him to the main sitting room and peered around. It didn't seem to have changed.

'I will have a lot to get used to,' she said. Usually, spaces appeared smaller when she visited them a second time. But not this one.

'You will settle in, and let us hope the monotony isn't tiresome for you.'

'Monotony. Matrimony. I have not found them to go together, but it would be a pleasant change.'

'I hope it is. I wouldn't have asked you if I'd believed it would be otherwise.'

They stood together, and it was the same as a hug of encouragement between them. 'I will try to be the most monotonous wife in the world.'

He chuckled. 'I will summon someone to show you about,' he said.

'You don't need to,' she said. 'I'm more than happy to find my way on my own.'

He inclined his head, clasped his hands behind his back and walked with her until she grasped the stair railing.

He stood behind her, watching the swirls of her skirt hem as she ascended the stairs, while every whispering ripple of the cloth spoke to him of what he'd never had from her, and what he could never have.

He averted his eyes, refusing to let his mind wander. But when he heard her pause, he glanced up.

She'd stopped at the turn, holding her reticule loosely, which had bobbed beside her steps and had fluttered at her skirt.

Then she rolled the ties around her hand, shaking her head, as if she couldn't believe what she'd done this morning.

'Don't fret,' he called up to her. 'I'll be a good husband.'

He stood there, waiting for a response. She pondered his words and gave him a wistful smile. 'But you've never been married before.'

'I've seen what *not* to do in a marriage. A considerable amount.'

'I've only seen it once. Up close.'

He waved away her words. 'But if we don't get on well, we can let Nettie and the governess carry the messages and do our feuding for us. We should not extend our energies on something so trivial.'

'I will bear that in mind.' She met his eyes and hers were truly smiling when she left his view.

He remembered they'd never kissed, other than that debacle of the one she'd given him when telling him goodbye.

He was wed, and he'd never kissed his bride other than a goodbye kiss.

Susanna was her own person, and perhaps someday they would share a chaste kiss of commitment between them. But not until they were a long-married couple. Otherwise, passions could arise, and those could not be introduced into the house.

But he couldn't stop thinking about the image of her walking from him.

It was no crime to have your wife's image stamped in your mind.

It was no crime, but it was folly.

His promises to himself would keep his life steady. And he'd always worked hard to make a better life for himself, especially when he'd had to become educated.

Now he had a wife who fit into society well, but who'd never truly noticed him when he was Quinton Langford.

And who would not have accepted his proposal had he not inherited so much.

Chapter Six

On Monday, the housekeeper, Nettie, summoned Susanna. 'A visitor, my lady.'

A sliver of disappointment touched Susanna that Quinton wasn't requesting her presence. She was wearing her new perfume in hopes he might notice. She didn't like it, but to her it smelled lordly, or similar to something a physician's wife might wear, almost like medicine.

'It's surely for my husband.'

'Yes, my lady. But you might wish to see her.' One of the housekeeper's brows twitched up. 'I'll fetch her.' She rushed away, not giving Susanna a chance to speak, but then the older woman paused and her attention returned to Susanna. 'I think she would be best meeting you in the main sitting room used for society people. Not the patient room. Do you know which one it is?'

'Yes,' Susanna admitted, disconcerted. Quinton had a small gaming room and he'd directed Nettie to have ill people wait for him there. He'd changed nothing of the old earl's furnishings, but the cabinets now stored his medical supplies.

'I'll let you get settled first, my lady,' Nettie said, her voice both cautioning and instructing Susanna. 'And then I will show her to the sitting room.'

'Of course,' Susanna agreed, and following the not-so-subtle guidance moved into the unfamiliar area, aware the notice of the marriage hadn't yet appeared in the newspaper.

She didn't recognise the plume or the feminine voice which floated into the air when the housekeeper showed the visitor to the room.

'Quinton?' a melodious voice called out before she even stepped into sight.

The sound of Quinton's first name on the other woman's lips scraped against Susanna's skin. 'The Earl should be home before long. May I give him a message from you?'

'You live here?' the woman asked. Her eyebrows nearly dislodged her bonnet.

Susanna felt a strength burning inside her that was so much stronger than any a perfume could add.

'Of course,' Susanna answered, voice soft. Assured. Calm enough to instruct troops into battle. She clasped a hand over the iron wedding ring so its plainness wouldn't be noticeable. 'Where else would I live since my marriage? The Earl swept me off my feet. He's so gallant.'

The woman observed Susanna, eyes as blue as a perfect day and the lashes that fluttered around them like fronds blowing in a gentle breeze to make the baubles beneath them more azure. 'Oh, of course. I'd heard some whispers that he might be married, and I so wanted to meet you.'

An amazing accomplishment that she'd known Quinton was married, as she'd practically stumbled when she heard the fact.

Susanna finally recognised her: Madeline something or other. Recently married to a viscount. All bosom and beauty and sadly—brains.

'I'm not feeling well, and I know the Earl can help me.' Madeline put a glove to her forehead. 'He always has in the past.'

'I'm sure.'

The woman removed her wrap and, holding out an arm, dropped the feather-trimmed garment into the sofa. A great deal of white flesh came into view, almost causing Susanna to wonder if the bodice of the woman's dress had also been accidentally removed.

'I have been feeling so dreadful.' She fanned herself with her glove. 'I must see Quinton.' The woman's words oozed with much more sincerity than anything else she'd said. 'He has been such a dear whenever I have been ill, saving me from death many times.'

Irritation prickled Susanna's skin. 'My husband truly is brilliant.'

'He is *divine*.' Madeline squeezed every second out of the word *divine*. She breezed by Susanna, staking her territory, and watched the open doorway.

'Oh, he is,' Susanna admitted. And for a moment she felt the same strength as she had had before she fell in love with Walton. 'I do hope you have not caught some disfiguring, dreadful disease.' Susanna sighed. 'That would be so unfortunate for you.'

Madeline stiffened. 'I am fine. Except I need Quinton.'

'Oh, I am so relieved.' Susanna put all the society manners she could muster into her voice.

Then Madeline examined a pair of sturdy candleholders. 'Those are just unlike anything I've ever seen. Are they from your side of the family?'

Rather rude of Madeline to snigger after the comment.

'I believe I was told they were a gift to the family from King George II. It's so hard to remember all the little anecdotes associated with the Earl's estate.' At least, she'd heard that something somewhere in the house had been a gift from George II.

'To think, I am able to reside here with these lovely things, in my husband's home, among all the most notable people of London.' She studied the third finger of her left hand, still making sure to keep the actual ring covered, and gazed adoringly at it.

'And we are all so very, very happy you are here,' Madeline purred, almost in the same way she might have commented pleasantly on the taste of ants or caterpillars or toads.

Susanna waited, amazed at how long she and Madeline could both smile insincerely.

'I do believe I heard my husband's carriage.' The relief Susanna felt at having Quinton home mixed with a sense of unease.

Madeline flowered. 'Wonderful.'

'Yes. It's so difficult for me to be separated from him.'

'Well, I hope that doesn't change.'

'I can't imagine anything or anyone changing it.'

She heard Quinton's footsteps. 'Ever,' she added.

'Mrs Nettie informs me I have a patient waiting,' he said as he strode inside. His eyes sparkled with humour. 'With my wife.'

Susanna watched as Quinton gave them both bows and then Madeline somehow swooned upwards—and then collapsed down onto a chair, plopping her bosom out even further.

He moved to Susanna, and his glance held all the adoration a woman could ever wish for. 'I hope I wasn't gone longer than you expected. I was delayed, but I told them I'm newly married and must get home as soon as possible to my dearest wife.'

She swallowed, momentarily at a loss for words. Never

had anyone looked at her with such devotion. Her mind went in a thousand directions, none with a usual stopping place.

'Oh, Quinton…' she answered, pulling herself back into a world with vocabulary in it. She meant to brush off his response. 'It was of no…' Then his eyes flicked a warning, and she did a Madeline flutter and completely changed course. '…no concern because I knew you would be home soon.'

She reached out, and her hand swept over the forearm of his coat. 'I did miss you. Terribly.'

Madeline groaned theatrically.

His eyes complimented Susanna.

'Oh, I almost forgot… Madeline. Are you well?' he asked politely.

'I will be able to go on living,' she said, patting over her heart and nearly causing the curtains to wiggle from the breeze she was creating.

'What is the illness today?' Quinton smiled and walked forward.

'I fear it is too delicate to discuss in front of another woman,' Madeline said. She glanced at Susanna. 'I would not want to disturb you.'

'I'm sure of that,' Susanna answered. 'Just pretend I am not here and I will not hear a thing. As a physician's wife, I must get used to hearing of all sorts of noxious, foul ailments.' She wasn't even sure what *noxious* meant, but she knew it fit the woman. 'And I so am looking forward to learning more about my husband's life.'

Madeline didn't waste any acknowledgement of the statement.

'I was lifting my puppy and I fear I have injured myself.' She stood.

Susanna clenched her jaw as Madeline swayed closer

to her husband. Susanna put a lone, curled finger across her lips, trying to act as she should and keep her silence. Madeline could take a lesson—the trollop barely had the ink dry on the special licence with her *own* husband.

'I see nothing to concern myself over,' Quinton said. 'I would only worry if you lose all sensation in your arms.'

She stripped off a glove. 'Well, now that you mention it, I do feel numbness in my hands.' She fluttered one in front of Quinton for his examination.

He took her fingers, studying, frowning, and then he contemplated her.

'I would put a scant drop of the spice mixture I gave you in some brandy and take that for two nights. Three days of staying out of the sun. That should clear it up. And I would get one of the footmen to lift the dog in the future.'

'You always make everything feel so much better,' Madeline said as she draped herself on his arm and tried to trap him against the wall. He sidestepped, and appeared unaware of what had just happened.

Susanna closed her teeth onto her tongue. That was her husband Madeline was panting over.

'Would you be so kind as to see me out?' Madeline asked Quinton. 'I don't know if I can make it down the stairs…without your help.'

'Certainly.' He smiled, but Susanna couldn't exactly read his expression. They exited.

Susanna forced herself to remain in place, and heard a feminine squeal and Quinton's comforting baritone response. Susanna just hoped Madeline had had the good sense to wait until the last step before she accidentally stumbled against Quinton.

Susanna crossed her arms and tried to remain unconcerned and forced herself not to peek down the stairs.

Quinton finally returned, and he frowned.

'When Nettie told me that Madeline had arrived, I was pleased you were with her. And that perfume she had on—' He shook his head.

Some invisible enclosure seemed to surround them, and all Quinton's movements jostled her insides.

He'd not spent that much time seeing Madeline out. It could have taken a lot, lot longer.

She'd not known he could smile in such a relaxed way, melting her heart and making it beat faster all at once. But he could—a brief one, fading from him but remaining inside her.

It shouldn't feel so astonishing to be with him. They were married.

Now he wasn't looking at her like a stranger.

'I almost didn't catch on at first.' Susanna smiled, and a little ray of happiness burst into her. 'She's one of the people you wanted me to help distance you from.'

'Yes. You're correct. Nettie is to interrupt when anyone arrives here for unneeded medical help and lingers more than a suitable time for a diagnosis. That helps, but I'll also need to host events, and I want everyone to see that I have a home.'

'You do,' she said, uncrossing her arms and adjusting her stance. 'And a wife.'

'I thought you were going to choke there for a bit.' He chuckled. 'You didn't seem to know which way to run when I first arrived.'

'I beg your pardon. I was just startled a moment.' She'd believed his look of adoration, and a little arrow of sadness hit her heart. Having Quinton look at her with such devotion was a treasured moment, even if it was false.

'Nettie is adept at preparing me for visitors,' he added. 'I don't think she likes Madeline being here.'

'Well, Nettie does seem wise.'

'She is.'

'But you might think of hiring a butler. For society's sake. And to help reduce Nettie's chores.'

'I will think about it.'

But she could tell he wasn't going to dwell on it. 'A butler is a sign of your status.'

'You've a point, but I have altered my life enough for the time being. Nettie took care of my bachelor's residence. I want to keep her in charge of the household. I've known her a while and we get on well.'

He indicated her left hand with a nod. 'She did wonder if the wedding ring you wear has additional value not obvious at first glance. I suppose I should purchase you a nicer ring. People in society will notice if I don't.'

Susanna stared again at the pitiful little band. 'True.' She brushed against her finger. 'But… I don't know.' The memories of her husband selling her first wedding ring gouged at her. She had replaced it with something smaller. She seemed destined to be wearing rings of no value, and she would just have to get used to it.

'You select something new,' he pressed.

'Well,' she said. 'I might. Something suitable for a loving couple.' Then she laughed. 'But do you mind if I keep this a little longer?'

The lightness left him. 'I don't want people to think our marriage is insincere. That's important to me.'

'I was just thinking.' She removed the band and examined it, somehow pleased the hint of it remained on her finger. 'And I would not lie, but this reminds me of something you might have given me when we first met… A ring a young man might present to a young girl to fill her with happiness.'

She flashed the ring his way—only the poor token could never sparkle.

'Well, since we must be honest,' he said, holding out his palm, indicating that she give him the ring. She dropped it into his clasp.

'We did meet at a picnic when we were children, and we could promise to always keep it a secret of the moment I slipped it onto your finger. A pact between us.' He studied the circle a moment, then held it out and took her hand. He slid it onto her finger again with studied care, then held the ring finger to his lips, letting the back of her hand touch his face.

'You outshine the biggest jewel in the land, and to have you as my wife is the greatest honour that could ever be bestowed upon me.' He followed his words with a pause, sealing the moment into their memory.

He had such sincerity in his eyes.

Watching her, he said, 'My wife, the woman above all others. The one whom even I, as a youth, could see the true treasure in.'

Her knees almost gave way, and she met his gaze. He'd called her a treasure. 'You could be so dangerous.'

'Pretty words are just that. It is the actions which are the true worth of a man, a woman, a marriage and a family.'

And those were the loveliest sentiments she'd ever heard. She clasped his hands and could feel his strength, and instead of feeling threatened, she felt protected.

She wanted to hold him close, to feel the comfort of his arms and rest against him. To feel safe, to experience the cherishing she could sense he'd bestow on her and be stalwart by his side.

'A friendly kiss to seal our deal?' she asked, holding herself still, fearing he would refuse her.

He didn't say a word or change one flicker of expression. In fact, he seemed to turn to stone, and not a welcoming one. No matter.

She tiptoed up and put the chastest kiss on his lips, then released his hands.

He touched her chin with one finger and their lips met once more—wine flavoured, moist—and she fell into his touch, savouring the senses flowering between them, bodies awakening.

He stepped away.

'Oh, my.' She clasped his hands again to hold herself upright.

'My apologies,' he said awkwardly. 'I overstepped.'

'No. You only returned a friendly kiss.'

He gave her a lopsided smile. 'Friends.'

'Yes.'

But friends didn't keep secrets, and if she became closer to him, he'd likely discover she didn't read, and then he would know that she hadn't been honest with him. She'd kept something important from him, and misrepresented herself.

His treasure would have turned to rust, but she could not destroy the moment.

If there was one thing she excelled at, it was smiling. Distracting people. Leaving a room as if she owned the world—not letting them see beneath the veneer. She stopped, looking back, and immediately knew she shouldn't have.

He was checking the cuff on his coat as if he didn't even remember their kiss. And she would never forget it.

Chapter Seven

The next day Nettie appeared, holding a triple-folded sheet of notepaper in her hands. 'This just arrived, my lady, from a footman. For Quint—I mean for His Lordship and for you.' She rotated it. 'I feel it's important, and he is out. It's from Her Grace the Duchess Wallburton.'

'But it's sealed. By a duchess.'

'You are Lord Amesbury's wife, my lady.' Her streaked silver hair didn't move as her brows almost bumped her hairline. She thrust it at Susanna and turned to leave.

'I could never—' Her words stopped Nettie, and the housekeeper studied her. Susanna returned the missive to Nettie. 'Put it where it will be seen by the Earl.'

Nettie pursed her lips and took the letter. 'It's not sealed that well. And Amesbury is not one to be overly private about his correspondence. He leaves it all lying about and I straighten it.'

'But I am sure you do not peruse it.'

'Who has time?' Now only one brow rose. 'At least not more than once. I've got chores enough.'

'I wonder what it concerns.'

'Well, open it. Reseal it somehow. Say it arrived that way. Say you didn't notice your name wasn't on the front.

Say if you find out which staff member did it, you will let them go. Say the wind came up and must have ripped it open.'

Susannah laughed. 'I could not!'

Nettie held up the paper, squeezing it so that it opened enough that she could peer inside. Then she moved to the window and squinted, holding it and moving it about. 'I think—just in case—you should be prepared, in case I am reading this correctly, for him to travel to the duke's tonight, as they're having a small event.'

'You cannot be serious. This is all far too sudden. Invitations go out in advance.'

'Not when you're a physician being summoned, or a duchess who doesn't want her husband to know she's meddling.' Nettie's lips firmed. 'Now, you'd best be thinking about it, my lady. I'll send a maid up. And I'll let His Lordship know the moment he returns. This will be important to him.' Her other brow rose. 'And you could be just what the physician needs.'

The older woman sighed. 'We can at least get preparations started. I'll summon you when it's time for the two of you to leave.'

Susanna stared, mouth open, after Nettie's departing form. No wonder Quinton didn't want a butler. Nettie was more than competent to run the household.

Susanna heard Quinton arrive home, and shortly afterwards a maid summoned her.

The thundercloud behind Quinton's eyes dissipated when he saw Susanna. 'Nettie was right,' he said. 'I never expected you to be ready so quickly.'

He held out an arm, and she took it.

'I'll let you in on a little secret. That message wasn't sealed very well. I hope you don't mind,' she said.

'It was for both of us,' he said. 'The news that I'm wed has travelled as quickly as I had hoped.'

He led her to the carriage, they departed, and the wheels hardly seemed to turn before they arrived. She hadn't grasped before how near his estate was to the duke's home.

The instant she walked inside, she spotted an acquaintance and then remembered her friend had recently married into the ducal family.

'Do you know Sally and her husband?' she asked Quinton, and when he said he didn't, she was quick to introduce them, and tell her friend that she'd recently married.

'How wonderful that you have both found love. My husband and I are so in love.' Sally's words tumbled over themselves. 'Love is just the greatest thing ever.'

Quinton had been lifting a drink to his lips, and at the statement, he'd appeared to have trouble swallowing.

Susanna reached over and patted his back. 'We met as children. And then we reconnected recently, and both realised what a treasure we'd missed out on. Isn't that so, dear?' She gave him a stronger pat. He needed to breathe.

Quinton took another sip of his drink, lowered his glass, swallowed and gazed at her. 'Of course.'

She reached out and threaded her arm around his. 'Our marriage has been all I could ask for.' She shivered in happiness and squeezed his arm.

'And I feel the same,' he said hurriedly.

'Isn't it so grand to be in love?' Sally asked, eyes adoring as she gazed at her husband.

'We don't talk about our deep feelings—our devotion—because it's so private. Personal. Such a recent discovery.' She smiled at her friend. 'But I am sure you understand. Marriage is something indeed.'

'Oh, I do. Love…' Sally gave another entranced look at her own husband and fluttered her eyes at him.

Susanna turned to gaze at Quinton. He needed another nudge. She stepped sideways a bit, jostling him, and gripped his arm harder. 'And what does my dearest husband have to say to that?'

Apparently not much.

She turned back to her friend. 'Sometimes, I can just look in his eyes and see all the wonderment at the remarkableness of our marriage.'

'I'm a very fortunate man. Beyond words.' He'd finally found his voice, and it carried an honesty no one could doubt.

'Yes. Beyond words.'

Their eyes caught, and a moment of triumphant victory was shared.

He put his hand over hers, covering the wedding ring. 'Besides, like Susanna, I would rather save our endearments until we are alone.'

'Oh, Quinton. That is just like you. So romantic. Remembering our first kiss, and I am sure you even remember our second.'

'I remember every kiss with you, sweeting.'

She peered at her friend. 'I do like him.'

'I like her too.' His voice rumbled in a way that touched her heart, and truly did cause a happy shiver.

She regarded him and smiled. 'Is that not the most appealing way for a husband to secretly tell his wife how much he adores her?' She turned back to her friend. 'And I do give him a little squeeze on his arm to just emphasise all the joy I have at being his wife.'

They spoke a little longer, with Sally telling her once again the happiness she'd also had in marriage, and then she left to dance with her husband.

'Sweeting,' he said, whispering against her hair. 'You can loosen your grip now. Else I am about to lose all feeling in my arm.'

'My pardon,' she said, gazing up. 'I thought you were going to choke again and I might need to hold you up.'

'Well, I was just beyond words.'

'I could tell, because of our deep conversations with each other in the past.'

'Deep. Except that one with Lady Matilda whatever, and about that elephant with the talking bird. I could have missed that.'

'Nonsense,' she said, releasing his arm and taking a glass of lemonade from a nearby table. 'You were hanging on every word I said.'

'I'd never met anyone who had a doll with an imaginary pet before. Whatever happened to the animals?'

'Oh, Mother said she opened the door and sent the elephant and the bird away and I was not to search for them or I would have to dust and sweep the house every day.'

'I must thank your mother.'

'Oh, she would not like to be reminded of them either.'

'Perhaps I meant to thank her for you.'

'Oh, that is… You must remember to say that if someone asks again about our—you know.' She finished her lemonade.

'Well, if you will excuse me.' He took the glass from her hand and held both glasses. 'I will get you another.'

He stepped away. 'And I really will thank your mother.' He lifted his glass in her direction, tilting the rim in a silent toast to her, and their eyes locked. He took a last sip of wine before turning away and going to the refreshment table.

It was so much more pleasant to be at the event with Quinton. The perfect night. Glorious. And if the duchess had been watching, she would have believed them to have been deeply in love—and then the night ended and the carriage took them away.

'It's been a long time since my mouth has been tired from smiling,' she said. She settled beside him. The inside of the carriage really wasn't that large, and it made her feel they were tucked into a little haven of togetherness.

Quinton propped his elbow on the side, rested his jaw on his folded knuckles and noted, 'You were certainly comfortable.'

'I didn't realise how much I'd missed Sally,' she said. 'We shared a seamstress before my marriage, and she was the absolute best. Sally said she's still at the same place and I'm thinking of returning to her...if that is acceptable?'

'Why would it not be?' he asked.

'The expense.'

'I'm not concerned with it and neither should you be. I doubt the duchess we spoke with tonight frets over costs either, but she certainly worries over the duke.'

'What did you find wrong with the duke?'

'He shouldn't get so upset at his servants and shout at them. It's causing him hoarseness, and not doing his health any favours. The duchess told me what's been going on—it's why she'd summoned us earlier in the day. Made things easier. Just wish I'd not had to waste an entire evening for that.'

'But the food was divine. The company was elegant. And, um, your adoring wife was there.'

'Yes.' He clasped her hand. 'Perfection. Beyond words.'

She sat a little taller. 'Oh, Quinton. Quit jesting now. We don't have to pretend anymore.'

'I like that phrase,' he said. *'Beyond words.'*

'Well, you gave quite a performance after you choked.'

He leaned his head back onto the wall of the coach. 'True. The duke and duchess believed the appearance we presented. It will protect us. Madeline will get the message that she is wasting her time. Other people who wished me to woo their daughters will understand I am not interested. People who expect me to do unwholesome things will see that I have a lovely wife to go home to. It will be best for everyone.'

'It just seems odd to me how honest you are, and how much it feels false.'

'It didn't feel false to me. It felt the way a brand-new marriage should be portrayed in public. Maybe a bit much, but still, we are behaving socially as we should, and we should present such an appearance at first. We are a united couple, not a couple who could be corrupted by combativeness, belligerence or disputes.'

He stared out the window into the darkness. 'I couldn't *not* go tonight. The duchess had summoned me. I just didn't know how long the evening would last.'

It hadn't really lasted long to her. All she'd had to do was chatter and agree and be pleasant. It was like being a pair of matching earrings and slippers that completed the perfect dress.

'One must do what one is good at, I suppose. In your case it is medicine,' she said. And in her case, it was smiling.

'Yes.' He took in a deep breath and she heard him slowly exhale. 'Though it was good for us to be invited to the duke's, even if we barely had time to get there. I would have preferred a quiet evening at home.'

Alone. She didn't complete the thought for him but when she peered at him, she could feel it.

He yawned.

She felt ignored, relegated to a cupboard along with his medicines to be taken out only when needed.

'Everyone was convinced we are entranced with each other,' she said. 'And if you fall asleep right now, you might feel a little bit of irritation from me. I will sing you a lullaby, and if you've ever heard my voice, I fear it will harm our marriage. Possibly irreparably.'

He took her hand. 'I will not fall asleep before we get home. And you may sing if you wish.'

'Oh, no. I also have ears so it's decidedly unpleasant on both sides of them.'

'I bet you sing like a dream.'

'No, I don't.'

'Neither do I,' he said. 'But you appeared so comfortable tonight. It was so providential you were at home that day I visited your house.'

'I have no complaints,' she said. 'I am truly fortunate.' Fortunate that she could flutter and dance and make mindless conversation so easily. But sometimes, she wished she was able to speak with people about things that mattered.

She hugged herself. In her haste to select a favourite dress, she'd not brought a matching wrap. 'I didn't expect the evening to turn chilled, but I should have known that nights can still be cold.'

'I'm sure there's a carriage blanket.' He moved to lift the seat top across and reach inside to the darkness. He lifted a dark object, held it to his nose, and dropped it back in, closing the lid again. '…which smells like it wasn't taken out once during the previous winter.'

He began to remove his coat. She clasped his arm, stopping him, aware of the warmth of his sleeve. 'Absolutely not. I need you to stay well. We can't have you getting ill.'

She dived between his arm and his body, snuggling into the warmth. 'Do you mind?'

He stilled. She burrowed against him.

He finally answered. 'I'm beyond words again.' After a pause of stillness, he gave her a squeeze, settling her against him.

'People appreciate you. When we were talking alone, Sally noted you have on handsome boots.'

He put his arm across her, clasping his other wrist. 'So you were talking about my boots?'

'Of course. Not everyone can wear boots like yours and not be overpowered by them.'

'I believe my boot maker neglected to mention that. I must be grateful as I was merely thinking they would help keep muck off my legs.'

'Truly?'

'Yes. It was wonderful to have you at my side. Still is,' he said, momentarily tightening his clasp. 'Are you warm enough?'

'Almost.'

'I will direct a fresh blanket to be placed inside the carriage from now on.'

'Thank you. But please be sure it is washed in your soap,' she said. 'That will make it feel even better.'

He brushed his hand over her arm several times, the friction causing a warming sensation. 'Are you sure you don't want my coat?'

'I'm certain, if you don't mind sharing your shoulder with me.'

'No.' He ended his word with a kiss on her hair. 'But my coat would keep you even warmer.'

'We may be about to have a disagreement.' She slipped an arm around his waist and nestled close.

'I'm too tired tonight. You will have to just make do with my shoulder and no argument.'

'I think forgetting my shawl was a good idea,' she said. 'Do you think Nettie planned that?'

'I've no complaints if she did. As I said, she is normally quite adept at her duties.'

The carriage rolled to the entrance of his house and she heard him grumble. She sat up straight, seeing what had caused him to tense.

Nettie stood at the open door, a lamp in one hand and a satchel in the other.

Quinton ignored the sunrise peeking through the clouds when he arrived home the following morning and woke Nettie with a light rap on the door. She usually waited for him in the easy chair by the entrance, and let him in, then took his satchel.

He was blasted tired, and Nettie needed no explanation.

They didn't speak but went their own ways. Almost the mother he'd never had, he realised, trudging to his room.

A woman's husband had been cut by a broken bottle the night before. The bleeding had stopped, but she'd wanted Quinton to take a look at it. That meant he'd had to leave for the stews right after returning Susanna home from the duke's residence.

The accident had been minor compared to most injuries he'd seen, but then the man had pulled out a unbroken bottle and wanted him to stay.

He'd no more been able to refuse his patient than he had the duchess and duke, and he'd delivered a lecture about taking care with the drinking and saving a physician from overwork. They'd parted in the early morning, but perhaps the man would take more care in the future.

Now he was exhausted. When he stepped into the sitting room, he immediately sank into the most comfortable chair, reclined back and closed his eyes. He felt his attention fading into sleep.

'Amesbury, are you awake?' A little voice commanded his notice, causing him to start.

He opened his eyes in the darkened room—the morning light outlined the shadowed boy in front of him. 'I am now.'

'Do you bandage people?'

'Sometimes.'

'What about horses? Can you bandage horses?'

'If I need to.'

'Mother said I could try to catch a bird in the back gardens. I saw a lot of them.'

'You can if you want, but they're pretty fast.'

'Do you want to play soldiers?'

'Why don't you get your mother or Celeste?' Quinton asked.

'She doesn't like playing soldiers when the blood oozes out and the men take their last gasp. She only wants soldier dolls where all the men go to soirées after the war, and they all line up in rows and beg pardon for shooting each other.' The sound of a sputtering disagreement followed his word.

'Perhaps that's right,' Quinton said with a hidden smile.

'But, Amesbury.' He held a toy aloft, waving it. 'It's not as much fun. Mother does not know how to play war.'

'What other games do you play?' He still found it odd that Susanna was interested in such an activity with her son. He'd expected Susanna to leave most of Christopher's care to the governess. After all, it was the servant's duty.

Christopher dropped the toy, then stood and folded an arm across his stomach and one behind his back and bowed. 'Dancing. But no one gets hurt.'

'That is a good thing, isn't it?'

'And when I asked Mother again to give me my soldiers, she called me a bad word. When I called Celeste it, I had to sit in the corner.'

His own mother had hurled all the oaths in the English language at him. His jaw tightened. 'Sometimes our mothers say and do things we don't understand. But we still have to do what is right.'

'She won't read to me like Grandmother did, and left all the stories at Grandmother's.'

That was more like what he expected of mothering. 'Perhaps some night I will read to you.'

The child had lost a father, and Quinton understood that.

'You have stories?' he asked eagerly.

'Yes.'

Then a flurry of raps sounded on his private sitting room door. 'Quinton. Quinton,' Susanna's voice called out. 'We can't find Christopher. Have you seen him?'

'I'm here. I'm here, Mother.' The boy ran towards the sound.

She opened the door, voice tight. 'You are in so much trouble, young man. You are supposed to get Celeste or me when you wake up.'

The lamplight drew attention to her hair, not yet piled on her head but hanging over her shoulder in an elegant plait, and she had on a dressing gown large enough to cover her twice over, but her face reminded him of an angry bee.

He braced himself.

Christopher held up his toy and he splayed the fingers of his free hand. 'I was showing Amesbury how my soldiers *dance*.' He dragged out the last word.

'That does not excuse you for leaving your room.'

'But Amesbury might have needed help. He can bandage people just like you said. So, I can play war and he can fix my soldiers.'

'Young man, if you do not behave, I will be taking your soldiers from you and you will not be playing with them for a long time.'

'Mother… Amesbury can fix anyone.'

'No, I can't,' he told Christopher.

'Now tell Lord Amesbury you are sorry that you interrupted him.'

'He wasn't doing anything. He was just sitting in a chair.'

'Christopher. What are you supposed to say?'

'Beg pardon, Lord Amesbury.'

'Go apologise to Celeste for worrying us.'

The boy rushed away, and she didn't even swing out her arm to box his ears as Quinton's own mother would have done when he ran by her.

Quinton expected her to follow Christopher, but she stayed at the doorway.

'I am sorry for his interrupting you.' She straightened the lapel of her dressing gown and pushed her plait out of the way. 'I know you had a long night. The carriage returning probably woke Christopher, and I didn't know he'd left his room.'

He just stared at her for a moment, untangling his feelings.

'Truly. He is a good boy,' she added.

'Yes, he is.'

Susanna stood at his door in thick night clothing, hair plaited and emitting an unexpected warmth which wasn't all coming from her lamp.

'He is growing up, and I suppose it is good for him…'

'I want only the best for the two of you,' he said, hearing the truth as he spoke.

'You do not mind, then…that he may grow to see you as a—?'

'An earl.'

'Oh,' she said, almost taking the words like a blow and he wondered if that's what she'd been going to say.

He took an extra moment, aware of the lamplight on her face. How flawless she looked. Forcing the traitorous thoughts aside, he pushed himself to his feet. And it wasn't a dream. She was still standing there after he'd blinked.

He stretched, but his eyes didn't leave her. 'I needed to get up and go to bed anyway.'

She took in a breath. 'I will tell him not to leave our floor of the house again, and I will make certain he understands why.'

'I'm an adult, Susanna.' His voice lightened. 'If a small boy is disturbing me, I can easily tell him to leave. Don't concern yourself with it.'

'But we agreed to keep to different areas of the house except when there are visitors.'

'If he does something I don't like here, I will send him to Celeste. Fair enough. I don't mind him discovering what is inside the house. It would be odd if he didn't want to explore. Boys, from what I recall, have to know what is around them. It's part of growing up, and survival. Besides, I said I would not visit your area without a written request. You may roam about as you wish, just like Christopher.'

'You don't mind?'

'No. Not at all. But I am sleepy, so if you'll excuse me…'

Having her standing there in his doorway disconcerted him—she seemed so innocent as she clutched the ties of her robe. She couldn't be as delicate and fragile as she appeared. She had a little boy. She'd been wed.

Susanna realised who was being asked to leave. Her. Not Christopher, but her. He was right in that he had no trouble removing someone he didn't want in his room.

'I apologise for the interruption.' She stiffened and started to pull the door closed.

'My pardon,' he said. 'I'm not used to—'

'You wanted to get married. You just didn't want a wife.'

The phrase had slipped from her mouth. Silence engulfed her. He didn't offer a platitude but seemed to distance himself from her. She was sorry she'd said it, but she'd been unable to stop herself from speaking.

'It's true, isn't it?' she asked.

'I'd decided against marriage early on.' He yawned, seeming to shake himself awake. 'Just didn't seem particularly necessary for anyone to do except for the parenting of children. A forced bond. An illusion for other people's benefit. Sometimes the impression is useful, though. I decided I needed it. And I enjoyed it last night.' His voice lowered. 'Surprisingly.'

The air had stilled, but a whirlwind of dismay hit her. When she'd suggested he didn't want a wife, he'd whisked out a few remarks, making it sound even worse. An illusion. It was true she'd not wanted to marry again when they'd decided to wed. And she still wasn't sure of it, but to hear him voice the words aloud emblazoned the syllables in the room—inside her—and made her shiver.

They'd had such a pleasant night, and it had surprised him. It had *surprised* him?

It was one thing for her to not be settled in a new marriage, but another to hear the man she'd wed say the same. She shouldn't be amazed, though. She'd not succeeded at much in life except dancing and laughing at soirées. That, she was good at.

'I admit, it fascinates me to see a tidy, peaceful life inside a house,' he said. 'And I do want this to be a happy place for your son also.'

She instantly forgave him for not wanting her company, and he again rose to the heights in the same manner he had when he'd rescued her doll.

He waved aside the conversation as easily as a dust mote. He would always be able to avoid a squabble. He only had to bring out the charm, the smile, the illusion of an answer while he put a cloth over the question and whipped it from sight.

She took in a breath and made sure her voice was soft. 'I appreciate that we wed. It almost seemed I didn't have a choice.'

'Do we ever truly have choices?' Quinton asked. 'Or must we always just do the right thing?'

She'd never even thought of that, which was no surprise.

Her shoulders dropped. 'I did make a decision once, and made the wrong one, and it led me to a world without many options. Everyone thought my husband caring.'

His throat rumbled, and Christopher would have been

punished for speaking back to her if he'd made such a sound.

'I could tell what a wastrel he was,' he said. 'All shining teeth and pomade hair, and tripping over his own feet to get to you. He probably told you all about that love nonsense.'

'He wasn't so much in love with me as—' As desiring her. As wanting her to agree to his every whim.

Then she grasped Quinton's words. 'You think he was a wastrel because he wanted to wed me?'

'No, of course not. I think him a wastrel because he acted all fluttery around your family, but out of sight of your house, with his friends, he'd drink and turn vicious. He stomped on a man's hand once so hard that I had to straighten the fingers as best I could. That man was no saint either. But I started hearing more talk about Walton even before he had the accident that killed him.'

The talk didn't surprise her.

'We had a few hours of a happy marriage, longer when I pretended, and then I moved back in with my parents. They thought I was being immature. They really didn't want me to return home. He was their golden son-in-law. He still courted them, and in front of them, treated me well enough to stay on their good side. But I didn't like him anymore.'

She'd always tried to hide how much smarter everyone else was than she. After meeting Walton—for the first time in her life—someone had seemed to understand her. She'd confided so much in him. He'd told her reading wasn't important. He'd told her she was clever at all the things that truly mattered.

That should have warned her he wasn't to be trusted. Then he'd told her after they married that rabbits were the most senseless creatures on the face of the earth, and he'd started calling her his little bunny when they were with family, particularly after she spoke, and everyone had thought him so affectionate. He hadn't been.

Quinton's speech softened. 'Our union was an awkward solution. But it made things so much simpler. For me. For you. I received a family which, in everyone else's eyes, gives me the appearance of the stability I need. It's important for me that everyone understands I am upstanding, even if I am not always to be found in the best of places.'

She nodded. That was Quinton—thinking things out. Using his head for something other than a place to put a hat.

She could see the benefit of a marriage for him. He was aware of her family's reduced circumstances. It was obvious to everyone.

Quinton didn't want a real marriage. He truly did want a divide between himself and all the callers. She'd been in his home long enough to grasp the steady stream of visitors. An additional one would arrive and the prior one would then decide to be on his way. In a sense, Quinton would be trapped by people and have to hope for time to rush out between them if he wanted to leave his house sometimes.

'You like your privacy, don't you?'

'It can be hard to find.'

She stiffened her shoulders and clasped the door to pull it shut. She determined to give Christopher strict instructions not to visit Quinton's rooms, and she would do the same. She would only enter the main sitting room when he had callers, as he'd requested, and not his private one.

He called out her name, stopping her in the doorway. 'Yes?' She hesitated.

'I don't mind you and Christopher being in the house. I truly don't. It's just taking time to get used to it. Sometimes I hear your voices through the walls and I'm reminded you're here. You're both usually so quiet that the reminder is good for me.'

'I understand.'

And she did.

Quinton only wanted her to provide more privacy for him, and respectability, and she certainly didn't mind the solitude, although sometimes she felt she was missing something.

Something she'd always yearned for—a deep bond. But she doubted such a thing existed for her. She just wasn't a person to talk long hours into the night with. She was a woman who could dance and laugh and say the right meaningless things, not the meaningful ones.

Life was full of barriers. Walton's were ones of deceit and pretence, and for her that had been a life-altering awareness of human nature. Quinton was far more honest and straightforward, but his barriers were even more impregnable.

She lowered her lamp so she couldn't see the distance in his eyes.

'Pleasant dreams,' she said, but she wasn't even sure he heard her as he walked into his bedroom.

She lifted the lamp and took one last look around his sitting room, feeling curious about his life, the man he was in his own environment.

Unappealing medical prints on the wall, books all about, not put on shelves but strewn open as if he read all of them at once. A stack of clean, folded cloths she assumed were to be used as bandages.

She left, closing the door. She didn't belong in a room so sombre, so full of knowledge and intelligence.

She remembered Quinton from her youth, who'd also had a distance inside him, but he had sought her out. She was certain of that. And she'd always been pleased to see him.

She could understand her childhood friend, and she could understand the man at her father's home. She could understand the illusion of the Quinton at the duke's dinner table.

But the Quinton in his sitting room was a stranger to her. And she knew the man behind the walls of his house, and the walls of his smile, was the true man she'd wed.

He'd wed her for respectability. And she'd not grasped that she'd wed anyone but the Quinton whom she'd once known.

She hadn't even comprehended how intelligent he was, or how handsome. She'd only thought of him as her childhood friend until Sally had appraised him so matter-of-factly and complimented her on her delightful good fortune.

She had truly been cold in the carriage, and he had provided warmth. She didn't have to try to remember the feeling of being in his arms.

But it seemed like that Quinton had been left behind, and the physician had returned inside the house. He hadn't wanted to linger with her, but had gently wanted his solitude.

She must remember to keep her distance from him inside his house. He had requested it, and so had she. And crossing those barriers, alone, would be devastating for her—especially when he walked away, as he had that night.

Chapter Eight

Susanna's maid had reassured her that nothing was out of place in her appearance, and Susanna had hardly been able to attend to anything Christopher had said that day. Her mind was taken up by the soirée she was to attend with Quinton.

In truth, she'd been preparing for it all day, and had started thinking about what she would wear right after Quinton had sent the maid with a message two days ago saying he would like to attend. She must go. She had to uphold her part of the marriage agreement. She'd alternated between nervous excitement, worry, dread and anticipation of being able to enjoy soirées again—and concern about how alone she would feel after the event ended.

Taking her gossamer shawl, she absently folded it over her arm. She didn't want to risk it getting creased before she reached the event.

She'd moved to his sitting room when she was ready to leave, and his door was open, wide.

He stood inside, a fortress of a man. Sombre. Dressed in black. But when he saw her, his eyes lightened. 'You are perfect,' he said.

She flicked away his words with a toss of her head, felt pleasure bloom, but then admitted, 'It's only taken three staff members, days of thought and a full day of preparation.'

'It would take more than a lifetime for anyone else to try to appear as lovely as you, and they couldn't succeed.'

His words rang with a sincerity she'd not believed possible, and suddenly she wasn't nervous anymore. 'Oh, you're very good at making people feel better.'

He gave a brief smile of acknowledgement and held out his elbow for her to take. 'The carriage is awaiting us.'

She walked beside him to the vehicle, knowing they both appeared their best, except he did have darkness under his eyes, and his coach had only returned home a short while before.

Settling beside him, she noticed the crisp cleanliness and a medicinal smell. They sat close in the tight interior of the vehicle, but then she didn't think there were many vehicles made that his legs would fit easily inside.

And she didn't feel the same as if she sat close to a stranger. True, they were married, and she liked him, but she didn't really know if he thought more of her than he might a porcelain doll on a shelf.

Well, she knew how to appear that way. She'd learned it easily.

She wondered if he would ask her to dance. She considered it, and was certain he would. A happy couple would partner each other, surely?

He seemed to be moving sideways away from her, and she watched him. He was nodding off, and he caught himself. Then his clothing rustled again when he crossed his arms and rested against the seat.

His eyelids dropped. She slipped her hands around

his arm, snuggling against him, and he opened his eyes, smiled at her, and dozed off again.

By then the carriage was closer to their destination, and she expected a bump would wake him, but it didn't.

They were nearing their stop.

'Quinton,' she whispered. 'We're almost there.'

He opened one eye halfway, took in a deep breath and then shook himself. 'I brought a baby into the world last night, and I found the father today and gave him a talking to about responsibility and not neglecting his family. And here I am, neglecting mine.'

'You aren't,' she said. 'Even knights need their rest.' She held her hands in a pugilistic pose. 'And I am your shield, protecting you.'

'Exactly what I needed.' He took her hand and kissed the wedding ring.

Her heart fluttered. The Romans must have been right about something on the third finger of the left hand reaching the heart. She'd felt it.

The coach pulled in front of the residence and came to a gentle stop.

The driver helped her out, and Quinton followed.

Stepping outside, no one would have been able to tell he'd been half asleep only moments earlier. 'You are quite devastating to tender sensibilities,' she said.

'I don't know what that means, but I'll take it as a compliment.'

'You should.'

She unfolded her shawl to wrap over her shoulders, and he put out his hand and raised his brows.

She gave the shawl to him and he carefully draped it around her—such a simple movement, the silken fabric caressing her arms, and his proximity adding a warmth. She glanced up at him, and again he held out his elbow.

Oh, she would have wed him for that moment alone.

Then she saw Madeline Trotter go inside, and Susanna didn't feel so strong anymore.

'Don't fret.' She heard the masculine rumble at her side. 'You're a countess.'

'Yes. But she's taller, and wider, in the places that people notice.'

'Well...' He walked beside Susanna. 'You could lift a puppy without hurting yourself. That means a lot to a physician.'

After they walked inside, she could feel the moment Madeline noticed him, and he leaned closer to Susanna, a hand on her back, seeming to hold her completely in his clasp as he said, 'Did you say something?'

'No.' She peered at him. 'I was just thinking really loudly, I suppose.'

Their vision connected, and his voice rolled around her. 'Not so loudly that anyone else might hear, I hope, sweeting.'

He was acting the devoted husband so well she had to remind herself not to believe it, and then she reconsidered. It would do her no harm to enjoy the evening as if she were with a devoted suitor she happened to be wed to, and when they returned home, she could put away the pretences along with her gossamer shawl.

'Thank you.' She clasped his arm. 'I will enjoy tonight.'

'I hope so.' His whisper touched her hair.

Then someone walked up to them, and she wondered if he'd meant the sentiments or was only voicing the words a devoted husband would say. They stood so close that his arm brushed against hers.

She peeked at him, and he caught her eye, and the regard in his gaze was just for her.

She glanced away as her heart blossomed, causing an extra warmth inside her.

A man greeted him, and from the corner of her eye, she caught sight of another familiar face. Then she fought to keep smiling. Her former father-in-law.

It hadn't occurred to her he might attend.

Well, she was a countess now, and he was a part of her past. She would uphold her bargain with Quinton and make him proud. She would not let her father-in-law disrupt her happiness, and she would continue with what she was good at—being agreeable.

She knew Mr Walton would speak with her before the night was over, and she had no choice but to be pleasant and say all the usual platitudes.

Quinton sipped a drink and then finished it. The years had only improved on Susanna's perfection and seemed determined to keep doing so.

He noticed tension in her face that he'd not been aware of before, but it was tiring to attend an event in society sometimes.

Quinton had no trouble letting his gaze follow her every step and brushed a kiss over the back of her hand as he led her into a dance.

The only concern he had at the moment was that she acted the part of devoted wife so well, and his body didn't appear to care if it was an act or not. It was believing every smile, every brush of their hands and every upward curve of her lips.

His attraction to Susanna was all falseness caused by a lonely bedroom. A man wasn't made to live without a woman's comfort, and yet he saw all around him how well that usually ended. He did not want his life disrupted.

He did the required dancing, perhaps spending more time with her than he should have, but it was all to promote the idea of a true marriage—or so he told himself—and then he stayed at the other side of the room and talked bunions to an elderly man who had a deep interest in them.

He tried to keep his mind from his wife.

He could not think of soft curves, of the tender parts of Susanna. Of how she would feel in his arms. He already felt the pull of his body to hers. But intimacies meant nothing. They were a physical action that would make him feel better temporarily but would add naught inside him—an action that risked far too much and depleted the soul.

He'd assumed it impossible to exist in a celibate life, but he had, refusing to let his body manipulate him. He'd stayed far from the old places he'd visited and poured himself deeper into his studies, bettering himself. He'd not known how his life would turn out, but he'd known that he needed all the knowledge he could amass.

And he was the aberration in his life, but Susanna would help him overcome the resistance to his acceptance.

He was a man who lived among society but was truly an outsider who'd claimed his bloodlines but could not turn his back on the past.

The atmosphere of the event suddenly changed. He heard titters and looked around.

Madeline held a small book with a poem in it that was considered bawdy. Some of the ladies were blushing and an older duchess grumbled. Susanna did what one did in situations like that—she excused herself to the ladies' retiring room.

Quinton listened to the men who'd lowered their voices

so they could comment on the tameness of a poem compared to real experiences.

They muffled their laughter, concealing their statements from the ladies, but no one could have been fooled by the hushed sniggers of the men that they were discussing anything proper.

Quinton noticed an older male leaving, and his senses heightened. He was wandering in the same direction Susanna had taken.

The man appeared familiar. Quinton recognised him from the past, but couldn't place him, positive their encounter hadn't been friendly. Then he remembered. As a youth, Quinton had tossed him from the brothel after he'd caused an uproar. His aunt had been furious that a man from society had acted worse than the lower classes. She didn't allow anyone to abuse the women.

Quinton was behind the man in an instant and followed him from the room.

When the man moved into the hallway and stopped, he still wasn't aware Quinton stood close enough to prevent any sudden lunge forward.

Susanna stepped into the corridor.

Her eyes took in the tableau. She tensed, taking a step back. Then she saw Quinton and she let out a breath of relief. The man turned, following her eye movements. He jumped aside at the look on Quinton's face.

'Sweeting,' Quinton said. 'Is everything fine?'

Susanna introduced Mr Walton.

'It seems you're all right,' the man said to her. 'I just wanted you to know I wish you well, Countess.' Then he nodded to Quinton and hurried away.

After a few moments, she spoke. 'My former father-in-law is detestable.' She shivered.

'He is never to speak with you if you don't wish him to. I'll tell him,' Quinton said grimly. 'And he will listen.'

'It's fine.' She waved away his words.

'Just let me know if he does, and I will take care of it.' Force resided in his voice. 'It will be nothing to me.'

Susanna gazed at him. 'What do you mean?'

'You were afraid when you saw him. I won't let anyone hurt you.'

'Oh,' she said, half laughing. 'I saw him and didn't realise you were here, and for a moment I just thought two men were blocking my exit. I didn't know what was going on. I was very relieved when I saw it was you.'

'I'm so sorry.' Quinton reached out, offering her the haven of his protection. She moved closer. 'I would never ever scare you on purpose. I knew he followed you.'

'Well, I don't like him at all, yet he's all puff and bluff. But we can't go back into the room and appear that we've been fighting,' she said. 'And you appear ready to throttle someone.' Susanna put her hand on his arm.

'I'm fine,' Quinton said. He glanced down at her and decided she might have been calming herself also.

Blast. He'd not experienced such a rush of awareness since he'd seen her dancing down the stairs at home.

Now he didn't want to go back to the soirée.

'Just give me a moment and we'll go back together,' he said. It was important that everyone knew they were getting on well.

'Oh, Quinton,' she said, and gave him a brief kiss before stepping away. 'You will always be my knight.'

He was locked in place.

The smile she gave him spoke of family. Of rainbows he'd never seen before.

'I've mussed you.'

She reached out, adjusting his cravat, then patting his

waistcoat into place; she even put a hand on his chest and used her other to straighten his hair.

'I noticed it in the carriage,' she said. 'But I didn't want to change it. It makes you look so rugged.'

He couldn't say anything.

Standing there letting Susanna fuss over him, he felt completely foxed, but he knew he'd not had more than the one drink.

Then she peered over his shoulder. She spoke softly, eyes shining. 'Madeline was watching. She's gone now,' she whispered.

He felt a part of him had just been amputated.

Turning, he held out his elbow to escort her back into the room. The hallway was empty.

'And I think you're quite a good kisser,' she whispered.

He stopped, and her eyes danced up at him.

'The feeling is mutual, Countess.'

Chapter Nine

The next morning, Quinton woke late and sat in his room after breakfast, stilling his mind to everything, trying to reason himself into keeping his distance from Susanna.

He'd heard enough tales of women falling for the wrong man. In fact, from listening to those tales during his childhood, being the right man seemed to dissuade women from being interested in them. He didn't understand that, but the women who'd worked for his auntie had told so many tales of surrendering their affections to a scoundrel that it had made it much easier for him to be celibate. Having an affection for someone was about the worst thing one could do to keep a friendship.

Susanna had been the most proper wife so far: Appearing when guests arrived. Welcoming them. Making them feel valued, and since they couldn't really boast or jest or ramble on in front of his wife, the visits had been the length of a usual call, and not a settling place.

And if the visitor brought his own spouse, then Susanna stayed in the sitting room, and he'd noticed that as callers lingered longer, she'd been so gracious. And then the other wife would suggest to her husband that they had other visits they must make, and they'd take their leave.

Susanna had lived all her life among society. Her

mother had ties to a duke. True, distant ones, as the young Susanna had explained to him, and then she had told him about the titles the other children would inherit, and had even known that his father's brother would become an earl and had a son.

But more importantly, she'd acted as if she belonged among the elite. Her speech was polished, never slipping into another inflection.

And one of the dolls she'd played with that day had had on clothing that matched hers. His mother's sister had struggled just to see that he had clothing suitable to wear when he visited his uncle.

Now he could more than afford living on his vast estate. He'd offered to find a better house for his mother's sister, but she'd scoffed at him, refusing, and he could see her point. She took in children no one else seemed to care for—ones the prostitutes would tell her about, either their own or from women they knew. But she was happy, and so were the little ones. And his aunt didn't want to live in an area where her neighbours might give the children short shrift.

He rang for Nettie, hating to disturb her, but he wanted her to see that a carriage was readied for him.

Then Quinton heard the squeal outside his window, followed by feminine laughter. He glanced out, but couldn't see her. He heard a screech. More laughter.

He wondered what was happening in the gardens.

The shouts had captured his interest. A celebration he'd not been invited to…in his own gardens. Another squeal.

He stood, tossing the pen onto the desk. The temperature was increasing in the house with the first blast of summertime. Perhaps the shade outdoors would be cooler. He heard a rap on his open doorway and glanced up. Nettie stood there, a basket over her arm.

'Yes?' she asked.

'Could you summon my carriage and let the driver know I'll be a little longer? The weather is so nice today, and it's a bit warm in here. I thought I should go outside to stretch my legs before I leave.'

'Well, you might not be alone. I was taking a basket out for little Christopher to have some treats.'

'That is considerate of you, Nettie. I can take it.'

She left the basket for him, and the twinkle in her eyes said she was happy to do so.

She dashed away before the scent of bread wafted to him, and he grimaced, waving his arm as he tried to dispel the tainted air.

Outside, Quinton held the basket away from himself. At least he'd not had to cook it.

Then he saw Susanna, facing away from him, arms outstretched and appearing a little wobbly. She was wearing some ridiculous cap, her hand reaching out and slapping the air. And Christopher was running around her, dodging—darting one way and the next.

Anger enveloped Quinton. Little Christopher was only trying to jest her into a better spirit, and she was slapping out at her son. He vividly remembered when he'd dodged his mother's physical anger. It had never occurred to him that Susanna might act as his mother had or he wouldn't have brought her into his home.

Christopher was now darting around her in a circle, and she was swinging her arms at him.

He would put a stop to such behaviour. She would not behave so to her child.

He opened his mouth to shout 'Stop,' but then he saw she wasn't wearing a cap but a handkerchief tied over her eyes, and she reached out, caught Christopher and pulled him into a hug, laughing.

She rocked him back and forth and he squirmed, squealing with evident joy.

Blast. Had she lost her senses completely? Had he?

Quinton instinctively moved his head closer, eyes locked on the scene in front of him, making sure he was seeing what he thought he was seeing. He touched his forehead.

'Finally caught my slippery little eel,' she said in triumph, letting Christopher go and then removing the handkerchief.

Then Susanna spotted Quinton watching them. Her cheeks reddened as she dabbed the handkerchief at her face, then tried to brush back the hair that had been disarrayed by the cloth.

'Did you bring us jam and bread?' Christopher asked eagerly, and ran to the container.

Quinton gave Christopher the basket, and the boy took it, then scurried to his mother, giving it to her. He selected one of the rolls and held it up. 'I'm a slippery eel eating, and I'm going to hide under the bridge.' Then he ran to the garden bench and knelt under it, nibbling away at the bread.

She held out the basket to Quinton. 'Would you...'

The last thing in the world Quinton wanted was bread, but he took a roll. 'Thank you.'

'I didn't realise you were still home,' she said. Little frazzles of hair framed her face, and she reminded him of the little girl who'd lined up her dolls so carefully. 'We were just playing a game he likes. I hope we were not too loud.'

'No. Of course not.' He spoke softly, and he wondered if his betraying senses were causing him to murmur as an excuse to shorten the distance between them. He stopped moving. 'Could you see from under the handkerchief?'

She grinned and made a shushing motion with her lips,

and the rest of the distance between them diminished. She touched his sleeve, capturing him with her attention. 'It's one of his favourite pastimes.'

Then she shut her eyes briefly, moving closer so her soft words could be heard only by him. 'Although I confess I do sometimes get a bit tired of it.'

'You and Amesbury can have the bench, Mother,' Christopher called out. 'I'm going to leave some crumbs in case there's rabbits and birds and foxes and owls, but none for spiders so don't worry…'

Then he ran to the edge of the gardens, tearing the rest of his roll into tiny pieces.

Quinton watched the boy but his attention was on Susanna. He could smell her soap, a cleanliness purer than anything he'd ever sensed.

'Can you feed my roll to the birds, also?' Quinton called out, and Christopher darted forward, taking it and scurrying back to tear it into small pieces.

'I don't really like bread very much,' he said, content to stand beside her and savour the moment of new sensations.

The world had tilted when he'd seen Susanna slapping the air, only it hadn't been from anger, but so she could play a well-loved game with her child.

It wasn't that he'd never seen a woman caring for her child. He'd even delivered quite a few children when the midwife couldn't be found in time, and he'd noted that each birth was different. Each mother.

He was standing like a fool, more aware of the woman beside him than he'd ever been of anyone or anything.

He had to get away. He couldn't fall into some web sprinkled with fairy dust that had tentacles, some dream that only he could feel or see.

'Amesbury. Mother doesn't let me run in the house so I have to chase her outside. I race well, though. Look!'

The little boy ran from tree to tree and repeated the movement. 'I'm running fast. Faster than you can run.'

Then he paused. 'Race with me, Mother.'

'Very well,' she said.

She put the container onto the ground, nestling it into the grass.

She waved to Christopher. 'Come here.' She pointed. 'But stop there.' She indicated the basket. 'Whoever fetches it wins. And Quinton can play as well.'

'I don't think so.'

He heard a squeak of disapproval from her. 'You can shout *go*. Your job will be to shout *go*. Whoever picks up the basket wins.'

'Go?' Quinton said. 'That is my *job*?'

'Yes.' She clasped her hands, eyes wide. 'Is that too taxing for you?'

'Perhaps I should practise first, to see if I can get it right,' Quinton said. He touched his cravat.

She batted away his words with a flick of her wrist. 'I will let you know.'

Christopher touched his tongue to the corner of his mouth and bent his knees. 'I'm ready.'

Susanna lifted the sides of her dress and bent her knees like Christopher. 'I'm ready.'

Quinton watched her. Sunshine in human form, with golden laughter that would make even the poorest man feel wealthy.

His wife. He felt proud, then defeated. He'd seen how emotional encounters ended. The women had cried buckets of tears to him about men they'd once loved who'd abandoned them, and then they'd cursed the men. So much for love.

But he and Susanna were just playing a simple children's game, and it would go no further.

'On the count of three,' he said.

They found their places. 'One. Two. Two and a half.' They both started. Susanna stopped. Christopher surged ahead and grabbed the basket, and Susanna's lips turned sideways. A teasing little swirl of displeasure—and challenge—sparkled in the eyes that viewed Quinton.

'I was practising that time. Pardon,' he said with a teasing wink.

She put her hands on her hips. 'You didn't say three. It doesn't count. That is not fair, Quinton.'

'I'm counting it,' Christopher said, 'but we can race again.'

'So, Countess Sunshine, are you quite ready?'

Susanna's mouth opened and her eyes widened.

Quinton cupped a hand at his ear. 'I think I heard a yes, and I know I didn't hear a no from Lady Amesbury. Did I?'

'You didn't,' she admitted, cheeks brighter.

'Get ready for the next time,' Quinton said.

Susanna lifted her skirt a few inches, then kicked a hatpin-sized stick out of the way. She crouched, her dress accentuating her bottom in a way that made Quinton nearly forget how to count. Quinton said, slowly, 'I will count to three this time, but you must listen and pay attention.' Her dress tightened more.

'One.' He waited. 'Two.' It wiggled faster. 'Six.'

She glared at him.

He smiled. 'My error. Apologies again... Three.'

She ran. They both reached the basket at the same time, but he could see she let Christopher grab it.

A lock of her hair fell out of her plait, brushing past her view. She put it back into place.

'You race with us this time, Quinton,' Susanna said.

Quinton peered at Susanna, flushed from running, and he felt an answering awareness.

'I'm afraid I need to be on my way.'

'Sounds to me as if he's afraid we'll both outdistance him.' She half closed one eye and peered at him.

'I should be seeing a patient.'

'An excuse,' she said, then sighed and glanced at her child. 'Can you believe that?'

She lowered her lids and challenged Quinton. 'It would be hurtful for you to be beaten by the both of us, neither of us nearly so tall as you.' She grabbed the sides of her skirt in both hands and lifted it a tiny bit. 'And you wearing boots and me wearing these floppy slippers.'

'It doesn't have anything to do with footwear, it has to do with leg length,' he said.

She turned to her son. 'We will run with him once just like your grandfather taught us. Just like Grandfather does.'

Christopher bit his lip, eyes smiling, then said to him, 'I can run faster than my grandfather.'

'My legs are longer,' Quinton said. 'If you wish to take the chance, we will compete—truly race. But I will not let you win. Trust me. I will get to that basket first.'

'We are a team, so you will have to challenge both of us. And a wager might be in order.'

'A wager?' he asked.

'Yes. The winner gets to ask Cook to cook a special treat of his or her choice.' Her eyes turned to Christopher. 'And I will run like Grandfather.'

Her son giggled.

'Sounds like a challenge,' he said. But it wasn't. He already knew the outcome. Besides, she could already ask Cook to fix a special meal. But he was not going to forfeit the game. He would get the basket, dart out of the garden, around the corner of the house and take the basket to the carriage with him and see the patient. 'But I must bid you farewell in advance.'

He lowered his chin and met her tough pose with an exaggerated stare of his own. 'In place. On three.'

He let them get ready, then put one boot behind the other, and said, 'One. Two—'

At the same moment he said *two,* she called out.

'Three,' Susanna shouted, jumping to block his path. 'Run Christopher.'

Quinton darted sideways, but Susanna threw herself in front of Quinton, arms outstretched. 'Run Christopher,' she shouted again, preventing Quinton from moving forward. 'Get the basket.'

Little legs scurried, but it was the dancing woman in front of him who dazed him, wrapping her hands around his arm and ploughing into him almost head first but then twisting and corralling him. 'I've caught him.'

She hung onto his arm like a trap and his brain stopped functioning normally. She didn't even look at him but called out to her son, 'Get it, Christopher. Get it.' She pulled at him and she stumbled. He caught her waist.

If he could have raised his arm, he would have lifted her off her feet, but she had him trapped with all the strength of a woman's body.

Christopher grabbed the basket and held it. 'That's how Grandfather races. He doesn't run.'

'Christopher won. I won. And somebody lost. Who would that be?' The eyes gazing at him made him forget his name. 'Unfortunately, you didn't make the rule of no cheating, so we were allowed.'

She was still pressed against him, doing a little victory dance.

'Defeat, Quinton. How does it feel?' Chin out, she challenged.

Pretty damn good.

'I think I need to summon the magistrate and tell him two highwaymen are in the area,' he said drily.

'Let's do it again,' Christopher said, jumping up and down.

'I dare you,' Quinton teased. But she must have seen something in his eyes because hers darted away.

'I will happily settle for one victory. Well, two. Mine and Christopher's.'

'And I will expect the highwaymen to share some of their treat with me.' Quinton left his hand at Susanna's waist a moment more.

'We did not agree to that.' She moved away.

'I need to go see a patient.'

Christopher tugged at Susanna's arm. 'Mother. Let's run again.'

Susanna glanced at Quinton.

It could become such a bad habit. 'Enjoy today,' he said, remembering the waiting vehicle.

'You too,' she whispered.

He needed to leave. The sunshine was affecting his intellect and working its way into his body. He'd never known the sun to be able to arouse a man, but it was. And making him more than lightheaded. Blast it. It seemed there was no simple cure.

Unless it was with Susanna. He imagined kissing her. Hell, he knew where that led. To ridiculous claims of love. To manipulation. To a ruined home.

Christopher caught her left hand, pulling her, but her right hand reached out and scorched Quinton's arm with her touch, and the impulses he'd all but extinguished in his body reignited.

Chapter Ten

Susanna sat at her dressing table, lifted the bottle of the perfume she'd not yet worn, tried to decide if she still liked the fragrance and wondered if Quinton would like it.

She always liked this time of night, although the dim room made the silence seemed more pronounced but peaceful, more secure than she'd expected. More alone than she'd ever been, but still…peaceful.

In addition to the nursery, and quarters for Celeste, she had a sitting room all her own, a bedroom, and an L-shaped dressing area, which she assumed had been added when the house had been enlarged.

The rooms were bigger than at her parents', and sounds didn't truly echo, but the walls absorbed and changed noises, in some spaces turning them into a hush, and in others, increasing them.

A tiny tap sounded on her door, and she called out to enter.

Nettie stood there. 'My lady, Lord Amesbury asks if you are awake whether you would visit him in the sitting room so he may talk with you?'

'Of course,' Susanna said, trying to make her voice sound like the mistress of the estate. 'You must send a maid to help me get dressed.' Then she stared in the mirror. 'And redo my hair. I already plaited it.'

'Um,' Nettie said, staring at her, eyes puzzled. 'I can assist you, my lady. But I don't think it's necessary. And he truly doesn't like to wait.'

Then Susanna remembered the other night. Quinton had already seen her with her hair down, and in her dressing gown.

'Will you ask Amesbury if it is acceptable to him if I visit as I am?' she asked.

'My lady.' The woman almost bowed her head, and Susanna was certain she saw a smile trying to escape. 'He's a physician. He has… He is… I think he will not mind that you are in a lovely dressing gown that covers you from head to toe. And your hair… The plait is most stylish for this time of the evening at home.'

Susanna let out a deep breath. 'If you are sure—' She stood without waiting for an answer. 'I will tell him myself that I will see him.'

Nettie darted away, and Susanna was fairly sure the woman was now fighting laughter.

She swallowed and moved to her dressing table, gazed at her reflection in the mirror, then left to find Quinton.

The door to his private sitting room was open, and she saw him hesitate when she walked inside.

Quinton's cravat had one neat, precise tie in it, and he could have stood in anyone's grand house in London and appeared at home. He could have stepped into the poorest hovel and been comfortable.

Susanna felt the heat in her cheeks as the soft rumble in Quinton's greeting rolled over her. She averted her gaze to study the pattern on the rug and distract herself for a moment.

He had the tiniest crinkles around his eyes.

She felt an unfamiliar tickle that heated her chest and didn't seem to want to stay in one place. She fought to push it aside. Those kinds of emotions had done her no favours in the past and she didn't want them muddling her life now that she was in Quinton's home.

She studied him—really scrutinised him. The determined stare. The strong jaw. A stance that made her insides liquid. He was in his shirtsleeves, but he still wore his waistcoat and cravat.

She could smell the manly scent of him mixed with the lighter aroma of shaving soap. She could see the gentleness in his appearance, but at that moment, she didn't care about the softer side of him.

She hated that she recognised Quinton's masculinity. It would not do.

She didn't know if she was losing herself again. She could not risk making another error much harder to recover from than marriage to her first husband had been.

She needed to increase the distance between them, but she could only do the opposite. He was her husband. She shouldn't feel she was being brazen by standing as near to him as she would anyone else. But she did.

'I apologise for not being dressed.'

'You're dressed.' His eyes widened. 'Completely. Don't concern yourself.'

She noticed his direct appraisal.

'I know you want a proper household,' she said.

'Yes. And you are.'

'Thank you.' She tugged at her dressing gown tie.

He flexed his jaw and let out an audible breath. 'Did your parents ever discuss my ancestry?'

'Not truly, though I did see the Earl's wife on occasion,' she said. 'She did mention your father going to fight and the last battle caused him to have frightful dreams. If not for your cousin passing on, you wouldn't have inherited. An original title was awarded for bravery in battle—'

'Wait,' he interrupted.

Now he understood why she'd seemed apologetic even though she was completely covered.

'And on my mother's side?' he asked.

'No. I don't think so.' She apologised with her eyes. 'My mother didn't speak with me much about people not of the peerage.'

'I would have thought my ancestry always a topic for conversation.' He shrugged. 'I suppose the laugh is on me.'

She didn't respond.

'Did you know I half grew up in a brothel?' he asked.

For a moment, he thought he might have shocked her into some sort of apoplexy, until she started breathing again.

'I suppose not,' he said.

'Are you jesting?'

'Not entirely. But I was comfortable there. I sometimes tidied up rooms for them if someone was ill. They made certain I had food when I needed it. One even taught me the alphabet. She was pleased she could read. A lot of them couldn't, except the bawd.'

'A bawd?'

'She took care of the lightskirts. If you want to call it taking care of them.'

If she had looked shocked at his disclosure at first, now she looked devastated. But she needed to know. He'd assumed she already knew. He'd not tried to hide it. 'Most people know, I am sure of it. I thought everyone knew.'

She didn't say anything.

'I was told that my father left London to fight because

he preferred fighting others instead of my mother. He wasn't pleased with my mother's behaviour, and when he returned, he drank a lot and they never lived together again. In my lifetime, her actions only worsened. She had a protector at first, but she never lasted long with anyone she took up with.'

'He just left you behind?'

'I don't ever remember seeing him many times when I was young, so I don't know that he left me behind, or just left.'

He would give her time to think about the information. 'I would have mentioned it before we married if I'd known you hadn't been told.' At least, he hoped he would have. He'd never hidden from his family's history, but then he'd only proposed once and he'd not given it a tremendous amount of thought.

She put hand on her cheek, her little finger over her open mouth. 'You don't even swear.'

'Not out loud. Usually.'

'A real brothel?'

'Yes. I'm fairly certain.'

'I wondered why you didn't have a butler. You're used to living in a house with all women.'

'I suppose so.'

'Was it rough?'

He shrugged. 'About the same as university.'

'Oh.'

'Being on the streets was most dangerous, but I knew how to handle it. I'd grown up there. I was fast on my feet as a child and could usually outthink any danger.'

She studied him.

'Does that change your feelings about living here?' he asked.

'No.' She stared at him, as if she couldn't understand

the question. 'It's a mansion, with candleholders that could have been a gift from the king. I have my own floor of rooms.' She raised her chin. 'No one has entered my storey without my permission. I feel free. I can do as I wish for the first time in my life.'

He moved half a step closer, expression intent.

'Free? Do you aspire to take a lover?' he asked roughly.

Her gaze widened and her nose wrinkled. 'I'm married.'

'What does that have to do with it? Are you going to pursue a lover?' he repeated.

She shrugged, then shook her head and shuddered. 'That didn't work out so well the first time. I married him.'

'Wasn't that what you expected?'

She peered at the ceiling for a brief second. 'Yes. It was, I suppose. I was so deeply in love. My whole being revolved around him. I was not using my head.'

His laugh was rueful. 'You were in love. What did you expect?'

'Are you making light of my marriage? I assure you it was nothing to laugh about.'

'No. Love.'

'It can be troublesome.'

'Yes.'

'You've been in love?'

'No. Of course not. The ladies at the brothel said love does more harm than good, and I agree.'

'I don't.'

'It's an ailment, but one that time always cures.'

'I cannot believe you would say such a thing, and you are supposed to be the best physician in London.'

'It's how I'm usually introduced to anyone. I never contradict them.' He apologised with a laugh. 'I think "Poor London."'

'You must be the most modest man I've ever met.'

He indicated a framed saying on the wall, the saying he liked above others. '*Primum Non Nocere.* First do no harm. That is the Latin phrase I try to use most, not just in my medical world but the rest of the world as well.'

She nodded. 'It's a good saying.'

'The reason I wanted to speak with you is that I wanted to ask you what you thought of this.' He held out a note for her to read from her mother, inviting them to visit and mentioning her father was unwell again.

'Mmm.' She moved suddenly, taking the paper and glancing at it, studying it long enough to read it twice. 'I want to think about it.'

He was pleased she didn't seem overly concerned for her father; he wasn't either, but it never hurt to make certain. She kept it in her hand.

'Fine,' he said.

She left the room, but he didn't feel right about her answer. Following her, Quinton called out, 'If we do go, we should leave first thing in the morning, but I need to see a patient first.'

'Oh, yes. Of course.'

'Is it acceptable to you if I take Christopher with me?'

She paused, giving him a chance to catch up, still clutching the note. 'You want him to see a patient?'

'A soldier. He has a few aches and pains, but he's a gentle person with a good heart. He's recovered but his wounds never will. We could leave after that to see your parents—just to make your mother feel better, I expect.'

'My mother. A visit to my mother. Yes, you may take Christopher to see your patient first, and I'll be waiting when you return. A trip out in the morning will likely make him tired, so he can stay with Celeste instead of going with us.'

He took the note from her hand, stepping back and folding it before slipping it into his coat pocket.

'It will possibly take several hours, and we can leave for your mother and father's right after I get home.'

She paced. Quinton and Christopher were late back from visiting the soldier. Very late.

She paced longer.

This was the kind of thing she would have expected from Walton—never being on time anywhere she planned to go. In fact, forgetting about her completely.

But this was important. Quinton had her son with him.

Oh, she should never have let Christopher go.

Quinton had said he'd grown up in a brothel. He must have been mistaken. Perhaps he'd known a woman who was a lightskirt and he'd considered that a brothel.

Yet, she still asked Nettie if he was normally late. She said not to worry. He was the best physician in London and that meant he often stayed longer to make sure his patients were fine.

'Do you think…' She started to ask Nettie about Quinton's thoughts of being raised in a bad place, but in truth, she knew he had grown up among toughs. He had told her tales several times when they were younger—tales of roughness. She'd thought him exaggerating a bit, but perhaps he'd not been.

And then Nettie said she would take Susanna a cup of tea to her room. Susanna declined. She would wait by the front door and insisted Nettie let her wait alone.

Susanna stood at the entrance, tensing each time a carriage rolled by. Finally, Quinton's carriage appeared.

Christopher jumped out and ran to the house. Susanna opened the door, and Christopher ran towards her.

'Mother, I don't want to grow up to be a soldier. I saw

a man with a walking stick and his leg hurts. Now, I want to be a physician.' Christopher ran through the doorway and stopped in front of her, bouncing in his excitement.

'Wonderful,' she said, relieved they were home, her smile firmly in place.

'Amesbury straightened a lady's nose,' Christopher said, stopping in front of her. 'He took his hands and—' He clasped his palms together, made a sharp right twist, tightened his teeth and made a breaking sound.

Quinton stepped in behind Christopher. His cravat was askew and had a brown spot on it. His waistcoat also had a spot of brown, and his hair was rumpled.

'You took him to see something like that?' Her voice rose.

Quinton blinked, his answer concise. 'Yes.'

She opened her mouth and took a second to speak. 'I can't believe you did that.'

'It was loud,' Christopher added, then his voice calmed. 'She screamed.' He put his hands over his ears.

'You let him see a patient's agony?'

Quinton nodded. 'We were out when someone saw my coach and waved for us to stop. It happens a lot when I am in the stews. Almost every time.'

'You—' Words escaped her.

'Amesbury says I might have to help someone when I grow up. The woman was happy. She fell down the stairs because her cane tripped her by surprise. Amesbury promised to take her a confection. And he told her she had to stop crying because sniffling wasn't good for her nose.'

'He's only a little boy,' she spoke to Quinton.

'I did not exactly plan for it to happen.'

Susanna averted her gaze to the window, unease wafting over her. She didn't know if it was because her son had seen something bad and been where she'd not expected him to go, or because he was growing up and would be out in the world—or even the realisation that she truly was wed and her husband could again go about as he wished and not keep her informed, and that could lead to all sorts of misbehaviour on his part.

Quinton truly didn't have to ask her about what he did. They'd had no agreement on that. And he still went to dangerous areas. He could be hurt himself.

'Can we visit the hurt woman again?' Christopher asked Quinton. 'I want to see her nose.'

'I will stop in on her tomorrow after I bring your mother home from your grandparents',' Quinton's voice rumbled. 'It will depend on your mother whether you can go or not.'

'I'm going to be just like Amesbury.' He put his hands together and again demonstrated the nose being adjusted and made popping noises. Quinton frowned and walked on.

Susanna bit the inside of her lip. Return tomorrow? She'd not realised they would be staying overnight with her parents. She'd have to ready some things quickly. If only it had been possible for her to learn to read, she would have been able to grasp what the note had actually said.

Quinton had been raised in a brothel and had not only acquired an ability to read, but also could understand Latin. He would think her an unsuitable mother if he knew she couldn't read, and she didn't want him to risk thinking her son had inherited the flaw she had. That wasn't fair to Christopher.

Her first marriage had been a disaster, and if she had kept the secret from Walton, perhaps he would have trusted her more when she'd told him that his father was using them all. But he had laughed in her face.

'Tell Celeste she is to watch over you tonight.' Susanna looked at her son and kept her voice soft. 'And tell her about the woman's nose and ask if she can find a treat from the kitchen for you. I need to speak with Amesbury.'

Quinton's head gave a quick snap to her, and his lips were firm. He'd heard the tension in her voice.

She smiled briefly at him, and he smiled back, and she could almost hear the click of their gazes locking.

Chapter Eleven

'I have to go to my room.' Quinton was aware of Susanna scurrying along behind him. Blazes. He had to change his waistcoat and cravat. Plus, he'd just had to listen to screams that were decidedly painful for both the woman and himself.

He'd learned with his mother that it was best to let another person's fury reside on its own, to give a soothing answer and try not to draw disagreements out.

Yes, they were going to be leaving later than they'd planned, and no, he couldn't do anything about it.

'How may I assist you?' he said when he reached the door.

'Christopher has been to the stews.' She raised her chin. 'I don't want him going there. It's not safe for a little boy.'

With one sentence, she'd ignited the brimstone of his life and thrust him into it. He spun away, the burning coals barely able to be contained. He'd thought he had toughened up enough to dust away any thoughtless or unkind words, but he'd been wrong.

He clamped his jaw tight and shut his eyes, taking in

a breath as he felt the flames. Where did she think he'd spent his entire childhood?

'Quinton,' she pressed. 'Quinton? We must talk about it.'

He fought the hot coals, extinguishing them.

He opened the door to his private sitting room, swung his arm wide and motioned her in.

He discerned her tension and the grim lips. He would have preferred not to have the next conversation, but no matter.

She moved inside and he shut the door.

'Out with it. You don't have to mince your words with me. I grew up in those stews myself.'

'You cannot understand.' She gasped in a breath. 'I don't know why I expected you to.'

Yes, he'd been mostly raised in a brothel, and that was that. She needed to stop being so sensitive. The world was not all perfume and nosegays.

At least his world hadn't been.

Quinton clasped the top button on his coat, unfastening it. Then he undid the second button, and the third.

'And how may I change the past for my wife?' He watched her reaction to the biting words—a bit of shock. 'Yes. We are married. I was there. I can attest to it.'

Her attention flickered to his hand. Then she averted her gaze.

In that instant, awareness flooded into him that he'd never discarded his coat in front of Susanna and they'd been married a fortnight.

He unbuttoned the fourth fastening with a flourish and lifted the garment's lapel from his waistcoat before tossing it onto the sofa. He could take off his own coat in his own home in front of his own wife.

She stared at the floor. He refused to ask her if she'd

never seen such an appealing rug before because she did seem to want to look at it.

'It's a rug, Susanna. It's under our feet every day. We walk on them to get to better things. That is what people do all the time. We must be aware of what is in front of us that we can grasp. Not what is behind us that we can't change. We should take care of what is beneath us and not destroy it, as just because it is under our feet doesn't mean it doesn't matter.'

'Did you learn that at university?'

'From one of the women who came to live at the brothel but was offered different employment which she preferred.' He did not tell her the woman's name: Nettie.

She took in a breath and stood tall.

He pointed to the sampler he'd paid one of the ladies to sew for him. 'I've mentioned it before.'

She stared at him, lips tightening.

'*Primum Non Nocere*. First do no harm. I think it should be in all homes. In all lives.'

'Do you read Latin well?' She spoke slowly, almost as if she felt the words.

'Of course.'

'And you say you grew up in—'

'I had a home, but it wasn't that far from the ladies, and I knew I could go there whenever I didn't know what to do next. Whenever I needed something—like food.'

He slipped his waistcoat off. He remembered how his mother had left his baby brother in his care when he'd not been much older than Christopher. She'd told him he must take care of his brother. Not that it mattered. He'd always watched over Eldon.

Then his mother just left them. Auntie had visited, and said he was doing as good a job of caring for Eldon as she could. One day his aunt told him his mother had died, and said she was going to do some travelling, and if anyone came looking for her not to help them. It had been months before she had returned. Later she'd told him there'd been a fight between his mother and a man, and his mother hadn't won. Then there'd been another fight, this time between the same man and Auntie, and Auntie had feared the man might not survive so she'd left, letting things calm down.

He'd never hidden his past, but he'd never dwelled on it either. No one could hurt him with it if it was out in the open. Besides, the other students at university had been in awe of it.

'I started at an early age taking care of my brother, and I've always taken care of people—when I didn't pick their pockets.' He shrugged away her surprise and held up his hand, rubbing his thumb against his fingertips. 'The only skill my mother ever taught me.'

Susanna seemed not to know if he told the truth or not.

He stepped away and found a fresh cravat in the dressing area and a different waistcoat. He returned to the sitting room, put the waistcoat on the sofa and slipped the cravat around his neck while holding his collar out of the way. He deftly tied a simple knot; he didn't need frills.

'You distract the victim. Either with pressure—movement—conversation. I tried it the first time I met the Earl... I was a youngster and I didn't know who he was, except he claimed to be my uncle—my father's elder brother.'

He donned the waistcoat, buttoning it as he spoke.

Quinton had known opportunity when it stepped over the door frame, only he'd interpreted the prospect wrongly. 'I lifted Eldon and held him out, jostling him, and I wagered my uncle's right waistcoat pocket would be the one with his purse. He'd had no choice but to take

Eldon. I picked his pocket.' He laughed. 'Hardly worth it. I expected him to carry more funds.'

But the clasp on the purse had been made of silver. He'd had a rough time deciding whether to try to melt it down or if he could get more to sell it as it was.

He'd found his auntie, thinking she'd be pleased. His aunt had informed him he'd made a horrible, horrible mistake, and had gone on for hours and hours and hours about unwritten rules in life and starvation and little fools and people who could help. Then he'd found out that his uncle had sometimes sent funds for him. She'd said his uncle, whom she'd called a cantankerous old fool, was the only halfway decent person in his life, and he must return the purse with every penny intact.

'I found my uncle's house and talked the butler into letting me wait for him. I returned the purse, told him he must have lost it when I handed him Eldon. We both knew *how* he lost it.'

His uncle hadn't said a word except to tell him to get out, and Quinton had bowed and left.

He'd been proud when he walked home—like a man. Returning the takings had felt so much better than stealing it. He'd never done anything dishonest ever again.

'I never contemplated him having anything to do with me. But later he returned and invited me to a picnic. He told me I had to clean up, and if I stole from any of his friends, he would personally see that I was going to gaol and I would not be in the first group to the noose but would have to wait until the last and watch everyone else until it was my turn. I believed him.'

Quinton had tried to keep out of view of everyone at the picnic. At the end of that event, his uncle had offered to let Quinton live with him, but he couldn't bring 'the bastard brat' with him.

Quinton had refused to leave Eldon.

His uncle had shouted, then sent him back to the stews, but Quinton hadn't cared. Eldon was his brother.

About six months later, his uncle found him again. Questioned him. Annoyed him. And his uncle had started inviting him to dinner on occasion, or rather, telling him what time to be at his house. And he'd given him books.

He said if Quinton sold the books, he could spend the rest of his life in the stews. But if he learned the information within and returned the volumes to the butler, he'd get more, and a true education. He was a Langford, after all. He said Quinton had a choice between becoming a barrister or a solicitor or a decoration at the end of a rope.

Quinton had barely been able to understand the books, and he'd had to learn quickly. 'My auntie was a survivor and she taught me to be, too. I always called her "Auntie" because she didn't want anyone knowing her real name.' He shrugged. 'A lot of people in my life didn't want anyone knowing their name, but a few didn't mind. Auntie even paid one of the prostitutes to tutor me in reading.'

'A lightskirt?'

'Yes.'

'Are you certain?'

He studied her. He thought a bit. 'I'm certain.' His lips firmed on the last word.

She watched him lift his coat and put it on. He rather reminded her of a rector. It did not seem at all possible that Quinton had grown up in a brothel. He just did not appear that way. True, it did appear as though he could have been visiting one in his unkempt state when the carriage brought him home some evenings. But he fit in among the Ton so easily. He was even rather prudish when he was with her, as if he had ricocheted from the brothel to sainthood.

'You grew up in such a place, and yet we do not have intimacies in our marriage?'

His blink was a strong indication of banked emotions. 'I don't know what unpleasantness it might release in our home.' He put his hand behind his neck and rubbed it. 'Having intimacy with a woman has never brought me closer to her. It has always lessened her in my mind.'

'Lessen? Is that possible?'

'Very. Think of your marriage. You did not grow closer to Walton, did you?'

'But—'

'You are growing every day in my estimation. No one else would I choose to share my life with.'

'Yet you don't want to—'

'Risk what I have.'

'Oh.' A quiet word. 'I understand. I do not want to risk losing anything either. One more quick question—' she put a finger to her bottom lip '—do you…"visit" your old friends occasionally?' She slipped that in—quietly, softly and with the subtlety of a blacksmith's hammer striking a forged metal.

His hand dropped from the back of his neck and he drew himself up, examining her, but his voice held no ire. 'You think I—' hhe touched his chest '—might have to pay for a woman's favours?'

'Well, I assumed you're getting favours from somewhere.' She pretended an examination of a picture on the wall, but quickly returned her glance to him.

She couldn't help it. He pulled her gaze more than anyone ever had.

'Sweet Susanna, that might be a question of a rather personal nature.'

'I never said it wasn't.' She drew her shoulders forward a second and then gave half a shrug. 'And you said I could ask anything.'

'I meant it. That is a far more innocent question than most I have received.'

Fingers bent, he rested his thumb near his mouth. 'I'm not a virgin, if that's what you're asking.'

She drew herself up, blinked and then crossed her arms, a high tilt to her chin. 'Neither am I...in case you were wondering.'

'I figured that out when I realised you had a son. I'm a physician. I'm trained to watch for such things.'

'So do you visit the friends from your past?'

'Never as a customer. I do not pay.' He let out a deep breath. 'I never thought to pay for anything offered to me at no cost.'

He paused. 'Once, Auntie found me at the brothel when I'd decided to...partake, and gave me the only backhanded slap from her I ever received. Then she tossed the lady out.' He sighed. 'I never returned to the place. I didn't want anyone else hurt.'

'But have you visited...recently?'

'I have friends there, and they were at times, good friends, but in case you are wondering, as you seem to be, I am not visiting a brothel for intimacies, or having any other kind of encounter with another person that might even raise a brow.'

He held up a finger. 'I've never, ever paid for a woman's touch. I just paid attention. That is a currency, though not always as valuable as coin to them. But I have given them funds on occasion. I simply kept them from having to work for a few hours. To laugh with them. To eat with them. I paid,' he said, 'to have the life around me I wanted. I'd decided money could buy anything.'

'But what about love? Everyone wants affection—a sincere love.'

'You're jesting.'

'Well, I thought I was in love once,' she whispered.

'And see what happened. The word *love* is really a tool to get someone to do something you want them to do. It is a jest.'

'You're not, um, spending time in someone's bed?' she asked, repeating herself but unable to stop.

'No. Nor anywhere else, for what might nicely be called relations.' He shrugged. 'It's hard to think of the gentle words for what we are discussing. The crude ones come to mind, but I have tried to polish my thoughts as I polished my manners.'

'Truly?'

'Yes.' He buttoned his coat. 'I'd had quick encounters as I matured. The lads at university wanted those type of relations with women, and I had seen too much of that. I wanted something far harder to receive, society ways, and yet, it was given me the opportunity to have it.'

He glanced around the room. 'See what I have now. Everything. Everything a man could want. A household. A family. I have it all, and that is what I wanted. I don't want to lose one fragment of it. The tidiness. The cleanliness. The peacefulness. And I have a wife who is a society jewel.'

'Are you forgetting about my disastrous first marriage?'

'No. You're still a society jewel regardless of Walton. I have eyes. People respond to you. You make them happier simply by bestowing a smile on them.'

'You are mistaken.'

'No. I'm not. But we should be going. I expect Nettie

is making sure the carriage driver has something to eat, but he will want to get home to his family also.'

'Of course.'

A chuckle burst from him. 'If you have any other questions, at any time of day, feel free to ask.'

'I suppose you could not stop me.' She peered at him with challenge.

'I would not try to.'

His voice held a reassurance that made her feel lighter, and she believed she could ask him anything, and more importantly, trust his answer.

'We must be on our way,' he said, losing his smile. 'If you've no other questions.'

'Do you miss having intimacies?'

'I didn't say I had to answer,' he said coolly, reaching for his valise.

Quinton could not risk destroying the serenity around him, and he didn't know what remained inside him that could devastate his new-found family world—the one which was better than he'd ever imagined.

He was exhausted, and his willpower was suffering. Last night had felt like the longest since he'd taken that vow of chasteness. At the time, the blasted vow had seemed like a wonderful idea.

Quinton studied the room. His life. His wife. He wanted to keep the serenity around him. He must. He'd seen too much of the uproar that was caused by misplaced passion. The senselessness. The foolishness. The women truly ruined. The men genuinely as lost as the women.

He had no idea what might be set free if he held her close.

For years, he had worked to embrace celibacy instead of a woman who did not hold him dear. He had promised himself he would never again lie in a bed with a woman who didn't feel an emotion he could not believe existed.

But the demons of desire were collecting around him, panting, reminding him of what he could feel.

Only the reminder of the meaninglessness of the encounters kept him safe. He might die if he awoke from a night with Susanna and discovered that she'd added him as a meaningless conquest.

He had to remain vigilant.

Against his number one and only true adversary.

Himself.

His task was not to desire her. Well, that battle had been well and truly lost.

She stared at the valise. He realised her things might be heavy and put the case down. 'I'll fetch your bags.'

'I can bring them.'

'I'll just go to the top of the stairs,' he said, irritated that she didn't seem content to let him merely collect her things. He'd stayed away from her area as he'd promised.

'It will be fine,' she said, lips tight. 'If you will just wait on me, I will be right there.'

Well, he would keep his word.

But just because he'd lived in those stews it didn't mean he couldn't be trusted.

He had the family around him that was many times over better than what he could have dreamed of.

He'd married one of the beautiful Adair sisters.

And he didn't have to concern himself about someone else's child being passed off as his own as they didn't share a bed.

Sometimes he did not believe his fiendish good fortune.

Chapter Twelve

Quinton waited for her in the vehicle. She was being fussy in his opinion, and he wasn't happy about it. Apparently, she was taking her time to punish him.

Finally, she rushed out with her portmanteau.

He stepped out and took it from her to lift into the carriage, but noticed it wasn't closed well, so he fastened it and slipped the strap through the buckle. It was as if she'd waited until the last minute to gather her things.

He expected her to sit facing backwards, but instead she sat beside him. Blast—she was feminine from the curve of her lashes to the fullness of her lips to the delicacy of her hands.

She didn't have to try. She woke up that way and went to sleep that way. He was certain of it.

He really had chosen perfection for a wife. But not perfection for celibacy.

She wasn't wearing a shawl or spencer, and he doubted one would have fit in the portmanteau with the clothing she would need. It could be cold in the mornings and evenings, and likely they would return later in the day. Her parents had invited them for the night.

He hoped the carriage driver had done as asked with

the new blanket. If the weather turned cool, keeping her warm all the way home would be cruel to his own body. But he would make the sacrifice.

Perhaps the blanket hadn't been added. He might not mind holding her close.

'Don't worry; I don't think it's anything serious,' he said.

'What isn't?' she asked, voice short.

'Your father's condition.'

'It's not serious?' she repeated, then seemed to catch herself, and shrugged away her own words. 'I didn't think it was.'

She peered out the window. 'What do you think is wrong with him?'

'From your mother's letter, it sounds as if he's been trying to help the workmen too much and isn't taking time to recover.'

Although, Quinton had wondered if it was a ruse by her mother to have them visit. He hoped so.

'Oh.'

He was confused. It almost seemed she didn't know her mother had invited them to spend the night or that her father was struggling. She'd read the letter he'd given her slowly but the light had been dim in his room.

Or maybe she hadn't been able to read the letter at all...

A lot of the lightskirts didn't read, but it was unusual for a woman of society not to. She should have been taught.

'You're fairly certain it's not serious?' she asked.

'Yes. But I won't know until I examine him.'

In fact, she was watching out the window, and sunshine was flickering onto her face, yet she didn't seem any more concerned about her complexion than a child would be. But her skin was perfect. He'd never before noticed how truly unspoilt she appeared. She'd not even brought a bonnet. Or gloves.

She settled, fluffing about, getting comfortable and relaxing.

His memory tweaked. 'What word did Christopher call Celeste that he had to sit in the corner for?' And that Susanna had, apparently, also called her son.

He wanted to hear it from her lips—to hear the rudeness, the unpleasantness, and remind himself not to be taken in by the illusion of kindness and patience.

She shut her eyes. 'Well, I know it was my fault because I said it to him first. But then he said it in anger to Celeste and we cannot have that.'

'What was it?'

'Beetle bum.'

'Beetle—' he studied her, trying not to laugh '—bum?'

'Yes, that's what I call him sometimes when he's slow to do what is expected of him.'

'Beetle bum? You call him that?'

'Yes, but not in anger, of course. If he's in trouble, I call him Mr Christopher. He knows I mean business when I do that.'

'Sounds to me like you can be a strict parent.' He put his arm around her.

'Well, it breaks my heart to see him upset, so I have been known to sit in the corner with him. But that turned out differently than I expected. He felt badly for me and cried. I can never do that again. It was too difficult for both of us.'

'I'm sure he learned his lesson.'

She gave that little contented wiggle. 'The carriage rides always seem shorter when I'm sitting beside you.'

'I don't know that I could say the same,' he muttered.

'I'm sorry.'

'Don't be.'

'Well, you can go to sleep if you need to, and I'll be quiet.'

'You've been keeping me awake, but it's fine.' The recollections of her had been lingering like a wafting mist in his mind, changing the air around him, making it more vibrant and letting him absorb so much more.

She reached out and tugged his lapel. 'The last thing I'd want is to disturb you. Your duties are so important.'

'And so are yours.'

'What duty? To be at your side during a soirée?'

'That wasn't what I was thinking of. I was thinking of motherhood. But having you with me at soirées certainly increases my standing. And if not, I don't care.'

'You have always been so considerate to me.' She snuggled against him. 'You will ever be my knight.'

Then, after what felt like a lifetime of her snuggling even closer, she finally fell asleep in his arms, and he hugged her close and dozed, dreamless, only waking to hold her closer.

The carriage stopped and he opened his eyes.

She looked up and the air stilled.

Their lips met—the most innocent kiss he'd ever experienced, and the most fulfilling.

He must stop this weakness. He must remember to remain in control and not be controlled by meaningless feelings. He cupped the back of her head and pulled her forehead close, putting a kiss on it. 'We mustn't get carried away,' he said gently against her skin.

'You are so right,' she said, giving him an extra hug.

Quinton stepped out, and with a wave signalled the driver to leave them so he could help Susanna disembark.

He reached for Susanna, and she alighted. He looked at their hands together, hers so delicate in his grasp.

He felt he had clasped an angel.

He looked into her eyes, and she must have seen something. She blushed, and he moved away, holding out his arm for her to take.

'I hope I didn't chatter too much for you earlier,' she said.

'Never worry about that, Susanna.' He paused, searching her face, searching for words to give meaning. 'It was like listening to birdsong.'

'Oh, Quinton,' she said, brushing his words away. 'That is so very kind. You didn't have to say it. I've already forgiven you for taking Christopher to the stews. I just hadn't really known that you…' She paused. '…would return safely with him. It used to be my biggest fear that Walton would take him from me. I know I don't have to be afraid with you. It's just hard to put everything behind me.'

He clasped her elbow. But she moved forward, taking the sunlight from his life that he'd not known she'd been putting there. Then she stopped and glanced over her shoulder at him.

'I know I was carried away talking,' she whispered. 'But I was quite pleased to be with you.'

Quinton saw the happiness in the butler's face when Susanna walked into the house. He greeted Quinton properly, but then his attention turned back to Susanna, and his voice contained the warmth of a grandfather for a granddaughter.

The butler told Susanna that her room was ready, and that Quinton's things would be put in the son-in-law's room.

Suddenly, it was as if a pane of glass had moved between Quinton and the others. He could hear them, listen and respond, but he was distant.

He was not a part of the warmth that swirled around them. The genuine fondness.

Nor had she appeared shocked when the butler had addressed her as Miss Susanna instead of Countess, and she'd thanked him in a way that seemed to tell him she'd missed him.

His greeting to Quinton had been formality itself, but not cold. Approving.

Internally, he shook himself. A servant's opinion, one he didn't know, should not please him so. But it did.

This marriage pleased him in ways he'd not expected.

He and Susanna had a deal, and he had the promise of a charade of a life that went with the earldom. He had so much to uphold.

Shoulders firm, Susanna continued into the house. 'I will show him to the son-in-law's quarters.'

Quinton followed her.

She pointed to one door. 'Yours.' And across to the other. 'Mine.'

Such a small thing of the nearness of their rooms jolted Quinton.

He would have to shut his mind to it, but the image of her swirled around him, a tantalising springtime cloud of promise, awareness and femininity. And he knew it wasn't false, but real womanliness. He liked it. He liked her.

Each step he took seemed to bring him into the Adair world. He didn't feel he was the Earl stepping forward, or the physician as it had been in the past, but Quinton from the stews, and he was in a foreign clime.

Respectable. There was so much genuine goodness around him that he had trouble believing in it.

The distance between him and Susanna hadn't mattered at all to him when he'd asked her to wed. Long ago he'd made a vow to himself that he would remain celibate because he didn't believe in love. But he believed in something rare—something he'd sensed at her parents' home the first time he'd visited.

He wanted purity in a marriage. Wholesomeness. He could see the innocence in Susanna's parents. And he wanted a marriage like theirs. Respectful. Correct.

He saw how much of a barrier stood between him and Susanna. Her own marriage had likely truly fallen apart because her husband had given in to his base desires. And Quinton could not risk their lives being shattered in a similar fashion.

In his youth, he had had dalliances with some of the women, and he'd not liked it when the women had pretended to care for him but had then given the same affection to someone else, or been open about not giving a whistle for him. He'd been almost controlled by his desires. Only his strongest will had allowed him to step away from the meaningless encounters.

He needed to keep the divide between them—of his past and the ocean of different experiences between the two, because if there was one thing that was certain, sharing a bed would change things. And he didn't want to lose the life he had right now.

Then his father-in-law limped into the room and patted his own knee. 'Thank goodness you are here,' he said. 'I bungled my knee something fierce when I fell off the ladder. But don't tell Susanna's mother how it happened because she told me not to do it. I told her I stepped wrong, and I did. But…'

Quinton examined his father-in-law's knee, while Susanna left the room and visited with her mother.

He told Mr Adair that perhaps he should stay off the ladder, but he reassured everyone later that the knee would heal.

Then they sat around the table for a simple but delightful meal of roast chicken and vegetables.

He noticed that while he seemed at ease with her parents, Susanna was more reserved, but her father began telling her about his renovation plans and after the meal took Susanna to show her the drawings.

Quinton retired with her mother to the sitting room, the scent of an orangery surrounding them.

He left the idle chatter aside. 'Did Susanna have any difficulty with reading when she was a child?'

She hesitated, thinking. 'Well, she's never particularly liked books in the same way Esme and Janette do. They would read aloud to us at night. Susanna flitted around.' She shrugged, sitting down and then taking up the linen square at her side.

'She was too active to sit still long enough to read, and would just refuse to be bothered.' She folded and refolded the handkerchief again. 'But she had the same governess as the other girls and the woman never complained of her inattention.'

He'd been wrong. He supposed it was because of his own youth that he'd jumped to such a conclusion.

'I suppose you mentioned this because Christopher is getting of an age to need a tutor,' she said. 'He should have had one over a year ago, but we were all so preoccupied with moving house and other things, like his father passing on.'

'Boys need an education.'

She put the mangled handkerchief aside and collected her sewing.

'I've heard about this wonderful man, Mr Marvin.

He's had some trouble finding a good position because he doesn't like leaving his mother alone and everyone wants him to live in. His mother can't see well or hear much, so he's limited in the possibilities open to him because he can't take her with him and doesn't want to leave her behind. And you know how costly it can be for someone to travel about.'

'I don't want a tutor living in. I know the house is big enough, but I'm used to a smaller staff around me and prefer to keep it that way.'

'I thought you'd say that,' Mrs Adair said. 'I'm so pleased you agree Christopher would benefit from more advanced learning than Celeste can provide.'

'Whatever you and Susanna decide is fine with me, and don't concern yourself with the expense. Just send the tutor to the house, tell him to ask for Nettie and explain things and she'll introduce him.'

She inspected the twist of embroidery thread in her hand and snipped a length. 'The two of you seem fine, and yet I get the feeling the past is still bothering Susanna.'

She paused, making sure he attended to her.

'We cannot change the past,' he said, words clipped, not pleased that his mother-in-law had just referenced his youth.

'Do not blame her. We encouraged her to wed that horrible little peagoose.'

He was surprised. She was talking about Susanna's past, not his own, and he was not going to enlighten his mother-in-law on any details of his own life unless she specifically enquired.

'Oh, he strutted fine, but that squawking grated on my nerves after I truly learned the nature of him. She tried to warn us after she married him but we didn't listen. It is my greatest shame that I encouraged her to go back to him after she left him. She refused.'

Leaning forward, she added, 'I'm not a perfect mother.' She shrugged. 'Perfect mothers are wasted on children because then children expect flawlessness the rest of their lives. And my daughters certainly learned not to expect perfection from me. But I overdid it with Susanna. That is my greatest regret.'

'You shouldn't have regrets. They do no good.'

'Well, it's been hard for her to get over…what happened. She cared for Walton. But not at the end.' She paused. 'I pray you are not offended by that suggestion.'

'Not at all.'

She frowned, threading a needle and keeping her gaze on the eye. 'And Susanna and I talked about Christopher's other grandfather while you were speaking with my husband. She said she's seen the old miscreant again.'

Quinton remembered the man at the soirée. 'Yes, she did.'

'He is a cheat—a scoundrel—who's even worse than his son. She said he was at a soirée you attended, and that he'd spoken to her.'

Quinton frowned.

'He's been here, too,' she said. 'But the butler… Well, the butler let him wait because it would have been a one-sided fight if our butler decided to toss him out.'

Quinton felt the anger thundering back inside him.

'You wouldn't….' She stared into the distance. 'You must promise me that you will not let that man cause problems for Susanna. And you will not…'

'I can promise you nothing where he is concerned.' Quinton snapped out the words, then caught himself when he saw the shock on her face.

He had reverted back to the ways of his childhood, when he'd promised himself he'd put it behind him for ever.

He stood and turned to the wall, then collected himself. His past must never injure his future because of his actions. If he couldn't control himself, he couldn't have the peace he wanted in his life.

'Please don't—' his mother-in-law began.

'Please *don't* worry about it,' Quinton reassured her, turning, soothing and making sure all the calmness he could pull to the surface was visible to her.

She relaxed. 'Let us all put the past behind us,' she said. 'As you suggested.'

He didn't answer.

'I'd hoped you might cherish her and she might grow to love you,' she murmured.

'I don't care a jot about the circumstances that led to my marriage, but I'm very happy to have Susanna in my home.' He walked over and took Mrs Adair's hand and kissed the air above it. 'How could I be anything but pleased about being a part of the Adair family? You are a cherished mother-in-law. And the family is welcoming.'

'I would say you're spreading it on thick, but I think it's the truth.' She pushed the needle into the cloth, squinting. 'I believe you are much happier with the family you've recently acquired than anything else in your life,' she added shrewdly.

'I have no complaints on either front. And Susanna is—' Fascinating. Captivating. Appealing. He was amazed to have her with him at events. To step out of the vehicle with her. She was a dream he could not have envisioned.

But when he'd said those vows, she'd been the treasure. He'd been keeping his distance from the society beauty, just as he had when he'd first met her. She'd been above his reach then, too, or so he had thought.

He'd once been right in front of her, and she'd chosen Walton over him. He'd returned to her house—to visit her parents, of course—and she'd hardly acknowledged him. She'd been too taken up with her beloved who was courting her.

He'd known then that she had meant it when she'd told him they could be friends.

She did speak to Quinton long enough to introduce him to her suitor, who'd sneered a greeting to Quinton. Barely. But all she could see was the worthless man she was betrothed to, and her eyes reflected the hearts she imagined around him—not the true person.

Only after she'd been widowed had she accepted Quinton's marriage proposal. That was harder to put behind him—perhaps the hardest part of the past. He could see in his mother-in-law's face that she grasped his inability to move forward completely.

His wife never saw him as a suitor before he'd inherited an earldom, and that reminded him to keep on his guard.

When he thought he had a weakness completely conquered was just when it could attack him and wreak the most havoc. He'd felt it with each kiss from Susanna. A lowering of his resolve. The weakness growing.

Back in his room, Quinton opened the door and stared across the corridor.

They were only a hallway apart.

He made himself comfortable in a chair and picked up a book, leaving the door wide open.

And he wondered if she was in that dressing gown, sitting alone in her room, thinking of…their kiss.

Or him.

Or the weather.

Like sunshine.

Sunshine was beautiful in all its forms. Sky forms. Human forms. Wife forms. Susanna.

If he crossed the hallway, he would be giving in to the weakness, a crevasse inside him.

Pushing himself to his feet, he trod the hallway, still holding the book. He would just ask her to read a passage to him. To be certain.

Rapping softly, he called out, 'Susanna.'

The door opened.

'Is everything all right?' she asked.

Again she had on the dressing gown which enveloped her, and her hair was plaited, and he knew what an angel looked like.

He changed his mind about the reading.

He tapped his knuckles on the book at his side, knowing that it wasn't that he'd been strong—just that Susanna hadn't been in his path before.

'Can you sit with me for a moment?' he asked.

'As long as you'd like,' she said, following him to his room.

He moved into his room, shutting the door firmly behind them, and pulled her into his lap in the overstuffed chair. He needed her presence to bolster him.

'You have a wonderful family. Two loving parents. It frequently amazes me. I didn't forgive my father—even when I saw what he'd done to himself. His drinking had destroyed him, and he couldn't stop. He died with a grip on the glass. As he wanted.'

He brushed a knuckle over hers. 'I watched while the servants put him to rest.'

'You were there?' she asked, hesitant.

She reached out, and her hand felt like a lifeline to him—a rope, tugging him to shore after a shipwrecked life.

Then she put an arm around him. He couldn't not

hold her, and hug her, and take comfort from her. He didn't need the sympathy, but she wanted to offer it and he wanted to accept her touch. He felt they were united, something he'd never experienced with anyone before.

'I didn't tell you much about my mother's sister, Auntie. Auntie had been sitting with me. She'd helped me with preparations and all the things I didn't know to do.'

She swallowed and stared at him.

'Auntie fetched me when Father was ill and his brother sent a message to her. She told me I must see my father and be nice to my uncle. She said he would not be grieving for the man we'd lost but for the man my father could have been.'

He let out a puff of air through his nostrils. 'Susanna, compared to many people's parents, you inherited the best. And you genuinely care about your son. But I don't know that I am ready to accept a true family into my household.'

'I will stay on my floor of the house. And I will tell Christopher he is to stay there too.'

'I can tell him no easily enough. I repeat, don't let that concern you. Don't keep him from knowing his surroundings. But don't expect us to have the same life your parents do. My duties as an earl and as a physician take up all my time. That is my first and second obligation.'

'Yet, you visited my parents with me today.'

'Your father may have needed my medical help. It would have been wrong of me not to check on him.'

'You seem to me to be arguing a point with yourself. I've not complained, have I?'

She cleared her throat in a delicate way. 'Perhaps you should listen to yourself, Quinton.' She turned in his arms and delicately rested a finger on his chest, her eyes on her hand. 'Do whatever you think best. I'm not complaining, nor have I been. And when I offer you sympathy on the death of your father, it is the same as I would do for any friend.'

Now she tapped the same finger to her cheek. 'And you invited me into your room just now. I am a little peeved with you. I am doing exactly as you request, and yet you are overexplaining how I must act.'

'I'm merely saying not to expect any deep feelings from me.'

'I have asked for none,' she reiterated. 'The marriage is merely on paper for the benefit of others. You and I are friends, and I realise that is the most important part of our marriage.'

'That's what I wanted,' he said.

'Only sometimes, I think a hug is good for you,' she murmured, burrowing against him again. 'And you do feel good to me—like a mountain of a man and respectability. Stalwart. Strong. Just think of it as if I'm hugging a monument and I don't have to worry about it toppling over or getting grime on me.'

He mustn't kiss her again. Not in this room. Their future could drift onto some unseen path that led them both to despair.

But when he saw her wet her lips, he cupped her head, letting a gentle kiss swirl into a deeper moment.

She didn't pull away but ran her hand over the contours of his face as if she was absorbing it into her memory.

He took her wrist, holding it and placing a kiss in her palm, and then letting their fingers intermingle as he lowered her hand.

'I'm not a child,' she said. 'If you think I must be protected as one, then you are very wrong.'

'Perhaps,' he said. But he knew she'd never see the truth of his past. Perhaps she could understand it, but the scars would always be there if she truly looked for them. 'Some things you can't unlearn.'

'If that's true,' she said, 'I hope this moment is one of them. I hope we have a lot of wonderful moments together that we can't unlearn.'

With two fingertips, he pulled her face closer to his, letting her breath caress him, feeling contentment in her presence.

'I don't know that you can understand what I faced to survive. I was fortunate to have the brothel to escape to.'

'I don't have to understand it,' she said. 'I'm not living in your past. I'm living in your present. That's all I have to comprehend. Don't overthink things. And don't live in your memories.'

He could have shaken her away, physically, but he'd lost all that strength—lost it in the sensation of her mouth. The darkness of her lashes. The tenderness of her skin. The sweetness of her voice.

Suddenly, he knew what peace felt like, and angel's wings brushing against skin. He knew what Susanna felt like and tasted like. She tasted like wine and innocence and happiness, and she gave him the feeling of seeing the daylight inside himself.

Chapter Thirteen

Susanna draped her arm over Quinton's shoulder and rested her head against his. The strands of his hair caressed her cheek, and she let her body bloom in his presence. It seemed she couldn't clasp him close enough.

Each crinkle of the fabric of his coat heightened her senses. It was just cloth, but unlike any she'd ever felt before because it covered him. Warmth burst into her, creating a delicious storm inside her, teasing her from head to toe.

She wanted to comfort him, to take away the pain of his past—to welcome him into her world and make her childhood a part of his. 'I know you can't forget the past, and I would never have wanted you to have the difficulties you faced…' She said the words against his hair. 'But it made you who you are, so it did a fine job. Or rather, the strength inside you did a fine job of combatting it.'

'Susanna…' His voice rolled over her body, rumbling like a distant thunder saying the storm was fading away, leaving behind dewdrops of rain sparkling in the air.

Again he put an arm around her waist, and he finger-combed her hair, brushing it over her shoulders. He let it fall gently against her skin and then he took a small strand, held it in his fingers and lifted it to brush it against his face.

Quinton leaned in to kiss her and she pulled the fabric of his shirttail free, slipping her hands between it and his body, pulling him close, the touch of his skin vibrating through her and taking all thoughts from her mind except the instant of holding him.

His lips rested against her neck, nuzzling, and the bristles of his beard brushed the sensitive spots of her neck. She shivered.

In one slow glide, he slid his shirt away, pulling it over his head.

Then he moved her to her feet, and he stood as well.

Untying the sash of her dressing gown, he opened it and held her against him. She savoured the sensation of having him surround her before he let the gown slide from her shoulders and tossed it onto the chair where they'd sat.

Instead of merely pulling the fabric of her chemise from her body, he touched the front and let his fingers glide over her breasts. Her nipples hard, she could feel the ridges of his fingers through the thin cloth.

Next, he slowly slid the garment down her thighs and let it glide to the rug.

She brushed fingertips over his chest, sending a deep awareness of her own femininity into herself.

She used her hands as if she were painting him into her mind, covering each particle of skin, absorbing him with her senses.

She looked up as he undid the buttons of his trousers, feeling his gaze—first on her eyes, and then travelling down her body with a reverence and a passion that she had no idea could have ever existed.

His clothing rustled to the floor.

She cradled his hair in her hands as he found her lips and gave her a kiss laced with promise.

Their kisses deepened, delivering on that promise, and they changed her body into a bubbling desire of need for Quinton.

Pressed close to each other, the world faded, until he scooped her into his arms and placed her onto the bed.

With her body against his, all the feelings she'd kept locked inside opened up and dashed into the world. Containing them in one body and one person was impossible.

He lay beside her and her breasts rose and fell with each breath.

With one arm he held her close, and with the opposite hand he caressed her body, moving in swirls down to the feminine *V*, stoking her innermost fires, bringing her to her peak.

She could not touch him enough as he rose over her. He was a muse of sensations. She was lost in something more powerful than he was.

She no longer breathed alone, but breathed with him. And there was a purity and innocence in caressing him, in taking him inside her body.

She'd waited her whole life for Quinton, and nothing mattered but that they hold each other.

He slammed his head against the pillow, pulling the world around him and trying to keep the feeling of dread from swamping him.

Her contented sigh reached his ears. She gave him a nudge with her body, and he responded automatically by putting an arm around her and letting her cuddle against him.

He tried to breathe normally, to calm the rush of feelings settling in his stomach.

He'd let his desire override his brain, and his brain was sending him all sorts of fluttery feelings that could destroy the perfect life he had around him.

If he stayed in the bed with her, he could not promise he wouldn't hold her again. He had to leave and hope for the best. But she was in his room. No matter. He had to leave. Where he'd go, he didn't know, but surely they had a garden. It wouldn't be the first time he'd spent the night alone outside.

He kissed her cheek, then her hair, hugged her and slipped from the covers, understanding why those men in history had taken whips and flagellated themselves.

He needed no whip to feel pain. He had his feelings for Susanna to do that.

'You're leaving?' Susanna asked incredulously from the bed behind him. 'This is your room.'

He stopped, his hand on his trousers. He turned to her. Of course. It was safer, and besides, she would not want him to stay.

She reached out to him.

That was unexpected. But then, she was his wife.

He digested the word. *Wife.* He had to admit that he'd not truly considered Susanna his wife before tonight, although he'd considered himself wed. Susanna was Christopher's mother. Her parents' daughter. The woman he'd dreamed of until he'd discovered she planned to marry someone else.

He lifted the trousers and hung them on the end of the bedpost, and then he took his shirt and hung it on the other and put the waistcoat over it. He would wait until she fell asleep to leave.

He crawled back into bed, putting an arm around her, letting her snuggle into him. He'd not known another woman who liked to burrow against him so. She did feel pleasant against his side—comforting, feminine, flowery and delicate.

She squeezed him close, then rested her palm on his chest.

He took her fingers and pulled them to his lips for a kiss.

'I really feel married now,' she confided.

He stopped, his feelings rotating like a whirligig had been planted inside him, disrupting everything he'd ever known.

They had discussed everything so correctly. They had a marriage document of a sort, although none of it was written down. It had all been stated plainly—much more than those actual vows in front of the vicar, where he wasn't sure of what he'd agreed to because he'd been watching her so closely.

But when he'd asked her to wed and she'd agreed, that was all the vow he'd needed from her.

What if she'd conceived tonight? Another child wouldn't be a bad thing, he told himself. The governess was already installed, a tutor around the corner. A mother to take some of the load from him, and a brother for the child to play with.

But he couldn't shake the memories that flooded into him: Caring for Eldon when he didn't know what he should do for the best. The hunger. Rainy days. Cold nights. Running out to ask the ladies for food.

He was on an island again—an island where he didn't know what direction the cyclone was going to arrive from, or where the boats were docked, or how deep the currents ran.

A man's heart was only so big. It could only take so many storms.

'Are we really married now?' she asked.

'I would say so,' he said. 'I have been from the first moment of the vows.' Truly, from before he'd said the vows. From his first glimpse of Susanna as a woman.

Susanna awoke, stretching her arms to the sky, feeling like a swan opening her wings for the first sunlight of the day.

Quinton was gone, but she remembered the kiss he'd given her forehead early in the morning when he'd left. She'd heard him moving about. In fact, he'd woken her when he'd gathered his clothing—the second time.

She dressed quickly, anxious to start the day.

Just the thought of Quinton and her world brightened. She had a husband, a son and someday, perhaps soon, she'd have another son or a daughter.

In the hallway, Quinton was returning for her.

'You're…' She met Quinton's blank stare. Eyes frozen over, showing no more recognition of her than he might have given a stranger.

Her feelings plunged so low she could not speak.

She'd thought after last night they'd had a chance at being better friends. Lovers. Caring for each other. But it seemed nothing had changed. Nothing. She was no more a part of his world than she had been before. Maybe even less.

She found her voice.

'Very well.' She fought her expression as she passed him. It didn't matter. It really didn't. She would have her family, of sorts. She just would accept the truth and take the good moments when she could.

And next time, she would ask Quinton to leave her bed before he had a chance to pick up his clothing from the floor, to *arrange everything neatly*.

'Susanna,' Quinton called out.

She hesitated and turned, seeing his expression. The ice in him had melted, replaced by something else. Pain? She wasn't sure.

When Susanna observed Quinton, she felt for the agony on his face.

'I need to say something.'

He appeared to pull his resources close, and intensity flourished behind his speech. 'I'm fond of you. I wanted you to know that. It doesn't matter how you feel about me, but I had to tell you.'

'I'm fond of you too.' She paused, and waited a bit, considering. 'I am truly very fond of you. I have the deepest kind of fondness for you.'

He lowered his chin. 'If you wish to leave me, I won't stand in your way. If you wish to destroy our agreement, and stay with your parents, I will still support you and them.'

'No. I intend to stay with you in our house. You will have to accept that. We are married and will remain so. I will honour my vows, no matter what our future holds.' She crossed her arms. 'I won't leave. You cannot prise me loose.' She let out a deep breath. 'I am staying, Quinton Langford. No matter what. I made my vow and I made it again last night, even though you didn't know it. I lo—' She caught herself. Quinton appeared as if she'd punched him in the gut.

From the bleakness in him, she doubted it would be anything they would be discussing for a while.

Telling Quinton she loved him wasn't working out so well, but at least he was fond of her.

His past gripped him like a leather glove that had been dipped in water and dried in the sun. 'You need to meet my auntie, the bawd.'

She gasped, and his eyes raked hers. He answered her unspoken question with a frozen stare.

Susanna heard the words and whispered, 'She ran the brothel?'

'She doesn't anymore.'

He'd created an illusion of his life, and his wife was almost as in the dark about it as her six-year-old son. And perhaps Quinton was as well...about *her* life, and the innocence of it.

'I need you to go with me to the country. To meet her.'

She paused. 'Me? With you?'

'I want you to see that part of my life. My auntie.'

'In a *brothel*?' She gaped at him, her mouth open.

He shut his eyes. 'No. She cares for children now.'

'A *bawd*?'

'Formerly.' But he knew Susanna had never met a woman such as his aunt. 'She's turned from that life, but she's not delicate. In fact, I would say she goes out of her way to make certain that it's apparent she's rough.'

'I don't know.'

'If she turns up on my doorstep, I will not have her sent away.'

Her mouth opened. 'She could appear where we live? In your home? With my son?'

'If you are to live in my house, and not stay with your parents, then it might be best if you know my family. My younger brother, who is a baker. My aunt, who is not, but might stir things up from time to time if the mood takes her.'

The air between them tingled and seemed to arise like cold air seeping from the sky on a dark, damp winter morning.

'My aunt has not stepped foot in my residence yet, and I don't know that she ever will. But I cannot tell her what to do, and I would never turn her away. She never turned me away. And I might hope that you would greet her warmly if she appeared.'

'But she's a...fallen woman?'

'She oversaw others at the brothel. She's not just a fallen woman. She once referred to herself as the queen of the palace of sin.'

'But I don't want—' She cleared her voice. 'I would not want my son to be exposed to such a life.'

Then he spoke again, all emotion in his demeanour concealed. His utterance had a bite. 'I was.'

'It's not... It's—not that I—' She rushed the words, apologising with her expression.

'What part of my life do you want explained to you?' He stopped her with his words.

She opened her mouth, soundless.

'I know,' he said, raising his hand to stop her flow of thoughts. 'That is how I dealt with it as a youngster. At university. I asked people to ask me any questions they might want answered, and I could and *can* do it. And I explained anything they wanted to know. I learned, also, how society-minded people think when there are no barriers to understanding.'

'You don't have the past completely behind you,' Susanna said.

'I do well enough.'

'Christopher knows the proper sound that is a response to that, and he would get sent to the corner for it, but I am an adult and in control of my actions, just as you are.'

He was in control of his actions, except when she hugged him as a friend. Then he wanted to be more. He wanted to be an upstanding husband, and he had to remind himself that he was. A decent one. Wholesome. A monument, if that was how she wanted to think of him. And they had a bargain, and he would uphold it.

But he was tired of hiding a part of himself from her. She needed to see all of his past, particularly the part of it that still lived and might show up at his door.

She examined him closely. He'd never appeared so cold. It was as if the man she knew had departed, and a stranger stared back at her. At that moment, she remembered the younger Quinton, the physician, who'd appeared at her parents' home. He'd been friendly, charming, polite and all things proper, but he'd had the same barrier around him as he did now. She'd not really known him then, nor even when she wed him. Or now.

Now, she saw the stern Quinton, the one who could straighten a nose without flinching.

Those eyes were levelled at her, and the man who owned them appeared to have no heart. Perhaps he truly did feel nothing inside. She would like to soften his heart—to let him know that friends helped each other with words and not just actions.

He was tough.

But she wasn't, and she couldn't reach him or understand who he was beneath the veneer.

The most important moments of her life, and she couldn't get them right. Just like in her studies. She sighed.

She deliberated on Quinton. 'You live in society now,' she said. 'And if your auntie appears at our home, I will invite her to tea and have a maid prepare a room for her.'

His jaw flexed. 'She could show up with three children and a nose full of snuff.'

She put her hands on her hips. 'Then I'll see she has plenty of handkerchiefs.'

'It's no matter, Susanna.' Then he almost smiled, and no one had ever smiled at her with such distance behind it. 'I learned to accept it a long time ago. I want you to meet my aunt. I don't want to just tell you about her, but for you to see her and form your own opinion. And don't pretend with her. If you don't like her, it won't upset her at all. Nothing like that does. She's nail tough and weather hardy.'

'I'll meet her,' she said.

'Are you strong enough?'

'I'm soirée tough, and perfume hardy.'

Quinton didn't argue or agree, and his expression didn't change. They may have been standing in the same space, but he had closed himself away from her.

She walked to him and held his lapels, staring directly into his face. 'And if I don't like her, it's not the end of the world. Sometimes I don't like my own family, so if she and I don't get on well, it doesn't matter. It only matters that you get on well with her, and if she does find her way to your doorstep, I will make her welcome and disappear into the house.'

He clasped her elbows. 'I wed the right woman.'

'Of course, you did. And don't you forget it.' She pranced away.

Chapter Fourteen

He had shared facts with his wife, but not the certainties and uncertainties that he lived with. To her, he had been Quinton the physician. Then the Earl's heir. Not Quinton from the stews, the boy in tattered trousers who carried a knife in his boot, whose mother claimed to her sweethearts that Quinton had been the one stealing funds from them he'd never seen, and who'd learned life's morals from his aunt, a bawd who kept accounting books and lists but who believed her business increased if the women played by certain rules of conduct.

The bawd who'd watched over him... The first person in his life who'd tried to teach him right from wrong and not to steal from a decent woman or a rector or on a Sunday. She'd wanted him to learn right from wrong so badly she stole a prayer book for him. He'd not been interested in reading it, and he'd not learned to read at all until his uncle had appeared in his life.

When Susanna had said she was soirée tough and perfume hardy, he'd understood his fear that she wasn't really strong enough to handle a meeting with his aunt.

Perhaps he was still getting educated as well. He remembered the young Susanna, opinionated with her dolls, but kind. The Susanna who had been at Sunday services and had made them so much more palatable after his uncle had visited his auntie and convinced her that Quinton must regularly attend. And she had received a stipend for sending him.

After he'd discovered Susanna was there, he'd not minded so much.

Why he had seen her as beyond compare, he didn't understand. Perhaps he'd had some of those daft flowery sweetness stars in his vision as well. That surprised him. He'd not considered himself capable of such drivel.

He remembered that the first time they'd met, she'd even told the other boys they had no idea what it was like to be as wonderful as Quinton. No one had ever called him anything nice, except tall for his age.

When his uncle had told him he must go to university, he'd learned that others had so much, and he'd wanted the best, right along with them. Later, he'd seen Susanna again, and he'd never observed a woman with such perfect manners and a caring family before. When he'd been a physician, her father had accepted him into their midst, but she and her mother had been distant.

He hoped the woman in his household wasn't the same person who would be impressed by a braggart's compliment on her slippers now.

Yet he didn't know how his wife, the one who wore her dressing gown snug and made sure her hair was plaited perfectly when she went to bed, could accept the little ruffian he'd been with a dirty face and torn clothing—the child with matted hair who didn't even know the words he used were improper until one of the prostitutes had told him.

It mattered to him that Susanna was able to accept his past.

He hadn't thought it would. But it did. A lot.

He would take Susanna to see the bawd. To see the straggling and scraggly children. To let her grasp the world he had known, and if she turned up her nose at it, it would show her in her true light. No one had ever weakened him with their views. If she showed distaste, it would only strengthen him.

Susanna settled into the seat, interlaced her fingers and kept her demeanour placid. Quinton gave the driver directions and she heard him say it would be a visit to Mrs Adams. She could tell that the man knew, without instruction, where he was meant to go.

When Quinton stepped to the door of the vehicle, he hesitated, then replaced his frown with a shake of his head and a smile she wasn't sure was directed inward or at her.

He still imbued the air inside the carriage with his vibrancy, but now he seemed to have coldness seeping from him.

The edges of his lips lifted, but she could tell he wasn't feeling humorous. 'If you don't like my aunt, it will not concern either her or me. But you should be prepared.'

The ride progressed in silence, a jagged-edged silence, and she didn't know what she'd done to cause it, but she could endure it. Goodness, that was nothing compared to the fury Walton could unleash on her. She'd often been afraid to move, afraid he would get even angrier. She'd not stayed with him long after she realised he wanted her to defend herself so he'd have an excuse to lose his temper completely.

'Auntie,' he spoke into the silence marred only by the vehicle creaks, 'rarely has a true kindness for anyone but the children. But she is fond of me too. If she were to send a message that she needed me at any time of day or night, I would immediately go to her.'

He looked down, staring at his flexed fingers before he relaxed them. 'I wouldn't have rushed to my mother's side as quickly. Auntie could be depended on. If Gwen, my mother, could see me now, she would certainly expect to be reimbursed for every crumb she threw my way—and she would demand payment many times over.'

'Your speech is perfect, you know. As good as any peer,' she said.

He leaned closer. 'Not if you listen closely when I'm tired. Sometimes, I hear a trace of the streets slip in, but I was taught to speak in a more educated way. In fact, the ladies insisted on speaking well. They said they earned more that way. It was a jest my auntie made. A woman could make a good wage with her brain and her mouth and her back working together. If she only used one, then it was only one earner instead of three. Auntie told my mother we must talk as if we came from society all the time. I carried on the rule with Eldon. And it did help when we were selling the bread. I tested it—using both accents.'

The image of him growing up almost alone, in poverty, slayed her.

'I once stepped into a world I didn't like and couldn't escape from, but it was much better than yours,' she said. 'Marriage to my first husband. I'd hoped for the best but received the worst.'

She'd believed that things would improve if they had a child, and had been anticipating the joy. But within days after she'd told him there could be a child, he'd complained of her appearance. Then, months later, he'd caught her straightening his room and thought she was rifling through his papers. He'd slapped her. And then she'd reminded him she couldn't read. And he'd slapped her again.

But if she'd been able to read, she suspected the notes she'd found would have informed her on how much money he was bilking from her father. She'd had no idea at the time, but she'd begged his forgiveness and when he'd calmed down, she'd brought him food, given him drink and slipped out the back door, cradling her stomach. She'd never spent another night with him after that.

She'd let her family believe that their flighty daughter had returned and not been able to make a good wife. But she didn't care how terrible a wife she'd been; she was not enduring his anger a day longer. She'd prayed her soon-to-be-born baby would never have to live with her husband, and she'd not wanted to alert her family to her grave mistake.

'I really just hoped for the best when I left him. And to be able to keep Christopher.'

In truth, she hadn't wanted her father to stop giving him funds. She feared her husband taking the babe if they didn't. He could have.

The only way she would have returned to him was if he'd tried to obtain Christopher, so she'd been cautious to never let him know how much she cared for her son.

'Hope is a good thing if you don't have to depend on it,' Quinton said.

She hid the shivers inside herself and crossed her arms over her midsection, gripping the opposite elbow with each hand. 'I agree. I was so worried Walton would use Christopher against me, but he didn't.'

'Susanna.' He leaned across the seat, holding her fingertips loosely. 'You're shivering again. I will hold you whenever you need it.'

She felt as protected as if he'd taken her in his arms.

'When you change your life, you should leave behind both actions and regrets,' he said. 'I'm thankful to know Christopher. He is helping me see how my childhood is behind me. But I don't want to care so deeply for a child again.'

He lightened the clasp but didn't release her. He half smiled. 'When Eldon was little, I was constantly scared senseless if he had a fever or fell or anything made him cry. I never knew what to do, except try to make him as comfortable as I could—pretty much the same as I do now for my patients.'

'You save their lives.'

'Some days I help. Some days I feel I'm just another form of poultice, and such cures are not something I'd want to depend on. Laudanum helps diminish pain. I have a few other cures for ailments, but I can't make someone see again, or ease nearly as much as I'd like.' He shrugged, but his fingers clenched. 'I do save a few people though, and I know it.'

She sighed, from deep within herself.

'What was that all about?'

'Because I… Do you think I'm like the women you grew up around?'

'What are you talking about?' He considered her.

'I left my husband.'

He snorted out a laugh. 'Susanna. You are not at all like the women I used to know.' Another soft chuckle from the base of his throat. 'Not a hair.'

'Did it ever occur to you that…that we made a bargain? A transaction of sorts?'

He reached across himself and tapped the third finger of her left hand. 'The ring. That's what made it different. That proposal. A commitment is different than a tumble.'

When he moved his hand away, she noticed the tarnish on her finger and held it up so he could see the stain.

He used his thumb to brush at the skin near the jewellery. 'This one…' He shook his head at her. 'I told you that you can buy another anytime you wish. I will have a jeweller bring you a selection.'

She examined her ring and also tried to brush the tarnish off her finger. 'I suppose it would probably be best if we had something more fitting.'

'What did you do with your other wedding ring, from Walton?'

'It went to the hackney to pay for the ride to my parents' home.' She sighed. 'I don't think he profited much, but he was sympathetic. He tried to give it back to me and I told him I'd send someone out with payment for him but I was not taking it back. And I meant it. He wished me well and left.'

'Your husband should have cherished you.'

'He should have, but he didn't.' She was angered all over again at the thought of Walton—of her innocence in believing his lies.

'I pity him.'

The sincerity of his words released her from the memories of the past. She'd never felt quite good enough for Walton, and yet she wondered if perhaps she shouldn't have blamed herself, or even him, but just accepted her mistakes and moved on.

She softened her gaze and couldn't help moving nearer to him. Instead of feeling alone, she felt connected to him when he studied her, as if what he saw pleased him. As if she were perfection in his view.

'The road is so rutted,' she said, 'and I keep being jostled against you when the carriage moves.'

'I don't recall any bruising.'

'Well, on the night that I snuggled against you in the carriage, I probably could have managed with the blanket. Or alone. I wasn't that cold.'

'The blanket was musty. Your arms were cold. I felt you shiver.'

'With contentment.' She pretended another quake.

Without thinking, she lifted her face to gauge his reaction, and time stopped. His eyes took her in, but his lips found hers. The liquid warmth of his kiss exchanged the tingles she'd felt before as an awakening in her body.

She clung to him, and when the kiss ended his lips stayed close to her face, until she lowered her head and rested it on his chest.

'We have to be careful,' he warned her. 'And not start something it would be hard to stop.'

'I know,' she said. 'But I'm afraid it's already too late.'

'It's not.'

Chapter Fifteen

Squeals of children's laughter filtered through the window, and the coach slowed.

'Let's put everything else aside for now,' Quinton said, suddenly recalling memories of being a child without enough clean water. Thankfully, the children here had plenty to drink and could wash as much as they wished to.

Then he jumped out of the vehicle before she could respond.

Several children ran from the edges of the rather overgrown garden, shouting, laughing and generally adding to the confusion.

The cottage itself was sturdy. Warm-looking.

'It's Mr Langford,' one shouted. 'I mean, the Earl of Something Buried.'

Suddenly three children, two boys in tattered trousers and a girl in a mud-stained dress, ran over to them.

He helped Susanna alight and watched her as the children surrounded them, dirty faces all.

She took in a breath and he saw her examine the cottage—a plain home with a window up and the curtain fluttering through, caused by a breeze from another

opening on the opposite side of the house. Chickens cack-
led. Three goats bleated. A burly dog raised his head, examined the situation, and fell back asleep.

'Who is she?' the littlest boy asked as Quinton stood
at Susanna's side.

'This is Lady Amesbury,' Quinton answered.

Another child called out, 'Did you bring us anything,
Lord Amesbury?'

Then he scratched his cheek, seeming to remember.
'My wife. But I am taking her back with me.'

'You have a wife?' the little girl asked.

'Yes.'

'Blast it,' the little girl said, stomping the ground.
Then she stuck her tongue out at Susanna. 'I was going
to marry him.'

Mrs Adams sauntered from the doorway, a woman
whose hair frazzled around her like a silvery, out-of-con-
trol halo. She ambled to them, holding a stick, but used
it to point to the children. 'Visitors, children. Be good.
Remember. He could be a magistrate.'

'Yes, Mrs Adams,' three voices chimed.

'But he's not,' the boy said. 'So we can talk to him.'

She tucked the stick under her arm and wiped her
hands on her brownish apron that could have started out
as white. 'Well, you've been a stranger recently,' she said
to Quinton. 'I figured I'd have to send Walter to say one
of us was dying to get you out here again.'

'You know I never let a month go by without checking on my favourite auntie.'

'I'm your least favourite auntie as well. And we
all know you only visit to make sure the children are
healthy.'

'Well, they do have to eat your cooking…'

She pretended to swing at him with her stick.

'Ah,' she said, after she propped herself back on the stick. 'A woman with you. Must be a new sweetheart? I do get tired of all the women you bring out here, Quinton.'

The older woman's voice held far too much innocence to be genuine.

Susanna gave her a generous smile in return.

'My wife, Susanna.'

The woman fluttered the side of her apron. 'Well, that's a surprise, you bringing her.'

Susanna didn't move.

A little girl had stepped closer to Quinton and slipped her hand in his. He'd not seemed to notice. Quinton switched the hand the little girl held, reaching to clasp Susanna with the other, holding her close.

His auntie smirked, then yawned, stretching wide. 'Well. I suppose it is what it is. A society woman visiting little ol' decrepit me.'

'Auntie. You should also mind your manners.'

'I would, but I'm forgetful and I left them somewhere. They were cumbersome.' She smiled in Susanna's direction. 'How do you put up with him?'

'We don't live on the same storey. I hardly ever see him.'

The old woman laughed. 'I live in a small cottage, but I hardly ever see my husband either. He lives somewhere else. Usually stops by on Saint Smithereen's Day.' The woman laughed. 'That's the day he's so far out of funds that he has to risk being knocked to smithereens when he arrives.'

'I wanted to show Susanna the rose garden and the memory tree,' Quinton said.

'If you must. You know the direction.'

Susanna watched as Quinton took a detour to walk

closer to Auntie and she made a fist this time and swung in his direction. He sidestepped with a dancer's step, but then he reached out and clasped her in a quick hug.

The old woman laughed and gave him a pat on the shoulder before she stepped away. 'I'm getting slower,' she said. 'Old age is creeping up.'

'No,' he said. 'You were still quick. I was just lightning fast.'

She chuckled, but changed her attention to the little ones. 'Stay here, imps,' she called to the children.

'Can I look in His Lordship's carriage?' a child asked.

'You might find a crate for Auntie in there,' Quinton said, taking Susanna's hand and leading her to the path.

Susanna walked ahead, expecting to see roses, but all she saw were weeds and briars and thorns. Birds chattered and flew overhead as she walked by. 'How far to the roses?'

'I don't know.' He removed a limb from the trail. 'I've never seen them. If you see any, please let me know. I think the path ends at a small village. Auntie said if you keep searching only for the roses, you'll never see the birds, the green of the leaves or the beauty of the sky.'

'A philosopher of sorts?'

'Yes. Even when she was watching the house, Auntie was always the more responsible one. Auntie tried to protect her younger sister. She kept her out of the brothel and guided her into marriage, but it didn't turn out the way she expected.'

'Are the children related to her?'

'Not by birth. In six months, it could be different ones. I've brought some of them to her and found homes and apprenticeships for others who were older. Some have mothers who hope for the best. Some don't. It just depends. This is a haven for the children. She truly cares for them and they give her a purpose in her life.'

Stopping, he led her closer to an old tree. Initials were carved around the trunk, both high and low.

'All Auntie's children get their name carved in the trunk,' he said. 'She didn't start it at first, but later we did.'

He moved aside.

'Are your initials in the wood?' she asked.

'No. It's only for the children.' He touched the initials. 'Auntie left the business when I had to go to university.' It just wasn't good for his brother to stay there alone. And she'd said she was tired of it, and wanted a new life.

He led Susanna to the beginning of the path. 'I could not ruin the chance I'd been given. I would never have such an opportunity again. I had to do well. My uncle had the funds. I had nothing.'

His aunt had insisted he take advantage of the opportunity; she'd said in the long run she would profit by it. Eldon would. She'd said it would be selfish of him to stay at home.

'At first, I was to be a barrister, but I convinced my uncle I wanted to study medicine.'

He took her hand and put it against his face. The bristles of his beard had grown just enough so that she could feel the roughness, and underneath that, the life of a man.

He nodded, causing her hand to rub over his cheek. 'My aunt told me she wanted to change her life, and she thought if I did, she would be able to survive better. She didn't consider her efforts matchmaking for my mother wasted, because her nephew was related to an earl. When I told her I'd inherited the title, she cried for hours. It was the first time I'd seen her tears.'

'She pretends to be a scoundrel,' she said. 'And perhaps she is, in a way, but no one can raise such happy children without a heart.'

'Auntie only has kindness where children are concerned, and for me.' Truth be known, her husband had probably departed for his own safety.

'Well, the children are what matters,' she said. 'And you were fortunate that you had someone to watch over your brother.'

A branch cracked as he pushed it out of their way.

'My aunt told me that I could make something of myself, but neither of us expected so much to be given to me. I had no choice, really.'

He walked farther along the trails, past a mire.

He took her hand to keep her from slipping in the mud. 'This would have been an easy childhood compared to mine.'

'Well, I would not wish for you to have had a struggle during your early years, but those years made you what you are, and I have no complaints there.'

The kiss barely touched her lips, but lingered, moist, drawing her closer against him as he dropped her hand and held her tight, fingers threading in her hair. His tongue touched her lips and brought them even closer, tingling and deep, and taking her back into an awareness of what could happen between them if this went any further.

He stepped away and lifted her, cradling her in his arms to swing her around until they were both dizzy, and then he deposited her and they stumbled against each other.

'I can almost smell the scent of the roses,' she said.

'I can see them.' His forehead touched hers. 'We should go back now.'

But she didn't want to let him go.

'I had so much, and I lost it.' She whispered the words. 'Mine was the horrible mistake.'

'Susanna. Mistakes are our past, present and future, but we must do the best we can and correct them. That is the measure of us. How we deal with and correct mistakes—our own and those of others.'

At that moment, one of the boys ran onto the path, laughing, patched clothes almost falling off his body. 'I followed you, Lord Amesbury.'

'So you did, my friend. So you did.'

'She allows them to be alone in the woods...?'

He nodded. 'This is safer than the streets where they would be roaming if left to their own devices. They're a family here.'

After Quinton returned them to the cottage, Susanna watched and listened. He and Auntie talked at length about the needs of the children and how well the cleric from the village was teaching them. Now the man's oldest daughter came once a day to give the children some instruction.

Most were doing well, but the boy Quinton had called his friend would rather run through the fields or fish or annoy the other children than study. They'd decided to give him more time to settle, and leave it be.

Susanna heard them fret about how the little boy was having trouble learning. Her heart went out to him. He probably read better than she did.

Susanna's own father had been a good father, but she'd never seen a man who took care of children as much as Quinton appeared to, and yet he claimed he wanted to keep his distance from them.

She noticed he often knelt down so the little ones could

see his face as he talked to them. One little girl pulled at his coat as he knelt speaking to the others. Instead of pausing the conversation, he held her close.

Auntie slipped to Susanna's side and waved her away from Quinton and the children. 'He's not the soft sort he seems.' The older woman crossed her arms. 'He always rescues people. Always. Even took a woman from the streets and gave her employment in his home. And you. He rescued you, too. Didn't he?'

'I guess you could say that. But I would like to think it was a joint venture.'

'That's part of his charm. He convinces others they are helping him, that they are the ones doing the grand thing. Do you really think I intended to end up with all the little ones? Not until my nephew convinced me it was my idea. And I let him think it still is.'

She swiped the back of her forearm across her nose. 'And yet he sees that my bills are paid, and clothes given to us.'

Susanna glanced to the tattered clothes of the boys.

The old woman guffawed. 'It's easiest for me if I don't keep 'em too polished,' she said. 'I never liked it when my own mother slapped me for getting a stain or a torn dress. I let them do as they wish. It's just a covering. Not worth an upset to either of us.'

Auntie raised a brow, and one side of her cheek matched the movement.

'Once Quinton saw a lad hungry on the streets and brought him here but told me not to give him second chances. I could tell within a day or two that he was trouble. He couldn't stay.'

She saw Quinton searching them out. She smiled. 'We don't always give people chances, do we Quinton?' Auntie smiled a feral glint. 'It's true, isn't it? You have no tender feelings for my sister and you felt you were better off without her.'

He agreed. 'I never trusted her after I had to take the knife away from her so she wouldn't hurt my brother.'

'Tell her what he did,' the aunt called out, laughing.

'She didn't like people to know she had children. And Eldon and I were not to arrive home until after her caller left. I saw him leave and I took Eldon into the house. She wasn't happy to see us.'

'But you're leaving out what horrid thing he did.'

'He called her Mother.'

Leaving Auntie's always put his past back around him. It was as if he stepped through a spider's web of memories as he climbed out of the vehicle, and he had to push at them when he left until he cleared his mind.

He'd been certain his auntie would have offended Susanna. His aunt had told him she'd changed from letting her outside be clean and her inside soiled to the reverse. She'd said it was too much for her to keep them both in order. He'd told her she was beautiful, and she'd sworn softly and laughed again, and said he wasn't too big for her to reprimand for lying.

The coach ride home started companionably enough. But as the wheels revolved, the years of his childhood stayed inside him.

'You seemed to get on well enough with Auntie,' he said.

'Is it true that your mother became upset because your brother called her *Mother*?'

'Well, it might have angered her because of the way he said it. It wasn't entirely an endearment.'

'I can't imagine such a fight.'

'I'm pleased.'

'Your mother only half raised you,' she said. 'Getting you to an age where you could take care of your brother and leaving you two to fend for yourself.'

'That's one way to look at it. Another might be she kept us there to get more funds from our fathers.'

'Which do you believe?'

'I believe she couldn't even grasp how to take care of herself, and proved it by dying. If someone lives in such a way as to destroy themselves, they can't take good care of children. Mother couldn't. Auntie can.'

He'd asked Auntie if she wanted to return to town, but she'd refused, feeling the children needed to see a different life. And perhaps some of them needed not to risk seeing their old families.

He kept his gaze from Susanna, and wondered if he'd visited Auntie, in part, to remind himself not to immerse himself into life with Susanna too deeply. To put his trust in her could be courting disaster if her attraction to family life waned.

He gave a half laugh. 'Recently, at home, I awoke in the middle of the night when it was thundering and raining against the window panes and thought I must get a pail so the water didn't drip on the bed. I stayed awake a long time, listening to the rain. Didn't know it could sound dry.'

'Until my parents' current home, I don't think I'd ever lived in a house with a bad roof. And Mother whispered to me that the man you'd sent Father's way would be correcting that. Thank you.'

'It pleased me to do it, like giving myself a Christmas treat in springtime. You had a good childhood. I admit, some days I enjoy the scars of my own. They give me a feeling of pride to have survived—to have lived though it when I didn't know I would have a better life.'

He touched his sleeve. 'The scar here. It's just fingernail marks. I broke up a fight once between Mother and Auntie. So when I saw inside your household, it was one of the most calm, well-ordered places I'd ever seen. It seemed odd to me that parents could take care of their children. Your parents may be naive, but they're good people. The best.'

'They are. And I care for them, but I'm the daughter who wed the true villain. It's always in their mind that I made a bad decision. And it's in my mind. Really, I sacrificed their future to protect my son. I didn't tell them how bad Walton was even after I knew. I didn't want him even more upset. I wanted Christopher protected.'

'They would have wanted him sheltered also. And you have redeemed yourself by wedding me to restore some of their funds, and I will do so.'

'I know. But I saw what I'd done to us all. I didn't like the reduced circumstances for my family. And I refused to put more of a strain on their finances than I already had.'

'Well, I don't want to completely forget my life of poverty. And I'm not stopping my responsibilities for the children. I know society might frown on Auntie, but she is what she is. The children appear a bit rough but they're healthy enough.'

'It's a part of your life as much as the earldom.'

'It means a lot to me that she's giving the children a haven,' Quinton said.

'Where do you feel at home?' she asked.

'Nowhere.'

Stricken eyes assessed him.

Then he remembered. 'Once, I felt at home.' He paused,

reflecting. 'When you first appeared at my doorway, in that dressing gown, covered from chin to toes, it was better than inheriting a fortune.' He shut his eyes and rested against the carriage seat, lost in thought. 'That was the best moment of my life.'

Chapter Sixteen

Taking the stairs in his house two at a time, he alternated between regret for his words in the carriage the evening before and a feeling of weakness.

He didn't truly know the woman in his house. She'd been a different person when they'd first met, and so had he. They both had changed.

Susanna had moved in and he'd told himself she was another staff member.

But she was not. No one else had ever made him feel the emotions she'd uncovered in him. They could go so deep that he might never be freed from them.

He'd known each time he'd walked into the house that it was different now. He had a wife and a stepson.

Emotions could run roughshod over people. They could pool in a stagnant place where they would grow like dank mould, destroying all that was fresh, but he told himself he could still divert his thoughts and keep them away from Susanna.

He'd left at breakfast and stayed away. It hadn't been easy, but it was the only path. To become embroiled in emotional intensity could destroy the family feeling that had begun to feel so precious.

Leaving at breakfast every day and returning late would be a good idea.

He'd proven to himself that he could be honest about his past. And if was honest about that, then he must also remember that emotions muddied things. They ruined people and lives. They were just impulses, like the sexual ones that caused men to do such foolish things. So much of a physician's work would be reduced without impulses that led people astray. So many children wouldn't need homes. So many families would be true families, and happier. Safer. Alive.

Yes, he had finally returned home. But he'd stayed away all day considering the future as he went about seeing patients and his brother. He'd returned with strength bolstered inside.

His life in his quarters would not change. He would do as he usually did. He would settle into bed, alone, and finish reading about Lemuel Gulliver, not that he really cared what that man did anymore.

The giant women had made Gulliver a plaything. Swift should have left that part out.

In fact, Quinton wasn't certain he would even keep that book in his house. He would collect it and give it to Nettie to do with as she wished.

From her easy chair, Susanna studied the nonsensical words in the newspaper she'd retrieved and had stared at most of the day. They made no sense to her. They never would, but they still made more sense to her than Quinton's childhood.

She thought back to his aunt insisting he tell her the bad thing his brother had done. His aunt knew—knew that it would be strange to Susanna to hear of a mother behaving so.

It was almost as if she was daring Susanna to accept him as he was, or perhaps telling her how much turmoil he'd had to move aside in order to be able to go forward.

Susanna had always known she was her parents' third-favourite child. But her mother had never minded being called *Mother*.

Perhaps she'd even told her mother of Quinton's proposal as a way to say that an earl was interested in her, that she was more than just Christopher's mother.

Nothing seemed to make sense any more. How could Quinton say she made him happy, and then immediately withdraw from her? He'd turned to the window, and even though he'd remained in the vehicle, he'd been further away from her than ever before.

He'd said the best moment of his life was when she'd stood in his doorway, but how could that be true?

She bit the inside of her lip, tightened her grip on the paper and ripped it. Christopher looked up at her from the floor where he played. She smiled at him, and he continued moving his toy soldiers around.

Then she folded the paper neatly and put it on the table beside her. The servants didn't need to see a paper ripped to shreds.

Quinton had told her once, then told her twice, what kind of marriage he wanted.

A distant one—a pure one—with her clothed from head to toe and distant. That made him happy. Or he thought it did.

She took her handkerchief and tried to remove the little smudge of black ink from her hand.

Some things you just couldn't free yourself from.

Quinton.

She liked him far better when they pretended to be married. When they really were married—off he went.

A knock sounded on the door, but she knew it wasn't her husband. After returning from his aunt's, he'd given Susanna the most perfect, chaste kiss on her cheek and moved away. Then that morning he'd left at first light. She was fairly certain he was at home now, but he was definitely not receiving visitors so late.

'Enter,' she called out. Nettie stepped inside. Christopher stopped playing with his soldiers.

'Countess, Lord Amesbury wishes for you to bring back his book if you are not still perusing it. He's asked that you return it, not me.'

'Please let him know I don't have his book.'

Christopher stopped moving.

'Lord Amesbury does not think it possible that the book departed his bedside table on its own, my lady. And he would also like to speak with you about another matter.'

Susanna hesitated.

'I forgot,' Christopher said in a small voice.

'You forgot—what?'

Instantly, Christopher scurried into motion, running into his room.

She turned to Nettie. 'Thank you. I will handle this.'

She took the lamp and followed her son. He fetched a book from the floor. 'I took it because I wanted to show my soldiers the engravings. I was going to put it back, but I forgot when I saw my soldiers.'

She saw the drawing of a man tied with ropes. It must have something to do with surgical needs.

'We will return it this instant and you are never, ever to go into Amesbury's rooms without being asked—particularly when he is not there. And you are not to take anything from anywhere without permission.'

'I like stories, Mother. Don't you?'

'Yes. But you are not changing the subject. The problem is that you took something you were not supposed to take.'

She took him by the hand and marched him to Quinton's sitting room. Quinton stood when she entered, rumpled, rugged and looking none too pleased.

'Are you looking for this?' she asked, and Christopher held out the volume.

'As a matter of fact, I am.'

She corrected her son with her eyes. 'Tell him you will never again take his books or anything else.'

'I won't, Amesbury.'

'When I returned home, I discovered that someone has been in my medical supplies as well.'

Susanna gasped.

Christopher bit his bottom lip momentarily and said, 'I needed to fix my soldiers. Just like you do, Amesbury.' His voice sped up. 'I want to be a physician just like you.'

'Christopher,' she said, shocked. 'When did you do this?'

'During my nap time. When I was supposed to be asleep.'

'You are not to do that again.'

His eyes were wide. 'I wanted Amesbury to play with me. But he was gone. He was gone all day.'

Quinton took the book. 'I have instructed Nettie to lock all my medical supplies away. We cannot have you practising medicine until after you are properly taught.'

She stared at her son. 'Tomorrow you will be helping the maid with chores all day.'

'It's not necessary to punish him. We both learned our lesson today. Didn't we, Christopher?'

He nodded rapidly, eyes wide. 'I did.'

'We will see about that punishment,' she said, tugging on his hand. 'And we are going to have a long talk.'

'Will you read to me Amesbury?' He said the words as one. 'Mother wants to hear the book too.'

'Oh, no,' she said, moving to the door. 'You are going to bed, and before that, you are going to tell me how good little boys should behave.'

Christopher's eyes widened, begging Quinton.

'I doubt he would like it, but you're both welcome to stay if you wish and I'll read it aloud,' Quinton offered.

'Please, 'Bury. I like it.'

'Christopher Walton, you are going to bed,' she insisted.

'Susanna,' Quinton called after her. 'Why don't you stay?'

'He knows what he did was wrong—'

'So do I,' Quinton said, letting out a deep breath. 'But we're humans. We don't always do what's best for us.'

'But he should not be rewarded for wrongdoing.'

'True. I will scold him if you'd like.'

She stopped. Christopher started sniffling. 'I don't want 'Bury to scold me.'

'He is to be addressed as Amesbury unless he instructs you otherwise.'

'Beg pardon, Amesbury.'

'Don't cry,' Quinton said. 'I will read to you. But you must not touch my medical supplies again without my permission. Agreed?'

He nodded.

'That was not much of a reprimand,' she said.

'He and I just made a deal. A gentleman's agreement. He's not going to bother my medical equipment again, and in return he will get no more scolding for it, and he will get read to tonight because he's going to remember what he promised.'

'Well…' She smoothed Christopher's hair, and he side hugged her.

She couldn't help herself. She was just as curious about the book as Christopher was. And it had been a long time since she'd heard any stories. Lamplight flickered. Raindrops sounded on the window pane.

'Esme and Janette used to almost fight to read aloud every night,' she said, trying to keep her voice unconcerned, making sure not to reveal how much she missed those stories.

Quinton held the volume so she could see the title, and she nodded.

'I thought I would like it when I discovered the main character was a surgeon,' he said. 'Now, I'm not sure.'

'Well, we really shouldn't disturb you.'

'You won't be.'

'I don't know that Christopher would like a medical book anyway,' she said. 'Come along, Christopher. We must let Amesbury finish his work. He has to know about medicine to help people.'

'Wait.' Quinton stopped her. 'I'm resting. It's been a long day. And having the two of you here, listening to me read, might help me relax.'

She appeared sceptical. 'Medicine? Aloud?'

He held the book and ran his hand over the first two words. 'Have you heard of this story?'

'I don't think so,' she said.

'It's about a man named Lemuel Gulliver and his travels.'

'Oh, yes. I remember now. I've heard of it. But it's been a while. I'd forgotten.'

'The two of you can sit on the sofa, and I'll take my easy chair, and I'll refresh your memory.'

'But—'

'Please...' a little voice piped up, and Christopher tugged on her hand, pulling her to the sofa.

'Both of you can decide if it's a good tale.'

She settled onto the sofa and Christopher slid against her. He was nodding off soon after Quinton began the story.

Quinton kept reading and she relaxed, shutting her eyes.

After a time, Quinton closed the book. 'I think you're about to fall asleep also. Let me carry him to his room.'

'Well...'

Quinton's voice was soft. He put the book on the stand beside his chair. 'Can you read?'

He'd not known he was going to ask her that, but she'd thought it a medical book when clearly it wasn't.

'That's a preposterous question.' She stared at him, wide awake now. Too tense.

The lack of a simple *yes* told him all he wanted to know.

'I don't care if you can tell me the title of the book or not.' He stood, body unfolding, eyes unemotional and voice unwavering. 'I don't care if you can read or not. It doesn't matter.'

She averted her face.

He stood, stopping near her, and knelt down onto one knee. Putting one hand on the sofa, he gently took her chin with the other one. He turned her head until his eyes locked with hers. 'My mother could read. But she never sat and listened to a story with me. She might have gripped my hair in her fist, but she never would have brushed her hand over my head while I slept without even noticing she'd touched me.'

She didn't respond.

Lips full, but unhappy. He could not bear that, not for something so trivial.

He pushed himself to his feet and lifted Christopher into his arms as easily as he'd lifted the tome. 'I promise you, it's of no concern to me whether you can read or not.'

'No one knows. No one in society. I've been very careful.'

'You've hidden it?'

'Yes. I can't learn to read.'

'How do you know?'

'I just do. My sisters learned so quickly, and I couldn't. Sometimes I worry that Christopher inherited my lack of ability. It's my deepest fear.'

'You're the youngest, aren't you?'

'But that's not why. It was just harder for me. I can't do it.'

'I taught my brother to read. It wasn't easy for either of us.'

She led him to Christopher's room. 'Well, now you know why you could never get a written invitation from me to these rooms.'

'And I thought it was my lack of charm.'

She did the sputtering noise and placed the lamp on the bedside.

'I'd like it if you learned to read. I can show you how.'

'Trying to teach me would be a waste of your time.' Defeat filtered across her face.

'No. It won't.'

He watched as she removed Christopher's boots and readied him for bed. She tucked him in, placing a tender kiss on his forehead.

He would never forget that image as long as he lived.

She stared at her son, sleeping peacefully. 'I've never been able to read him a story. And Celeste has trouble reading English. But it doesn't matter.'

She stepped back, almost into Quinton, and he touched her shoulder, stilling her. She put the lamp on the table.

'I can read him a story again another night.'

'You would not mind?' She spoke softly.

He shook his head, then shrugged. 'No. Not at all. If you would join us.'

She turned to him, almost stopping in his arms. 'I have missed the stories my mother read to us.' She rubbed her finger over her wedding ring, and once again he saw the stain underneath.

For some reason, that rust stain was more of a promise to him than any jewel he'd ever seen. He snorted internally. His wife had a ring that would leave a mark on her hand that was difficult to hide should she take it off.

'Will you please pick out a new ring?'

'No.' She clasped her left hand and stared at the ring. 'If I am to get a new wedding ring, you will need to choose it for me.'

'I don't know what you would like.'

'Then I will keep this one.' Her eyes caught his. 'Just like I will keep my husband.' She put a palm flat on his chest and brushed a kiss across his cheek before she hurried away into her room.

The next night, the vow he'd made was on his mind. Not the wedding one, but the one he'd broken—the vow of celibacy.

Susanna had sent Nettie to tell him she didn't want to intrude so she wouldn't be coming to listen to him read. And he had to be strong enough to remember his vows…to himself.

He rang the bell but stood staring at the ceiling overhead. He imagined raindrops leaking through, but he was content with placing buckets around. He didn't even want to think of what one tear drop from Susanna could do to him.

He'd seen how a woman with wiles could twist a man around her finger, put him on his back and pick his pocket.

But she'd appeared so sad when she'd said she couldn't read. He'd had to prise it out of her, and she'd been worried her son had inherited something from her that might cause him the same problem.

He heard footsteps but knew they weren't hers.

Nettie arrived with the tray holding a Sally Lunn bun. He tried to ignore the yeasty aroma, which reminded him of all the loaves he'd cooked, and waited as she put the tray on a table in his sitting room.

Still, he was aware he was crossing a boundary he shouldn't be crossing.

Susanna may have had a child, but she was too innocent for her own good.

In fact, he doubted he'd seen many women in society as naive as Susanna.

He was relieved he'd not had to fight off the feelings that her pushing her body against his would bring, but she'd kissed his cheek. That was so underhanded.

'Please let my wife know that even though she thinks it an intrusion, it isn't. I would like Christopher to hear a story and we will all have a treat.' He met eyes with Nettie. 'And if he overhears you telling his mother that, all the better. I didn't live in the stews without learning how to be tricky.'

Nettie grinned. 'Sir, I expect you will have company shortly.'

She bustled away.

He stood at the stairway, looking up while remembering the struggles he had had when he was studying Latin—the sheer determination that it had taken, as well as an instructor willing to spend extra time with him.

He'd somehow managed to fit in with the boys, as he was particularly good at many of the things the students admired. He'd been able to out-swear any of them in a variety of accents, and embarrassment—well, that had been a new discovery for him, but only in the sense that other people felt it.

A questionable engraving had surfaced that the boys had practically studied into oblivion, and he'd been dumbfounded at their inexperience. He'd been dared to say how he knew so much about such things, and he'd filled everyone in with all the details that were commonplace to him. His friends' innocence surprised him. He'd suddenly seen the world through different eyes.

He had also repeated Auntie's claim that he was descended from royalty on one side and the peerage on the other.

Afterwards, he'd been treated with as much reverence as any peer, but they'd been much more interested in discussions of the ladies than of him, and he'd been able to get others to help him with the more difficult studies because he could answer their questions about women.

The actual lessons in medical techniques hadn't been hard but had come naturally to him, and on that, he'd also had an edge over the others.

Even the instructors at the Royal Physician's College had been surprised at his comfort and ease with the different body parts.

The diseases he'd often seen up close in the stews. In fact, he'd often seen more than the teachers had of injuries as well. The instructors had been surprisingly sheltered, except for the ones who had been in the military.

The study of anatomy was just about a body, and the insides were best kept on the inside.

The ladies had complained of every ailment under the sun, and he'd been familiar with the aches and pains of life. He'd seen the rougher boys who ran the streets and heard the crack of bones breaking. He'd smelled the scent of the blood and seen how quickly a jest could evolve into death.

The brothel was safer most days, and he'd once held down one of the ladies while Auntie stitched a wound closed. He'd liked Auntie's confidence that they could fix the injury, and the act of repairing people.

Above him, he heard movement.

In moments, a bundle of energy bounded down the stairs, with Nettie behind. Alone.

'You're going to read to me again tonight, Amesbury? I'm good at listening.' He held up a small volume.

Quinton glanced up the stairs.

'Come on, Amesbury.' Christopher gripped his hand. 'I picked out a story today that Aunt Esme gave me.' He held the book high. 'It looks really good. See?' He waved the children's book. 'It's my first very own one, ever.'

He darted into the sitting room.

'Help yourself to the treats, and I'll be back in a moment,' Quinton said. 'I want to see if your mother would like to join us.'

And Quinton knew then that he was going to break his promise about not visiting Susanna's room without a written invitation.

He gave three quick raps on the door, but no one could have missed it.

The wood pulled back just enough for her to peer around.

'I'm here to fetch you for your reading lesson.'

'It's too late. I'm tired and I'm—sleepy,' she said.

He cocked his head, paused, lightly chewed on the lining inside his cheek, and said, 'Well, we will only read a short story then.'

She blinked. 'Don't worry,' she whispered. 'I'm very adept at hiding that I can't read. I've done so all my life.'

'I don't care how well you can hide it. I want to see how good I am at teaching.'

'I don't want to.'

'It's just a reading lesson. A children's book. Just listen. We can try the lesson after Christopher falls asleep.'

'No.'

'Do you remember how we first met, and how you helped me understand the peerage and the names of the people in attendance? You taught me and you were just a child.'

'It was nothing. Just children's play.'

'Not for me.'

She raised her brows. 'But I don't need to learn to read now. I've managed this long without it.'

'But for invites?'

'You receive the invitations first. And I'm completely happy with your decisions.'

'But what if you would like to engage in private correspondence which you would not like me or anyone in the household to read?' Those words surprised him, even as he heard them coming from his own mouth, and he knew what he truly asked. So did she.

Her eyes narrowed. 'Well, I will have no letters such as those so I don't need to worry.'

The door shut in his face.

He took the steps downwards and landed at the bottom faster than he could have fallen, but stilled himself before continuing to his room.

He'd liked her indignation at the thought of receiving letters from a suitor. And she already knew how to put an exclamation point on the end of a sentence. She'd shown him that with the door shutting.

He would think about how to proceed with Susanna. He could not go straight ahead, but had to tread carefully. She was well-entrenched in what she believed.

Making sure he reflected peacefulness on his face, Quinton strode into his sitting room and greeted Christopher again.

He read the book six times to the boy and did not once tell him to keep his boots off the sofa. Twice he had to ask him to move because he couldn't keep reading if Christopher's head was between him and the words.

Then he spent a few moments tracing the letters with Christopher. 'You can show your mother how well your finger can follow the letters tomorrow. Now, let's read about Lemuel Gulliver,' he said. In only moments after starting it, Christopher had curled into a ball on the sofa.

'And on the seventh try, even the little one rests,' he said, lifting the small, sleepy bundle. He hooked an arm under Christopher's bottom, letting him snuggle into his shoulder, and headed up the dark stairway.

He put Christopher into bed and pulled the covers over him.

Christopher woke enough to say, 'I'm still wearing my boots.'

'Do you care?' he asked.

'No.'

'I don't either. Tonight, you can be a soldier and sleep in your boots. But in my sitting room, a gentleman keeps his boots off the sofa. Do you think you can remember?'

'Yes.'

'Good.'

'Night 'Bury.'

'Good night, Christopher.'

'Mother would like listening to Mr Gull Liver's story again.'

'Perhaps tomorrow night.'

'Pardon me.' A prim voice interrupted his morning perusal of the newspaper in his sitting room. He'd left the door open. 'You know that last night you could have easily sent for Nettie to take Christopher to Celeste and she would have prepared him for bed.'

He lowered the paper enough to look over the top. 'I put him to bed.'

'In his boots.'

'He didn't mind. I didn't mind.'

'And now he thinks he should always sleep in his boots, like a soldier.'

He grinned. 'Why don't you join us tonight, and I will tell him it was only for one night?'

'I do not wish to learn to read.'

'Fine. And I do not want to read a children's book six times, one after the other.'

'That was your decision.'

'You're right. I never again intend to read one book more than one time in a night. I made that decision as well.'

'And the boots?'

'That is between you and Celeste. I'm fine with him wearing them to bed every night if he wishes.'

'Well, then I will tell him he must get Celeste or me when he is ready for bed.'

She waited but he didn't respond. 'And that question you asked me last night… I'm not sure it was a compliment.'

'I beg your pardon if it sounded improper. I was not pleased in that moment, and I surprised myself with the question. But your answer satisfied me.'

'It's the truth.'

'That's why I liked it. And I would like it very much if you would try to read again.'

'If I never learn to read, I cannot have private correspondence.'

'Very well.' He pulled the paper back in front of his face.

He glanced up again and had to keep himself from smiling. He understood where her son got that little way of inserting himself into Quinton's line of vision. Susanna stood peering over the top of his paper at him.

'Do you mind if I stay?' she asked.

He lowered the paper. 'By all means.'

'I would like to speak with you. If you don't mind?' Her chin went up.

She shut the door and sat on the sofa.

Oh, his wife was not wanting to learn to read this morning. She was wanting to give an instruction or her opinion—and he would wager on the latter. He held up the paper momentarily to make certain his expression was hidden.

He folded the paper closed. 'Say anything you want. Anything.' A dare, if she wanted to take it that way.

Susanna firmed her lips. She would say what she wanted. 'You didn't have to tell me that. I was going to anyway.'

'I know.'

His eyes had smudges under them. His cravat was tied, but only the barest knot—perfunctory or functional, but not stylish, which somehow made him seem even more assured and more in fashion than if he had a valet who'd spent hours perfecting it.

'I've spent my life pretending. No one can pretend better than I. I can dance. I can sing and laugh, and distract people, and pretend to be the person they think I am. No one notices all what I can't do. I can't read or do sums or anything like that. I could see my sisters' schoolwork and copy it. I could cajole Cook into giving me extra treats for the governess and she felt I was learning just fine. You wed me for what I can do, not what I can't.'

'If you can't read, that's fine. But I believe you can. And I would like you to try once more. Or perhaps ten times more. Because on the ninth, you might not make it. But on the tenth, you might surprise yourself. Even if you don't ever grasp it, the tenacity you exert for the attempt might mean more to you than the actual task.'

Not only could he look like a rector—well, a rather young one—but he could sound like one also. But he'd sent her thoughts in another direction.

His hands were larger than hers. Capable. His nails neat. Fingers ordinary. Yet she could see the strength inside him, contained in his body. Compressed. Anything he had chosen to do he would have been a success at, and he could never understand her limited abilities.

She closed her eyes and thought of their lovemaking. She couldn't throw herself against him. He'd think she was just trying to distract him. Yet he was certainly distracting her. He'd even made the newsprint and paper scent come alive. She shouldn't have moved so close to him.

But it had been impossible not to. He pulled her to him. It had taken all her strength to stay away from him the night before and she'd cursed herself, and then she'd waited for the dawn.

It hadn't been a surprise to her that she'd had to enter his sitting room that morning, only that she'd been able to wait so long.

She put a hand on the sofa and ran her fingers over the upholstery.

She was as trapped in the room as she was trapped in her inability to read. But if she had to be confined somewhere—near him was her first choice.

And she could have sworn she saw something warm peeking from his eyes before he sounded so direct.

She firmed her face, and she knew, without a doubt, even though he couldn't grasp her failure to read, Quinton would never call her a bunny.

But she would never be able to tell him she loved him. He wouldn't understand. That plunged more despair into her than not being able to comprehend spelling.

'I'm not going to be able to recite a book.'

'It's not about that. It's about making the effort.'

She shook her head and stood. 'I did. I couldn't, any more than you can change the feelings inside you that keep you from believing in love. And I can't change the feelings inside me either.'

Then she stood and stalked to the door, but once she reached it, she turned on her heel, marched back to him and kissed his temple, then touched his freshly shaven cheek.

His eyes registered shock.

'And *that* is how I feel about you.'

Chapter Seventeen

The next morning started with a door banging somewhere in the residence. A servant would not have dared, or so she thought. But the atmosphere of the home had changed. Everyone seemed to be in the midst of their personal storm cloud.

The day progressed slowly. Only Christopher was skittering around like he had wings on his feet, happily oblivious to the adults around him and letting his soldiers use his books for a fort.

Apparently, Quinton had been to the bookshop the afternoon before, and he'd spent half a fortune on every children's book he could find at Hatchards. Christopher had them strewn from room to room, and Nettie apologised but said that Lord Amesbury had given specific instructions that the maids were not to straighten them, and to leave them where it would be easiest for Mr Christopher to find them.

Susanna mentally repeated Nettie's words, finishing with a head waggle that she was sure Nettie had been thinking. She was equally sure Quinton knew just what he was doing.

When Christopher had found the books, he'd rushed

to find Quinton and they'd had a little reading session. Then he'd had to tell her of the great fun he'd had in helping his 'Bury read.

She had corrected her son during the day, telling him to say Amesbury, and he had returned later and told her that his Amesbury said he could call him 'Bury or Father or Papa if his mother didn't mind. But they would have to abide by her decision.

She clasped her right hand over the ring on her left and sat down.

For the first time in her entire life, she had a true husband. A man who—

Oh, she didn't know. She didn't know what she was feeling, but she turned her head so her son wouldn't see her eyes, and she wiped away the wetness.

Quinton had always been there. He'd been there when she'd wed Walton, and she'd never truly seen him. She wasn't entirely sure she was seeing him now, except through her love for her son.

And he deserved more. So much more. He deserved to be seen for himself.

They'd already accepted an invitation to a soirée, which he wasn't looking forward to attending. But he was friends with Carruthers's son, and more than once he'd been called upon for medical advice.

He appreciated the opportunity to attend. He needed to spend some society time with his wife, but more than that, he wanted to be with her.

All he wanted was for her to try reading once more. If she couldn't, that was fine, but not giving it a fair attempt wasn't. It may be harder for her, but harder was just the way of life sometimes.

Nettie had appeared earlier, a solemn look on her lips

but with the sides faltering occasionally. She held a small bottle in the palm of each hand, as precisely as a butler might hold a treasured wine for inspection.

'Her Ladyship would like to know which one meets with your approval.'

'What is it?'

'Perfume.'

He frowned, taking each one. 'Please tell the Countess I am considering both. I would not want her to make a mistake on something so vital. I may take some time. Considering…'

'I will tell her. I don't want her any more concerned about her appearance.'

'She shouldn't be. Just between the two of us, my wife is too beautiful.'

'I won't tell her that, or she may feel she has to change her clothing again.' She scurried from the room.

A few moments later, Susanna made her way down the stairs. Her hair was swept up with just the right amount of tendrils framing her face, and her eyes were luminous. The bodice of her dress was trimmed in ribbons and matched the ones in her hair. The clothing complemented her as well as any butterfly's wings framed its owner. She had a reticule on her arm and gloves lying across the top threaded among the ties.

'Which perfume?' she asked.

He had not complimented her enough to Nettie.

He was putting himself in a special kind of torment. 'Let's try each one,' he said.

She took one bottle, then tried not to truly get any on her skin but the barest amount.

She repeated the process with the opposite wrist and the other glass.

He took her wrist. Heavenly.

Then he lifted the other wrist. Sublime.

Blast it. He couldn't speak. He swallowed.

'Well?'

He reached for the nearest bottle and held it out to her. She smiled. He didn't really know which one he'd selected, and he couldn't really tell the difference.

'Oh, that is my favourite too.' She beamed.

She took the bottle top and daubed a bit more on her wrist and rubbed them together, then touched the bottle again and pressed her fingertip to each side of her neck.

He took the container from her and lightly clasped her elbows. He shut his eyes and breathed in, and on the exhale, he moved away, finding his reason and trying to remember what he should say.

She was pulling on her gloves. 'We must be going.'

That wasn't what he'd been thinking.

She swept out the door, the hem of her dress moving with each step, her delicate matching dancing slippers moving swiftly.

As he stepped into the vehicle to leave for the dance, he looked at her and said, 'You should know Mrs Carruthers always has a waltz.'

'I will so enjoy waltzing.'

He sat beside her. His glance flicked to her. He thumped the side of the vehicle strongly enough to vibrate the carriage, letting the driver know they were ready to leave. 'I'd rather be at home with—a good…book.' He substituted the words at the last moment. He'd rather be at home with her. 'Dancing is tedious.'

'I'm sure you would have a better time with Gulliver tonight.'

He reminded himself of his promises, of the safety of distance—that they were partners in a deeper sense than any physical touch.

'I do not want to be with Gulliver unless you are with us,' he said, aware of the lingering scent of her perfume and how the interior of the carriage was like a little slice of Eden.

'Make sure Christopher doesn't wake me in the morning at daybreak and ask me to read it,' he said.

'He did not do that!'

'This morning, I woke up when he dropped the book on my face. He was sorry, and I sent him straight back upstairs. And "Mr Gull Liver" is now locked away with my medical supplies. You have a powerful force of nature on two legs. And after I selected some other books for him, and read to him, I told him that I won't read to him at night anymore unless you are with him.'

'I know. He told me, and he pouted, and his favourite storybook is now with his soldiers until morning.'

'Won't you try to read?'

'The additional matter of my reading was not part of the original agreement.'

'It is the addendum I'm requesting.'

'Addendum?'

'Latin. "Something added."'

'Well, if I could read, I might know that,' she said. 'But I can't, which means there will be nothing added.'

The carriage ran over a bump, and it jostled her closer to him. She gazed at him.

'Try reading for me,' he begged. 'And if it doesn't work, it doesn't. Not everyone has to read.'

'I keep trying to tell you that.'

'Christopher likes books,' he said.

'But what if he has my learning difficulties?'

'He can tell the difference between the words *cat* and *rat* already. It seemed easy for him.'

The carriage was silent except for the turning of the wheels, the creaking of leather and the squeak of springs.

'He can?' she whispered.

'*Cat* and *Christopher* start with the same letter. He learned it instantly when I showed him. I have a slate and he enjoyed drawing on it. And he knew the word *rat* was different from *cat* so I let him read those words in the story.'

'Oh.' Quietly.

He shrugged. 'It was nothing. To him. Or to me.'

He took her hand closer to his body and indicated on the back of her glove. '*C*. A half circle...or sideways half circle, however it is easier to think of it. *Christopher* and *cat* both begin with it.'

'I think I knew that.'

'Didn't you enjoy the moments when you were listening to *Gulliver's Travels*?' he asked.

'Not enough to read it myself.'

He gave up. Arguing with her would only make her more determined not to give it a try.

'Fine,' he said. 'No addendum.'

'Will you waltz with me?'

'Yes.'

'Good. I like the waltz.'

The feigned innocence in her eyes amused him.

She sat so prim and proper. 'Oh, another bump,' she said, and jostled herself against him.

'I didn't feel it,' he said.

'But I did.'

He relaxed, stretching his legs as much as he could in the confined vehicle. He had received what he'd asked for. He appraised her again. 'This will be our first waltz.' He made up his mind. 'I am going to like it.'

'Are you sure?'

'Yes. I am.'

Excitement lit her smile. 'It's considered daring.'

'We will try to live up to its promise, then.'

Before the first violin sounded for the waltz, Quinton walked over, and with the bow of a gallant, he held out his elbow, and she clasped it.

When he took her hand, she felt the strength of his grasp through her glove and the other palm at her back, contacting softly—hardly a touch, more of a feeling, but covering her with the knowledge that he held her.

A flurry of violin notes surrounded them, perhaps an echoing flute lingering behind, and he pulled her closer. Not too close—not touching—but each time she moved, her back contacted his fingers, linking her to him. Her skirts swirled, and she knew when the fabric wisped against his trouser leg.

Her other hand rested on his shoulder, the crisp fabric of his coat between them, but when he stepped backwards, his shoulder flexed slightly.

The notes blended their feet. She twirled, and at the end of the swirl, their distance diminished, their bodies closer.

When the dance finished his eyes were shut, and he opened them in the moment her gaze locked on his.

'The most beautiful dance of my life,' he said, voice rough, and he paused to lead her into a final slow twirl. Her skirts rustled, not truly flaring but falling back into place as she slowed and he led her to a quiet corner.

As they separated, he took her hand. 'If you can show me how beautiful a waltz can be, can I show you what reading can be like?'

She held herself up with the power emanating from him.

'You truly are traitorous.'

'You have more than fulfilled the role I married you for. You have smiled at me with such devotion every time someone sees us together that I don't doubt for one breath that they believe we are as united as any two people can be. You could convince someone you could read every word Shakespeare ever wrote and translate it into Latin. But in our home, when we are alone, I don't want you pretending. Ever.'

'I won't. And I don't want to learn to read. Ever.'

He took her hand, pulled her palm to his cheek, and then kissed it. 'I didn't want to waltz.' Emotion billowed under his words. 'But it was magnificent.'

It was as if she could see stars twinkling around him and feel lightning in his body from centuries before, like she could embrace a moment of being one with him. She could not have refused him anything, even that.

'Fine. I will try to read. With you. If only to show you that I can't.' Immediately the happiness she'd felt wavered, and she wished she'd never agreed.

When he saw how difficult it was for her to learn, he would discover how well she acted her role, and he would be disappointed in the real her.

'We'll try for just a small amount of time, as sometimes I need a rest from medicine. If it gets exceedingly problematic for you, then you can rest. But not because it's hard. Difficulty is just the hurdle before success. And it doesn't matter either way about reading. It only matters that you try.'

She could almost believe him, and she didn't care anymore that she couldn't read, because what she could do was savour the nearness of Quinton.

Chapter Eighteen

For a moment, after she was seated and before he entered the coach, he spoke with the driver. They talked about carriage wheels and whether the ones on the vehicle appeared to be in top condition. The safety of the vehicle was important, but his delay tactic was vital. He was giving someone else his attention so he wouldn't be so captivated by her. But it wasn't working as it should. He could do no more than agree with whatever the driver said. If he'd said they needed a whole new carriage Quinton would have approved and his thoughts would have remained as strongly on Susanna as if he still held her.

He shouldn't have waltzed with her so intimately. He shouldn't have. She was too feminine and beautiful, and he had such a weakness for her…and now for perfume.

He told himself it was because they had married. It was not a weakness but a wifeness. But he knew he lied. Marriage had reduced his ability to retreat from his desires.

No matter.

He was a man, not a youth. And she was all lightness and warmth and treasure. But treasures had tarnished before.

She appeared like the sweetheart he'd never had, the girl whose gloved hand his seventeen-year-old self would have held so carefully—just as carefully as his mature self had done. He must gather his resources and keep his distance, and not let the seventeen-year-old inside him ever resurface again. Ever. He had a family to protect. A life. A household. Even the servants could be upended if the home became disrupted.

With his fortitude back in place, he moved into the carriage.

She reached out and clasped his fingertips. 'That was a lovely waltz.' She stretched out her legs, flexing her slippers. 'I hardly have any room over here,' she said.

His resolved immediately softened.

'Apologies.'

'If you put your arm around me I'd have more room, and I'll be warmer, and I won't have to pretend to be jostled against you.'

He put his arm around her, holding her close. 'I would not want to wager against you in any card game,' he said.

'Sadly, you would win. I don't know how to play cards.'

'I've heard that one before. Good strategy.'

'You're good at tactics too.' She paused. 'I just realised. I am completely surrounded by the staff you hire and I am never out of their path, so you likely know where I am at each minute of my life.'

'Mostly.'

'Mostly?' The silence in the carriage surrounded him. 'You think I am like the other women you've known. Don't you?'

'No.'

'You chose everyone who lives in your house based on—loyalty.' She gasped. 'I was separated from my husband, but still loyal, and even after he died… I never courted, or even attended any soirées.'

'I don't know that you're right. I don't know that you're wrong. I never thought about it much.'

'You don't have many males around. Except for your brother and my father, you keep men at a distance. You do seem to like my mother better than my father.'

'Well, I was raised around women, as you know. I'm used to that.'

'Well, then… I guess you must get used to me.' She was near fluffing about, making herself comfortable snuggled under his arm. That dashed perfume scented his nostrils and he had a feeling of being claimed—of being marked as hers. And it wasn't as dreadful as he would have expected.

'I almost feel I'm being toyed with,' he said.

'No. It's something different. Something you don't believe in. But it doesn't matter, because you are a man of honour and I am your wife. And you are very busy, and yet you want to spend time teaching me something I don't want to learn.'

'I had to learn, too, when I didn't want to. And I don't regret it.' He reached up and loosened his cravat, and then slid it free.

She took the cravat from his hand and folded the cloth, and then he saw the outline of her hand as she lifted it closer to her face, touching it against her skin.

The carriage stopped. His breathing seemed to stop.

'We should start tonight.' she said. 'Tonight is a good time to learn… . Perhaps for both of us.'

'Perhaps tomorrow,' he said cautiously.

'I will have an excuse tomorrow night.'

'I'm tired.'

'Like that one.'

'It's late.'

'I'll pick a good book, then.'

He stepped out, then reached back for her and helped her disembark. And in his clasp on her, he felt vibrancy, energy and sunbursts. 'Very well.'

'I certainly lost this argument,' she said.

He sputtered.

She walked into the house. 'I will be with you shortly. This dress is too tight.'

'You're going to put on your dressing gown, aren't you?'

'If you don't mind.'

'And you'll have your hair plaited?'

'Yes.'

He paused at the landing. 'I'll be waiting for you. In the ballroom. I think this is more important than reading. To hold you.'

She put her fingertips over his lips, and the touch held him immobile.

Her eyes rested on him. 'It is.'

One lone candle lit the ballroom.

She walked inside, feeling rather overdressed in her thick dressing gown.

He removed his boots, shed his coat and waistcoat, and held out his arms. 'One circle around.'

Then he undid the tie at her waist, and the garment opened, her knee length chemise under it.

He began to hum the rhythm of the waltz, bowed to her and took her at a most proper distance into his clasp, with only thin cotton between her skin and his hand. The dance began with a twirl and then a broad swing around the room, making her breathless.

Then he pulled her closer, and the circle became

smaller and smaller and slower and slower as he held her, and his humming became softer, more breaths than sounds.

When the circle diminished, he held her against his body, moving as one. The imagined music faded, replaced by the pounding of her heart, the scent of the warmth of their bodies heightened by the closeness and the heat a caress.

Eyes closed, his cheek brushed against hers, resting there. Lips traced her jawline, and he held her up with a dancer's clasp.

He pulled her dressing gown closed again, and led her from the room, and to his bedroom.

He touched fingertips to the pulse beat at her neck. Then the back of his hand slid to rest over her heart.

He kissed her, this time lingering along her lips. The kiss was a flavoured taste of male that turned her inside out and opened all her senses to him. 'After I touched you once, all I want to do is hold you.'

Her palms grazed the points of his shirt collar and the skin of his cheeks.

She tasted his kiss and felt the strength and hardness of his body as he pulled her close.

'You've totally demolished my willpower,' he said, then moved aside as he took her plait and slowly undid it, letting the hair ripple around her shoulders.

He placed her gently on the bed.

Then he took a moment to kiss her, before disrobing and lying beside her.

He touched her body as if it were a shrine he'd dreamed of his whole life, and perhaps it was.

Never had he had more gratification than when he listened to her gasps and knew that they had shared such glorious pleasure again.

* * *

Susanna lay beside Quinton. He'd said nothing. No tender words. He had held her close, but when she'd asked him how he felt, he'd not really said anything, but given a little murmur.

Perhaps he was right. Perhaps he didn't have the capacity to truly make love.

But then she glanced at the covers over them, felt the completeness of their bodies together—remembered his tender touch.

No man without a heart could be that gentle.

She paused, considering the consequences. Because she would continue to share Quinton's bed if he asked. She knew it without a doubt. She wanted to be his true wife.

And that could lead to another child. Quinton would never agree to his child living elsewhere like Walton had. They would be together for ever, in a way she'd truly never again wanted to be bound to anyone.

She would be taking irrevocable steps.

She studied the ring. It was truly little more than a blacksmith's nail. To be bound to a man who would put his child first could be pleasant because he would also be putting things in the right order—not himself above all.

Quinton might not believe in love. He might not grasp it. He might not accept it. But if he went through the motions… If his sense of rightness overrode everything else, then love didn't matter. Or she hoped it didn't.

To have someone she could depend on was most important. Loyalty instead of love.

But there was a little ache in her heart where love would have fit nicely.

He moved, not a lot, but just enough for her to be aware he was pulling away.

She felt like she'd been shoved to the corner. 'I have to know, and I have to hear you say the words.'

His jaw locked. Now she was going to ask him if he loved her. He would have to thank her for killing the sweetness of their encounter. Nothing she could say would work better than that.

'It's time for you to read the words,' he said evasively.

He picked up his trousers and left the room to slide them back on. He collected the slate he'd purchased, the chalk and the children's book, and sat on the sofa in his sitting room.

She stepped into the doorway, wearing her dressing gown, a determined look on her face.

He knew she was not going to stop talking until she spoke what was on her mind. He tapped the chalk against the slate.

'You are an earl, with wealth, and my husband,' she said. 'If I were to have a child with you, you would have all rights to it. I could not take it from you, but you could keep me from it. Would you ever do that?'

'Did I wed a barrister?' he asked, holding the chalk still.

He hid his surprise that she'd not mentioned the love nonsense.

He put the slate beside him and stood. 'Working under the assumption that you would always treat a child as compassionately as you treat your son, you would always have a place in my home with him or her, perhaps on another storey as now, with little contact between us. But if you were ever to take a lover, I could not allow him into my home. I just could not. You would have to meet him elsewhere, and not in front of my child. You and I would avoid each other also. My childhood did not teach me to share.'

'You would think, with my being the youngest of three sisters, I would have learned to share, but I didn't catch on to that any better than reading.' Studying him, she added, 'And if I were to remain faithful, would you?'

'Even if you were not to remain faithful, I would still remain so. It is my honour that I am entrusting my body with.'

'I don't really understand that, but I get the general idea.'

The house was silent.

'Can we consider this an addendum, agreed upon by both parties?' she asked. 'Faithfulness and not taking a child away or using them as a pawn.'

'And not just any child we might have together,' he said. 'If I grow closer to your son, I don't want you to ever use him in anger against me.'

'I won't.'

She stepped forward and clasped his hand, pulling his fingertips closed and herself against his chest, their hands locked between them as she rested against him. 'Addendum. Agreed upon by both.'

She raised her eyes to him. 'But I want you to write some letters for me. I want to see them. On paper. Not on the slate. At your desk.'

He frowned. 'I won't write anything I don't believe.'

He gave the chair a nudge with his foot and sat at the desk.

'It's for me. Not you.'

She stood behind his shoulder and dictated the words to him. 'Write, "The honour of your company is requested in my room…"'

He dipped the pen in ink and wrote the words.

'That appears right,' she said, taking the pen from him and putting a big flourish of an *S* afterwards with a swirl.

She presented it to him. 'A written letter of invitation.' She frowned. 'Or is that another addendum? I know it is not a letter of regrets.'

Smiling, he folded it, smaller and smaller, and clasped it, leaving it on his desk. 'Doesn't matter. I'll find my way there, and now, let's begin our lesson.'

She groaned. 'Are you sure you wouldn't like to explore my bedroom?'

Being in such close proximity to her, his hurdle was ignoring the womanliness of Susanna. But he was adept at directing his thoughts in the direction he wanted them to go. He'd had to be to survive. He focused on the task at hand.

Her reading.

But when Susanna was in the room, he wasn't Amesbury any more. He was Quinton, and she was the girl who'd needed her doll rescued, and who'd accepted him into society without question. Only he was older now, and he'd matured, and it had brought with it a multitude of other problems. He stared ahead, forcing himself to remember that she was his wife and he must treat her in the same manner one must treat porcelain, injured people and precious jewellery. She was fragile right now. He saw it in her gaze.

She hesitated, not moving closer. 'I can't.'

'Susanna,' he said. 'Don't defeat yourself before you've even started.'

He needed to say the same thing to himself.

Memories of the stews and the rashness of his past flashed into his mind, and the open doorway to the bedroom behind him taunted him.

The corner of the four-poster bed with railings rising straight to the sky. The coverlet. The mattress under it that had held them so perfectly.

He'd have to distance himself from her. This kind of thought never did anyone any good. It was a weakness of the body—a wonderful lapse, but a weakness.

He rose and shut the bedroom door without observing the inside again.

'No one will have to be aware. No one.' She walked closer to the table by the chair, absently straightening the scarf but making it more uneven.

'Except you,' he added.

'And you.' Her eyes were down.

'It doesn't matter that I know.' He shrugged one shoulder. 'Everyone has more things they can't do than they can do, but this one is important to you—important enough that you hide it away. That's the difference.'

'Only you're concerned about it.'

'You care. So I do too.' He smiled.

'Because you're trained to help others.'

'Then allow me to do as I've been taught.' He retrieved the slate.

She didn't answer.

'Let's start with this.' He drew an *a* on the slate, and held it where she could see it.

She responded with the correct name.

When he drew the *b*, she wasn't sure if it was a *b* or a *d*. He wrote the word *bed* on the slate. 'If you think of this word and imagine that it's a little bed, and how the letters look, and how it sounds, it's easier to remember.' He shut his eyes tightly for a second. Of all the words in the language, he'd picked the word *bed*.

'Fine.' She sat on the sofa. 'If you're not going to tax me too much.'

He sat beside her. She held out her hand. He put the chalk in it, but she switched it to the other and continued to extend her fingers. He clasped them and then slid back against the sofa. She immediately relaxed, and it was natural to put his arm around her and hold her close while she worked out the alphabet and he sat with her, assisting. She did the little wiggly thing when she moved, and he knew again his shoulder sleeve would be scented with her perfume.

'You're getting tired,' he said, after she started making mistakes.

'I know. I just don't want to quit.'

'You're not,' he said, taking the slate from her, but she didn't leave.

She melted into his arms. 'I think you're going to have to throw me out.'

'You can stay until you get a written letter of egress.'

'I wouldn't be able to read it. And I don't know for sure what that word means.'

'I suppose you can stay then.'

First one lamp sputtered out, and then a second one.

It was so easy to kiss her hair, to interlock their fingers and listen to the beauty of the silent night turning into morning.

He'd never done such a thing before.

The tiniest amount of light filtered in through the window.

''Bury. 'Bury.' A little voice called through the door. 'I can't find Mother.'

Instantly, she sat erect and called out. 'I'm in here.'

The door opened slowly with two little eyes peering around it.

Quinton shut his. Her clothing rustled. The sofa adjusted to the loss of her as she moved away. And the morning air turned cold on the side she'd left.

''Bury, you're reading without me. I want to hear the story.' He ran over to the table, picked up a book and wiggled and wobbled until he sat right next to him.

'I like this one,' Christopher said. 'What's it about?'

'We'll find out together,' Quinton said, and began reading.

When he finished the book, Christopher said, ''Bury, I love you.'

He tensed, standing. 'That's enough reading. Ask Nettie to read if you want another story.'

He left the room, donned the rest of his clothing and exited swiftly.

Susanna's knitting needles clicked together. Her son had told Quinton he loved him several days ago, but he hadn't responded in kind. Her son was used to hearing he was loved. His grandmother and grandfather were always saying such things to each other too.

But her husband confused the word with *hate*. In fact, someone could probably tell him they hated him and he'd not flicker a lash. They could possibly swear at him in any language they wanted, and he'd probably react better than he had when Christopher had said he loved him.

And if a child's tender words caused him to react so?

An uphill battle was still a battle, and she was not adept at fighting and didn't want to be. She'd promised Quinton he would not have to live in a contentious household. And he wouldn't. He'd given her son shelter and compassion, just as Quinton gave so much to everyone.

Except himself. He didn't really give himself all the credit she believed he deserved. She suspected he never would. That would be an uphill battle as well.

She raised her eyes to the wall decorations but didn't see them. Her first marriage hadn't been an uphill trek but a dash to a cliff edge. She didn't want a battle. That had worked out horribly in the past, and she didn't want to go back to hers any more than Quinton wanted to return to his.

He didn't even seem inclined to check on her.

For all her husband knew she could have expired days ago. Hopefully a servant would tell him, eventually, that she was still alive. Even Christopher had complained that he missed his Amesbury.

The needles clicked faster. She was making a cloak for one of the children at his auntie's. She ran a hand over the dark wool, imagining it keeping a little one warm, and smiled. Only one garment and she understood how the act of helping the children could become so important in Quinton's life. This was so much more important than a mere stitchery for the wall.

And she had learned it from Quinton.

Apparently, Quinton's heart was big enough for all the children, but not for his wife or her son.

She'd heard a carriage arrive earlier that morning and wondered if they would have a patient lingering somewhere, waiting for Quinton.

But the house was too quiet.

She went in search of Christopher.

She opened the door to her son's room. Christopher sat at his desk, feet dangling, and a man stood at the side.

Christopher's bottom lip stuck out. 'Amesbury is being mean.'

'Who are you?' she asked the thin reed of a man with checked waistcoat and a wilted cravat.

'I'm Mr Christopher's new tutor, Mr Marving.' He straightened. 'Your mother contacted me and gave me the direction, and when I arrived, Lord Amesbury hired me.'

'Where is Celeste?'

Christopher sniffled again. 'She said she is leaving

now because no one needs her. I have to be a big boy. And she said she doesn't need to be so close to me since I have a tutor and nobody told her about it.'

Susanna gasped.

'It is an adjustment when a child gets a new tutor,' the man said, tucking his cravat more neatly into his waistcoat. 'But in time, I'm sure Mr Christopher and I will become better acquainted. I am also to instruct any other resident of the house who requests it,' the man said.

Susanna's jaw clamped and her chin lowered. 'Did Lord Amesbury say who else might need instruction?'

'No, but he said it is to be known within the household that anyone who would like reading assistance is to have training each day.'

'Well, that's generous of him.' Only it wasn't. He was distancing himself from her.

Christopher sniffed. 'I have to learn Latin from the tutor. I don't want him to teach me. But Amesbury said I had to have a tutor and learn Latin. Amesbury's mean. He is not my 'Bury anymore. I told him so.'

'You're teaching a little boy Latin?' she gasped.

'Eventually, I will,' the man said. 'Once he is older and has learned to read and write English.'

'I want Celeste,' Christopher cried, jumping out of his little chair and away from his desk. '*Please*, Mother.' Christopher ran to her and hugged her tight. 'I want Celeste to stay with me.'

She knelt down and snuggled him close, the little boy smell of him touching her nose and his hair tickling her face.

She stood, still holding him, and forced her emotions below the surface. She would let the stranger go at that instant.

She spoke to the man. 'You may leave, sir.'

The tutor gasped, as crestfallen as if he'd lost his last friend.

'I need this post,' he said. 'The child from my last position went off to boarding school. I have to live with my mother, and we've barely kept off the streets. She was so happy when I told her I had secured this position.'

'Well, then you may stay…for now,' she said after a pause. 'But we will see whether you are to tutor him. I am still a little uncertain as to that.'

'Please consider it.'

'I will.' She turned to her son. 'Christopher, in order to keep Celeste, we are going to keep the tutor as well, and you must apply yourself in your lessons so you have plenty of time to play,' she instructed him. 'And Celeste will be with you, just the same as before. She will make sure he is not teaching you too quickly.'

Christopher sniffed again. 'I want new soldiers too.'

'We will discuss that, Christopher. Now, fetch your slate for your studies. Celeste will be with you both, supervising…and perhaps learning to read English as well. I will fetch her.'

She walked to Celeste's room, backbone straight, knocked and went in. She shut the door behind her. Celeste sat on her bed, a handkerchief clasped in her hand and tears running down her cheeks.

'You are leaving?' Susanna asked.

Celeste sobbed into the damp fabric. '*Oui.* I knew this day would come, but I'd so hoped there would be another child to look after.' She sniffed again. 'And then I saw how unlikely that was.'

A stab went into Susanna's heart. 'It's not completely unlikely,' she said awkwardly.

'It's not?' Celeste blew her nose on the handkerchief.

'Not entirely.'

'I'll never have another post like this one. The new

tuteur will be taking charge of Christopher's studies. I could not stop crying long enough to find you and tell you *au revoir*.'

'You are very much needed here. Even more than before. The new tutor needs guidance.'

Celeste gaped at her.

'Yes. You may stay as Christopher's companion and mine as well,' Susanna said. 'I do not know what that will entail, but I depend on you so much. You may keep your room, as it is the perfect location. And I suppose your payment will increase also with the additional responsibilities.'

'You are a saint.' She sniffled again. 'Oh, Madame Susanna, you are a saint.'

She stood tall. Celeste called her a saint, and she'd once admitted that reading English was not as easy as people pretended.

How dare her stuffy poultice of a husband put a stranger near her son without telling her! 'Do you happen to know when the Earl might grace us with his presence?

'He should be late tonight,' Celeste said. 'Mrs Nettie said she fetched the carriage driver to take him to his brother's home.'

He often stayed long hours with his brother or escaped there.

But this time she would be waiting for him.

'Would you please be so kind as to have a maid send some tea and biscuits to my husband's room, and later, a little wine, and some of the apricots, bread and some of the roast Cook was planning for me? I will be there until my husband returns.'

For the first time in her life, she truly felt like a wife while she waited for him. He had not hurried home. She'd had time to fetch the slate, practise her penmanship and return it to her room.

Now she ate another meal, enjoying the last taste of the apricots.

She contemplated the lack of decor in the room as she ate. Medical books. She spelled out the first word but she didn't know what it said. The others were just as difficult.

A coloured drawing of the internal organs, framed, hung on the wall. The intestines. One needed intestinal fortitude to observe that every day, she supposed.

She examined the other engraving, an outline of a body, with the brain nestled in place and lines with names written on them—in Latin, she assumed, because they didn't look like any words in the books she'd been studying.

And then she took the lamp to the wall, examining his possessions further. Goodness, Quinton had a strong constitution. She was pleased she'd finished her meal beforehand.

No wonder he spent so much time at his brother's house. Or his aunt's. Or her parents'. Or any place that was elsewhere. She would not take all of it personally. The decor was disheartening. Her room was almost as bland as his was unsettling. Then she realised she could change her surroundings however she wished. Quinton would not expect to approve her purchases.

She lifted a book. A heavy one.

Even the tomes were…intense. Her husband must be the smartest man on the face of the earth.

She moved over to examine a volume that appeared heavy enough to break a foot if dropped on it. She couldn't read a word on them. Again, probably Latin. She hoped.

Carriage wheels sounded. She placed herself as regally as a queen on a throne in his favourite chair. And she was wearing his favourite perfume.

Quinton would know she was there because no one would need to follow along after him to light a lamp.

The door opened.

'You did not tell me about the tutor coming.' She firmed her lips after she spoke the sentence. 'He said he is going to teach Christopher Latin. *Latin?* He's just a child.'

He stared at her as if she'd grown an extra ear. 'There is nothing wrong with learning Latin once he has grasped the English language.'

'He is far too young.' She rushed by him, intent on leaving once she'd had her say. 'And you cannot let Celeste go. I am Christopher's mother. I am to be consulted in all decisions about his life. I strongly suspect hiring the tutor was a ruse to get a teacher for me so you would not have to spend time with—.' She clamped her lips together and thumped her finger against her chest instead.

'Goodnight and pleasant dreams, Lord Amesbury.' Then she made for the stairs.

Chapter Nineteen

He rushed after her, calling her at the bottom of the stairs towards the upper floor. He could not let her go. She stopped, hand on the rail.

'Latin? Latin?' he said, each word bitten out. 'You complain because Christopher is to be taught Latin at the proper time? Do you know how hard that was for me to learn while I was having to learn everything else as well? What is wrong with you?'

Blast it. He was shouting up the stairway in his own house. He'd sworn never to be so uncontrolled.

'You are the expert. You tell me.' She seemed to lose her voice, and she had a lost look on her face.

He calmed. She stood above him, and yet, she appeared as vulnerable as a child.

He moved up the steps, took her hand, and gently led her back into his sitting room. 'This is not what you are upset about. You have already said Christopher was getting too old for a governess and that it was past time he had a tutor.'

'That's true, but that has nothing to do with letting Celeste go. Nothing. Even you seem to forget I am his mother and should be consulted on his education.'

'Your mother and I talked about it at length. She recommended Mr Marvin to me. I imagined you knew about him. You said you had talked with your mother.' He strode into his room and dropped her hand while he removed his coat.

Her lip quivered just as Christopher's did, and it hit him deep in the stomach.

'I knew intimacies with you would destroy our home,' he said bitterly. 'I knew it.'

'Don't be ridiculous. We are both perfectly capable of doing that without any help whatsoever.'

'Emotions are the devil.'

'I'm not being emotional. I'm being your wife. Yes.' A frown. 'Don't you look at me like that.'

'We never had one disagreement before.'

'I can't undo the past. Nor can you. But be assured I am thankful for you every day, just as my mother reminds me at length that I should be every single time I see her.'

She took in a breath. 'I am also thankful for what you have done for us. But it would be nice for once not to hear your praises heralded from one end of London to the other.'

He let his lids drop, took a step beside her, retrieved her hand and put it over his heart. 'You have crushed me.'

She hesitated, unsure of what he meant.

'Only London? I'd judged my praises were touted from one end of England to the other.'

Her mouth opened and she gasped in a breath. But he had her attention, and her hand.

'Perhaps you are right,' he said. 'Without realising it, I somehow make things that are not to be celebrated sound wondrous.'

'It is because you take moonbeams and spin them into gold. You make sick people well and have no heart to lose. You have no heart. After Christopher told you he loved you, you couldn't escape fast enough. That was unnecessary. We weren't going to chase you into the street saying that frightful word to you.'

'Susanna—'

He was still aware of her hand in his. The caress of his thumb over her hand seemed to calm her. 'This has nothing to do with hearts. They are merely organs that pump blood.'

'To you.' She touched her chest. 'I have a heart, for what it's worth. And I have lost it for the last time.'

'What are you trying to say?'

She paused. Her anger faded one small notch, and the words dropped to only a little louder than a whisper. 'Nothing. Just that I was not there when you talked with my mother about the tutor and I would have liked to be consulted.'

Quinton went through the door to his bed chamber, leaving it open behind him.

'I told you, I assumed she would tell you as well.' He pulled the ties of his cravat, loosening it, then slowly sliding it from his neck as he returned.

'Well, she did not.' She didn't look at him. 'And we still need Celeste.'

'My apologies. I will rehire Celeste, and he can have both a governess and a tutor.'

'You don't need to do that. I have already told her I'm keeping her on as my companion and expect you to give her a pay increase.'

'Problem solved.'

He left the room again. She listened to the muffled noises. The bed creaked. She heard a boot sliding from his foot, and then another. The bed creaked again, and she heard a soft clunk. The whisper of fabric.

He returned to the doorway without a cravat or waistcoat, in shirt, trousers and stockinged feet. He appeared taller without his boots on, which wasn't possible. He dismissed her calmly. 'Goodnight, Susanna.'

She stilled, secure in her decision to intrude in his life. It felt right.

'Aren't you going to have something to eat before you go to bed?' she asked. 'There's bread and butter on my tray.'

His gaze darkened. 'I had dinner at my brother's house.'

'I could understand you not wanting to eat in here with all the ghastly things around you. You have pictures of naked people on your walls. And you can see everything. All their bones and veins and everything.' She clutched her chest. 'They're not even artistic.'

'It's anatomy.' He batted away her concerns. 'I may have seen too much, but you saw too little of life.'

She stood, leaving the tray to be collected later by the maid. If it was in his way, that would be a bonus. How could she ever believe he would understand anything she said? The man had all the tenderness in the world when he was soothing someone or sending a patient on his way or speaking with her family—or anything but dealing with her.

Something bubbled within her. She had not done well at reading. She had not done well at romance. She had not done well at marriage. But she had a lovely child. She could find a way to discover if her husband had any kind of heart—oh, but it was just anatomy—towards her at all.

She sat down again and flounced out her skirt around her feet. 'What do you discuss when you are with your brother?'

He ignored her question, arms crossed.

She arranged herself more comfortably in the chair, blinking in question. So what if she discomfited him or interrupted his sleep or his reading? He should have taken that into consideration before he wed her.

'Having intimacies with me was not your mistake. Not telling me goodbye afterwards was your mistake. A big one.'

For a moment she just drank him in, watching him as if he were a painting to study—a painting that gave her goosebumps and tingling feelings inside and pulled her into it. But now she wanted to turn it against the wall.

He leaned against the doorjamb, but his stance didn't relax. 'Yes. It was. Goodbye.'

'Well, it's too late now.' She patted the chair. 'I'm comfortable here.' She pointed to his room. 'And I can be comfortable sitting on the side of your bed also.'

'In answer to your question about what my brother and I discuss—politics. The constellations. Sometimes I just watch the ovens for him or listen as he talks about his latest sweetheart or visit to the tavern. Does that answer your question fully?'

Of course. But that didn't mean she had to answer his. 'With my mother, we speak of her aches, her pains, the last treatments and what she is thinking of for the next ailment.' She cocked a brow.

He sighed. 'I didn't have real parents, Susanna, so I enjoy spending time with yours.' Just the slightest flick of his lashes.

'Oh.' She puffed out her cheeks for a moment. 'She talks about you often. She likes you.'

'She does.' He leaned forward. 'It's been a long day. I am planning to go to sleep now.

'And my reading lessons?'

'I thought the tutor could help with that also. As he

teaches Christopher, you could listen without seeming to. I assure you he is understanding enough not to mind if anyone else in the house needs assistance. I told him he may be expected to help the maids and Celeste as well, and he was happy with that.'

He took a leisurely step. 'You may stay as long as you like. Here. Sitting on the bed. Wherever. But this conversation is over.'

He quietly shut the bedroom door.

Chapter Twenty

The conversation wasn't over, and he knew it.

He grabbed the dressing gown he'd left by his bed the night before. He'd never had a valet. He didn't need anyone to hold open his waistcoat while he stepped into it.

Truly, he had been born with a silver spoon just out of his reach. He'd only had to stay alive long enough to be able to stretch far enough to clasp it.

He tied the sash of his gown, the roiling feeling inside him forcing him to remain on his feet. It didn't matter that he wanted to sleep because he wouldn't be able to. He grabbed the decanter on the mantel over the fireplace.

The sound of the liquid pouring didn't soothe him as it usually did. He put it to his lips and held the glass in his hands, letting the brandy burn down his throat.

'I have been very fortunate,' a feminine voice jolted him as she came into the bedroom.

'Yes.'

'I am free to live on an earl's estate. I never reflected much about it until today.'

He swallowed the dregs in the glass, not really enjoying the flavour but enjoying the taste of the money spent on it. 'I think of it once a day. At least.'

He'd moved right into the Earl's rooms. In the morning, no one opened those draperies but him.

'I was so upset when I walked into Christopher's room and saw someone I didn't know standing with him. I was jarred. Then when I discovered who the man was and that you had hired him, I felt so…upset that you hadn't consulted me. And then I was even a little more upset when he mentioned teaching the women of the household, thinking you meant me. Nettie reads quite well as you know.'

'Are you finished?'

'No. I'm considering how I should go on. At first, I dealt the cards, and they did not give me the hand I wanted. So, I lost the game. Now I don't like the game. I'm changing it. I am learning to read, no matter if you teach me or not. And I am learning to be your wife, whether you like it or not.'

'You might not like the next hand any better.'

'Then perhaps I should make certain of my cards.'

'I think you are at this very moment. There is a card in front of me right now I did not expect to be dealt. I expected to be asleep. Tonight. All night. Alone.'

'I don't like this room. It's grim and dismal at night and it really isn't any better during the day. I think it is improved by the darkness, actually. You can't say that about many rooms.'

He could see her studying her surroundings, outlines framed by the moonlight: the thick draperies, the heavy pieces of furniture that would never fit in a small area. 'I like it,' he said. 'I like it very much.'

'It was the Earl's bedroom…' she mused.

'Yes.' The word snapped from his lips.

Liquid sloshed.

'I played the cards that I was dealt,' Quinton said, 'and

when the deck landed my way, I ran with all my might towards the riches.'

'Are you my winning hand?'

'No. Christopher is. The station you have in life is.'

She pressed her lips together.

'You won,' he said. 'You won. In all the world, how many women do you think have a maid and live in such luxury?'

'You're right. You always are.'

'As a child, you had everything you ever wanted. More dolls than I knew existed.' A sound emanated from low in his throat. 'I don't know if I'd ever even seen a doll before yours except in a shop that I was tossed out of.'

The contents of the glass splashed when his hand moved closer to his mouth. He took a sip. 'You can stay or you can go. It doesn't matter to me. I was right in front of you and you couldn't see me, except to peer around me for that weasel you wed. I'm glad I don't get my feelings hurt easily.'

She walked over to the outer door, opened it and then returned to stand in front of him breathing rapidly—so close she almost seemed his height. Her words were terse. 'I was just like those women you grew up around. I made a mistake too. And you can forgive them, so why not me?'

'Perhaps. Perhaps not.'

'It is just as you said. We made love and you changed.'

'I would not use that word.' The controlling word. 'We were intimate. And I have not changed.'

'Then perhaps you should. Perhaps you are making just as big a mistake as I did.' She turned away.

He emptied his glass, then set it down.

She moved closer to the door once more and looked over her shoulder. 'Decisions in this household are to be made by both parties. I don't care if it is your inheritance. I am Countess Amesbury. You asked. I accepted. Deal with it.'

But he spoke softly. 'Do you remember when I asked you how you fared? The first time I saw you after I left for university?'

'Well.' She frowned, her voice softening. Movements stilling. 'Some things are hard to recall.'

'That was the first thing I said to you. The first time I had seen you after…we parted. Almost…a year before you married Walton.'

'I do remember that day, I believe.' She glanced down and to the left.

'You never even gave me the barest glimpse, but said you were well, stood up and left the room.'

'You were more distant towards me than ever before. You'd never visited us till then, and I had been at Sunday services and heard your uncle mention that you'd returned to London several times. So I knew…'

'When I did return to your house, it was about half past one on a summer's day. Afterwards, I was leaving around two and I heard you laughing. It was the first time I'd heard Walton's voice. He whined at the end of his sentences whenever you were around. And he warbled like a juvenile bird. "Yes. Yes. Of course. Whatever Miss Susanna wants. Yes, Miss Susanna. Of course, Miss Susanna. Such a wise idea to pair those two slippers together on your two dainty, lovely feet…" At least he could count.'

'I do remember that, actually. I had added matching ribbons to everything I wore so the colours coordinated with my dress.'

'I must not have heard that part,' he said. 'And that

first day, with the dolls, everything about you was so clean. So starched and proper. You could have been a doll come to life. I could not leave your side if I'd wanted to. I watched for your parents' carriage everywhere I went.'

She stopped, staring as she grasped the latch. 'You usually wore a dark waistcoat, with a coat which went well with it, and you'd always get a worn spot on the waistcoat. Your waistcoats still get that worn spot. I think it is from putting your thumb against the pocket. I don't know if you're even aware you're doing it. It's as if you want to make certain no one has taken anything from it.'

'Could be. But even if you noticed me, you were already caught by him.'

'He praised me. And I believed he…'

She left the room suddenly without finishing the sentence, but he'd heard the defeat in her voice and his weakness once again rose to the forefront.

He always wanted to rescue people in pain. But Susanna didn't need rescuing. She had a treasured child, a beautiful home and a husband—albeit, a husband whose sleep she was disrupting. And whose well-ordered life she'd catapulted into an abyss.

He clenched his discarded glass. He'd seen women leave breadcrumbs of desire out to pull the men along. He was married and he owed it to himself not to fall into some trap that would cause total upheaval in their lives.

A structured home with all parties behaving as they should would be best for everyone. He'd seen too much of the emotional dregs to think they were good enough for him, or for Susanna or Christopher. And now Susanna appeared to be playing some game. He didn't like it. She didn't know the risks of it. He shouldn't have made *love*—perish the word—to her. His life had crumbled just as he'd expected it to, but it would return to normal if he avoided her.

They lived in an earl's mansion and would live with all the decorum usual of the peerage.

He glanced at the size of the bed.

It was far too large for one person. He'd never noticed that before.

Well, he had a sofa, and he didn't feel like sleep. He didn't feel like he'd ever need to sleep again.

He turned on his heel.

He'd not hated working his way into the lives of the upper class. Really. He had only hated that without his luck he would have been fortunate to have a small confectionary shop of his own with a roof that rarely leaked.

Yes, he said, with his movements about London. *I was born* there *but now I am* here.

He understood why kings fought to keep countries, why Wellington was willing to risk the fate and the lives of so many, including himself.

They had been born *here* and planned to stay *here*. They had homes and wives and children here.

He now had a child. He'd not really considered Christopher his son in the early days of their marriage, but it was hard to think otherwise now. A son, but not a wife.

His chest was heaving with his breaths. By touching her, he had opened a Pandora's box inside himself, and it couldn't be closed.

He could not praise the virtues of honesty without searching inside himself and revealing truths that he had hidden from himself.

Emotions destroyed so much.

They claimed a part of his soul.

They weakened him.

She had invited him upstairs to her rooms. He had it in writing. And if that wasn't enough, she'd invaded his life down here too.

He moved into his now vacant sitting room and cursed at the emptiness.

The next morning, Nettie informed Susanna that the Earl wished for her to know that he would possibly be staying out all night as he had a patient with a brother in the north who needed him and he didn't think it would be right to force the horses and carriage driver to return in the night. They would find an inn.

He certainly did not need lessons on how to avoid his wife.

Susanna had Nettie fetch her a hackney. And she told Nettie she was going to her mother's house, in case the Earl returned unexpectedly and wondered. In case he asked—as if he would. And, if he didn't ask, Nettie was to tell him anyway.

She flounced out the door, Christopher's hand in hers pretending to be happy and all things perfection. But by the time she reached her mother's house, she was frazzled because Christopher kept talking about…not birds, but his beloved 'Bury and the books he'd read. She imagined Christopher had repeated every word of every conversation he'd ever had with Quinton.

Her mother quickly hugged Christopher when she saw him and glanced at Susanna as she walked into the sitting room, puzzled when she didn't see anyone behind her daughter. 'You're visiting?' her mother asked. 'What's wrong?' She rushed forward. 'You're leaving him? No. No. He's asked you to leave, hasn't he?' She put her knuckles to her lips. 'I knew this would happen, someday.'

Susanna squared her shoulders. 'Well, today isn't the day.'

Her mother studied Susanna. 'What happened then? Why are you here?'

'I was hoping Christopher could stay with you for a few days. He misses his grandparents. Celeste is getting acquainted with the new tutor. And perhaps Quinton and I need to get to know each other better without distractions.'

'Is that really wise in a marriage? Look what happened when you got to know Walton better.'

'I know you're still angry with me for marrying Walton because of all the things that happened,' Susanna said. 'And I wish I'd done things differently.'

'No. Not really.' Her mother twisted one of the silver ringlets at her cheek and then deposited herself into her chair, her skirts flaring around her as she plopped down.

'I think we were all victims of his horrible father. I shied away from talking about this with you—not because it was your mistake but ours. We let him into our house. We encouraged him to court you and for you to receive his attentions. If we could not see what vermin he was, how could we expect our innocent child to be aware?'

'I fell in love with Walton, who put his father first, and now I am…fond…of Quinton, who puts everyone else in front of himself, I think.'

'Don't blame yourself.' Her mother patted her hand. 'He makes up for all your past mistakes.'

'Thank you.'

She peered at Susanna. 'Yesterday, I heard at the ladies' tea that Walton's father has disappeared. No one can find him. Perhaps he was done away with.'

Susanna opened her eyes wide, as if it would help her with her hearing. 'I just saw him not that long ago.'

'I know. Quinton has visited several times and talks with your father about it. I admit, I told your husband about the funds Walton's father still owes us and he said not to worry about it. That did make me curious. Said he would make certain nothing like that happened again. I would not be at all surprised if he did away with him. Your husband is a saint.'

Susanna took in a breath, confused by the intensity bombarding her.

'Mother, you surely don't think Quinton could do such a thing?'

'Susie, he saved a patient's life when he straddled a man's back and did a leg amputation, all alone. The man survived. Quinton has an iron will.'

Susanna gasped. 'How do you know this?'

'Well, I've always shielded you because you're sensitive. But the ladies' tea is full of information. You should hear the tales from before his college days. No one dared anger him when they found out he was *that* Quinton. I admit, I did feel a little like you were our brave sacrificial lamb when you married him, but I thought you knew all about his past.'

'No.'

'Well, he is an earl. That makes up for a lot of things. And he's rich, too, and that makes up for even more. He's certainly handsome. He's just near perfect.'

'You think my husband is near perfect, and yet you say he might have killed someone?'

'Don't jump to conclusions.'

Susanna didn't answer, barely hearing her mother. She

felt the world slide again, and her knees weakened. Quinton had not known what would be unleashed inside him if he made love to her. Goodness, and he had all those books with horrific medical drawings in them.

He'd grown up in such a bad world.

'Mother. I love him,' she gasped, clutching her mother's arm. 'I do. I can't help it. And I don't know what to do about it.'

'It does my heart good to hear you say that.' Her mother's smile was the widest Susanna had seen directed at her in a long time. 'In case he needs an alibi.'

'*Mother*. I am certain Quinton needs no alibi.'

Her mother smiled. 'That's the way to do it. Be convincing.'

'He is a calm man.'

'Truly. It would take a calm man to dispose of Mr Walton.'

'Mother. You are drawing incorrect conclusions, I am certain.'

'Quinton is so fortunate to have you defending him. I am sure you can convince anyone that he was with you at the time.'

Quinton was intelligent. He could do such a thing and no one would be the wiser. Even her.

Quinton was a medical man.

She could just ask Quinton if he'd killed anyone.

She chewed her fingernail.

This would be hard to work into a conversation.

She would just have to ask him. He'd said she could ask him anything. But perhaps some things were better not to know, although he didn't have to answer.

Only now he wasn't exactly of a mind to talk with her. And such a question was unlikely to do more than put a bigger wedge between them.

If she asked, either innocent or guilty, it would anger him. Questions, he'd said, told him about the people who asked them.

She didn't know if she was in love with a physician who was a saint, or a man who had anatomical drawings in his sitting room, grew up among the lightskirts and introduced her to a bawd.

Again, she looked at her ring and wiped away the rust.

But she would have to ask him.

'I will talk with Quinton,' she said. 'And it will make—'

'Normally, I would recommend that,' her mother said. 'But this is Quinton we're talking about, and you. Perhaps you shouldn't speak too much. He is a physician, and has all that education, and well, silence might be your best option.'

'Thank you, Mother.' Susanna made sure her voice was pleasant. 'And I will take your words under consideration. Bu I must be getting back home now. In case Quinton returns.'

'I'll keep Christopher, and you can send Celeste for him later. Just remember what I said, dear, and don't talk too much.'

She kissed her mother on the cheek. 'Thank you for your advice.'

Chapter Twenty-One

At home, Susanna had had to take her thoughts from Quinton.

She, Celeste and Mr Marvin played charades, but none of them had their mind on the game. She'd rung for Nettie and asked for wine, and Nettie appeared a little sad when she arrived with it, so Susanna had insisted Nettie join them.

As the night went on, they'd simplified it somewhat and used shadows on the wall for the game, trying to act out simple phrases.

And she'd confessed to all of them that she couldn't read.

'I can't either,' Celeste said.

'I'll be pleased to teach you,' Mr Marvin said encouragingly.

'I met a lot of people early in my life and not a one has cared whether I could read,' Nettie said. 'Only time I was ever asked was when Quinton hired me to be housekeeper.'

She twisted her head around and studied Susanna. 'You can't read. You probably can't cook. You need help getting dressed in the morning. So what do you do?'

'I mainly just spend the day with Christopher.'

Nettie put her fingers against her cheeks. 'Well, what a disgrace. Do you think Quinton notices what a layabout you are? What with the little boy shouting out "Mother" in the hallway and your voices carrying hither and yon? And little Christopher telling Quinton his mother is the best mother in the world?'

'He didn't?'

'He did. When Christopher asks for bread for the birds, he always searches for his 'Bury and asks if he wants to help. One morning they were in the hallway while you were getting ready for the day and Christopher was chattering on about how his mother helped him make the best soldier tent ever and how his mother played chase with him, and his mother knew how to kiss away hurts.' Nettie laughed.

'That evening I took tea to Quinton and he said Christopher told him you could show him how to make sick people better even faster.'

'Oh.'

Nettie yawned so big her jaw popped. 'He's a good man.'

'But what if he committed murder?' Susanna asked.

'Don't worry. He would only kill someone who really deserved it. And I doubt he would leave evidence.'

'Oh…'

Afterwards, she'd not been able to stop herself. She'd discussed her former father-in-law's disappearance with Celeste, Nettie and Mr Marvin, swearing them to secrecy and asking their opinion on what she should do, as Quinton was already avoiding her.

And then she'd said the horrid words. She was in love with Quinton. Nettie told her that it could be quite the upset for Quinton and she could probably discuss murder with him, but not love.

Susanna had retreated, agreeing, and spent a fitful night, thinking about her husband and wondering if she knew him at all.

The next morning, Nettie interrupted Susanna right after she'd finished dressing and was sitting in Christopher's room where Celeste and Mr Marvin were now arguing over whether a marriage for love was best or a marriage of sensibility was preferred.

'A man has arrived and is asking for you, my lady,' Nettie announced.

Susanna's stomach tightened. 'What is his name?'

'He did not say.'

'Well, then I am not receiving visitors,' she said, puzzled. 'Do you think it is a magistrate?' she asked.

Nettie shook her head. 'No. I'm certain it's not. I know most of them. But the man appears well dressed.'

She remembered that Quinton would likely hear about the visitor from the servants. 'If he will not give his name, then he can leave. No suspicious characters in this house.' She lifted the folded handkerchief at her side and waved it like a flag. 'We are the most respectable of households. I spend evenings with my family and Quinton reads stories to us. That's where he was. Whatever day it was….'

Nettie moved downstairs, and then within moments Susanna heard the sound of scuffling feet.

'Lady Amesbury. Lady Amesbury,' Nettie screeched.

She moved to the stairway, Celeste and Mr Marvin behind her. Two sets of footsteps pounded on the stairs.

She inhaled sharply, recognising the visitor with Nettie behind him. He rushed towards her and stopped halfway up.

'Everyone,' she said, addressing Nettie, Celeste and Mr Marvin. 'Please do let us forget last night's discussion. This is…my father-in-law. And this may be the only time in my life I am happy to see him,' she said, meeting his eyes.

'Susanna, I must talk with you. The servant would not let me in,' he said breathlessly.

She marched directly into his path. 'For good reason. She is not allowed to let suspicious characters inside. And you would be first on that list.'

'Susanna.' He stopped, sweeping his cap off and holding it, then giving a nervous laugh. 'After I saw you at the soirée—and saw a smile on your face, and I remembered all the good times we had as a family.'

'That must have been interesting,' she said. 'So, nothing happened?'

'Susanna.' He stood, staring at her.

'I admit. I am very pleased you aren't dead. That is a relief. But I am not exactly pleased you are alive either.'

He stared at her with a nauseatingly sentimental look on his face. 'We have memories in common. My grandson.'

'No. *We* don't.'

She paused. Other memories returned, a downpour of them. The feelings for her former husband were nothing like her feelings for Quinton. Quinton was worth loving. Christopher's father hadn't even been worth propping up for a cup of tea. He'd managed to remain sober until they wed and then he'd only picked a few odd days a month not to drink, and on those days he'd helped his father bilk her family for every penny they'd had.

'I'm so sorry those investments for your father didn't work out. I lost money also. I was duped and now I'm penniless.' He shuffled his feet. 'I'm having to stay at my nephew's house and hide from creditors.'

'Sometimes we do things we regret,' she said composedly. 'It happens.'

'But it seems like you've done well enough without me. That husband of yours has provided you a fine living after your father, um, lost so much. We would have been even richer had those investments.... I was robbed—by unscrupulous men.'

She bent closer to his face. 'Men who had better cards than you, you mean? You talked your son into taking my father's funds for your so-called shipping endeavour, and then you gambled all the funds away. I admit, I was so desperate that I was willing to grasp that straw of him saying you would repay us. But I would actually have been better off with a bit of straw, because one little fake promise doesn't go far when the cards are marked.'

She raised her hands to the sky. 'You couldn't even win that card game with marked cards. And yes, Walton told me about it.'

Oh, he gave her such a pitiful peek from under his lashes. Goodness, Christopher's soldiers were better actors than him.

'I'm sorry. It was the biggest mistake of my life. The cur switched the deck on me and I didn't know it.'

'Yes, it was your biggest mistake. But it wasn't mine,' she said, backing up the stairs to increase the distance between them. 'Marrying your son was mine.'

Mr Walton took another step up the stairs. 'Susanna, you must give me funds now. You must. You have a son. I am his grandfather. I only need funds or a few jewels to help me get started.'

'But your son already took all my jewellery.' She raised her hand and held her base metal wedding ring high. 'Does this look expensive to you?'

He gasped. 'No.' Then he paused. 'The Earl is impoverished?'

'This ring is worth more to me than every jewel your

son took from me. I might even have forgiven the jewels, but not the disappearance of Christopher's silver rattle.'

She threw her handkerchief at him. He dodged. *From a handkerchief.* She sidestepped to the pedestal beside her and picked up a vase of reeds. With all her might, she hurled them at the stairs between them. The vase broke, scattering stems and glass. 'And that is for my mother's sapphires. They had belonged to her mother.'

He jumped one step. 'Susanna. I made a mistake.'

'Because you didn't invest the money from my stolen jewellery properly?'

'If you could scrape together a few coins now, I promise to leave and I'll not insist on seeing my grandson.'

'I detested you from day one. And you will not ever see your grandson, you crawling, slime-soaked vermin.' She took a step to the stairs, not lowering her voice. 'I'll tell everyone who you are and what you are. You should be hanged for those thefts, even though your son did it. He did it for you and for the drink.' She doubled her fist. 'And you will get not a penny more from anyone here.'

'Christopher is my grandson,' he shouted. 'My son's heir. And I will see him. He will know that I am his true grandfather.'

'Get out of my house.' She bit out the words. Celeste and Marvin moved to stand at her side. Nettie moved behind him, a broom in her hand.

He turned and darted down the hallway, knocking Nettie into the banister as he fled out the door.

'He is a—' And then Marvin said a word she didn't know. He repeated it with relish. 'It is Latin for something…um…very unpleasant and not fit for a woman's ears in English.'

Susanna gathered her poise. 'I must apologise to you for my most rude suspicions of my dearest husband.

Please replace the vase in case the horrid man returns. With something heavier,' she instructed Celeste. 'I am not jesting. Perhaps those candlesticks. They would work well for defence, and a king would be proud to help protect a family.'

Susanna glanced at the glass shards. 'I will pick up the glass while Nettie fetches us some tea. And biscuits.'

She lifted a shard and stared at it, then collected the others.

Because she had lost trust in Walton, and had seen how mistaken she'd been to care for him at all, she'd believed herself wrong about Quinton's integrity. She'd believed him possible of murder because Walton had been that disreputable—even challenging a man to a duel because the man hadn't liked Walton sweet-talking his wife.

She put the shards on the table and pushed her hair back into place.

Nettie returned with the tea and they gathered in the nursery.

Then she smiled, taking in a deep breath afterwards. 'We must all celebrate my marriage…to Lord Amesbury.'

She stared at the tarnished ring, moved it aside and looked at the almost perfect mark it had left on her hand.

Her husband was the treasure, not the ring, and they all carried the wounds from the past. Her first husband had lied to her even when the truth would have been no hardship.

But Quinton believed in truths. She could not fault him if he only disliked one little word. She needed to accept that her husband was so different than any other man—and the one she would always choose, over and over again. The one she had almost missed, and he'd been standing right in front of her.

She slipped the ring into place. It was just a bit of

metal, like most rings, and the jewels in them were stones. But Quinton was not made of metal or stone. Her husband. Her second chance. He had found her. And rescued her.

She would like to rescue him, with something he didn't believe in. But it didn't matter that he didn't grasp it. She did.

She raised her hand, showing the ring. 'My husband slipped this on my finger. He didn't have to, but he did. Even if he never places another on my finger...once was enough. I adore him. He may not like me very much, and may only be distantly fond of me, but I am so pleased to be his wife.' She shrugged and met the staff's eyes. 'Plus, he doesn't need an alibi.'

She glanced at Celeste. 'He wanted me to move here.' She turned to Mr Marvin. 'He did. My husband asked me to live with him. My first husband said he never even noticed I'd left his house, and he said moss had more intelligence than I have. Then he challenged a man to a duel and fell on his own sword and died before the fight even started.'

'Lady Amesbury, you are much cleverer than all the moss in the world,' Mr Marvin said. 'And that is one thing Celeste and I can agree on.'

'*Oui,*' Celeste said. 'You are a very intelligent woman.'

'Thank you, my dear friends. That means so much.' She touched her chest, lowering her voice. 'Quinton may regret our marriage, but he will just have to get over that, because we are stuck together now. Like, um, married people. A husband and wife. Isn't it glorious? And he will never fall on his sword. He is a physician and a lord and a husband and employer and more.'

With her right hand she gave a quick pat to her wedding ring, then a scrub of the rust underneath.

She waved the ring in the direction of where Mr Walton had departed. 'I am Lady Amesbury.' She twirled to Celeste. 'The metal might be rusty but it's strong. Can you believe it?'

'*Oui*,' Celeste said. 'The other man has made you appreciate Lord Amesbury.' Then she looked at Susanna's ring. 'Perhaps we should economise. If you need to borrow funds, I have set some aside. You do not have to increase my wages.'

'Perhaps that is a question I should ask my husband. I don't want to pauper him.'

Then she twirled around again, her ring high. 'This is more precious to me than any jewel I have ever owned.'

'Oh, you must have some wine, Lady Amesbury, for the shock you are clearly feeling,' Nettie said drily. 'I'll fetch it now. That ring is an embarrassment.'

'And please, Nettie, set out some wine for the other servants and Cook. Everyone is to be merry and celebrate my marriage.'

Susanna smiled, nodding. 'Oh, Nettie,' she said. 'I am so fortunate. Quinton has watched over me since our marriage, and he is not only the best physician in London but the best man. And he is so modest that he isn't aware of it.'

'I know. Not many men would have hired me to keep house for him.'

'Were you a lightskirt?' Susanna asked.

Nettie nodded, lowering her eyes. 'Not at his auntie's. And I could not bear it after a while. Didn't he tell you? I hope you are not concerned.'

'His aunt said he had hired someone, and it just occurred to me that it was you. I am pleased that you were here to offer assistance and understanding to him. You are truly noble. And you have earned my sincerest thanks.'

Nettie blushed and left.

'I will get the candlesticks and put them in place,' Celeste said, rushing away. 'Who knows when we may need them again?'

Susanna appraised the tutor. 'And Mr Marvin, is it possible my husband knew you were in dire straits?'

'I suppose he did. My mother is friends with the butler at your parents' house.'

'My husband likes helping people. He always does.'

She stared outside the window. 'He may not know what love is, but he said he is fond of me. And he cares for everyone. Everyone. He may not love me, but he cares. Is that not wonderful?' She clasped her ring. 'He is fond of me and I am fond of him. And he will be back.'

Celeste returned. 'Miss Susanna will protect us in the meantime, and we will protect her.'

'Let's hope we never have to do so again.'

Nettie rushed in next with a bottle of wine. 'I'll pour.'

'And let us all keep this a secret that my evil father-in-law was here,' Susanna said. 'Quinton has had enough upsets in his life, and the four of us scared the man away. We do not want to give Quinton more grief than he has had already. We want to be the perfect, calm household for him.'

She heard three utterances of sincere agreement. Her friends. And she also had a son and a husband—a husband who hadn't really rescued himself yet. But he would.

Quinton stepped into the entryway. Cook was there with a wine glass in one hand and a frying pan in the other, which she raised like a weapon when he stepped inside the doorway. But she lowered the pan when she saw it was him.

'They're in the nursery,' she whispered. 'Nettie said I am to stand guard.'

'Yes.' He was losing his senses, or likely Christopher had them all playing soldiers.

The nursery sounded like a good place to be. Susanna would likely be there.

He lived on an estate, and he must remember that and comport himself as an earl. His family was an earl's family. And they were to be as nearly perfect as could be. He would lead them with dignity and grace, and calmness.

He strode up the stairs, missing every other tread and noting that the vase with reeds had been removed, which was good as bits of them appeared to have been falling onto the floor. Candlesticks now sat on the pedestal.

Reaching out, he hefted a candlestick. An odd thing to put there. He returned it to its place.

Continuing on to the nursery, he went inside. Four startled faces greeted him.

'Where's Christopher?' he asked.

'With his grandparents,' Susanna answered, momentarily biting her lip. 'But I hardly talked at all with my mother. I just want you to know that.'

'You can invite her here and talk with her all you wish,' he said.

The tutor put his spectacles onto the table at his side. 'And that concludes all everyone needs to know about King John, and the Magna Carta, and Runnymede, and 1215 is a date that we must never forget. Thank you for enlightening me, Countess. It has been most edifying, listening to your vast understanding of historical events. Hasn't it, Miss Celeste? We have learned so much from Lady Amesbury.'

'*Oui*. Miss Susanna amazes me with her intelligence. It is *magnifique* to work for someone so wise.'

'We are just one happy, happy household,' Susanna said. 'With Nettie and the two of you, and Christopher and my husband, we have such a well-mannered, intelligent household.'

Quinton studied Susanna. Her face was too bland, but not bland at all.

He sighed, feeling his life was weighed down by more stones than a person could lift.

'I have been discussing the subjects Lady Amesbury believes Christopher needs to learn first. It is quite an undertaking she has assigned me,' Mr Marvin said.

'But I am sure you are capable, and Celeste has been helping with his French lessons,' Susanna assured him.

Four heads nodded in unison.

He could see Susanna had found her way in the household, but he wasn't sure where his was anymore.

Susanna caught Quinton observing her and smiled a trembling smile. 'We are all pleased you are home. And goodness, how dull this must all sound to you. So very dull. But calming. Mr Marvin is also teaching me, um, Latin.'

He raised a brow. 'What?'

'Of course,' Mr Marvin said. 'Latin. She is a natural scholar.'

Nettie rose. 'And her ideas on economising are so enlightening. Water anyone?' she asked.

'*Oui*,' Celeste said. 'That sounds delightful.'

'*Etiam*,' Mr Marvin said. 'I certainly would like a strong glass of water.'

Nettie bustled to the door. 'I will bring it.'

'Wait,' Quinton commanded.

She did.

He stared at all the innocent faces. 'Did something fall down the stairway?' he asked.

'Well, it was my mistake. Dreadful. I caused it all.' Susanna shut her eyes. 'I will not do so again, I assure you. Once was enough.' She glanced at her ring and smiled. 'Well, sometimes it does take a bit to get things right. But those candlesticks are perfect there.' She let out a happy sigh. 'And the water here. It's delightful. We should drink it more often.'

Three agreements. He'd never seen anyone get so enthused over water.

He had lost his home. His quiet, well-ordered life. She'd shredded it bit by bit and he'd not even seen it going on under his own roof. He'd known making love would destroy their home, and yet, he'd still hoped for sanity to reign.

Then Susanna smiled at him. Mr Marvin adjusted his cravat. Celeste had something absorbing her concentration on her fingernails.

And Nettie had pulled a cloth from her apron and was brushing the top of the table. 'My, my, my. Dust. Here. Imagine that. Atrocious.'

The whole lot of them seemed intently absorbed in amazement and relief that Nettie had found a dust spot that he thought she'd imagined on the table.

He'd feared touching Susanna would be catastrophic. And it had been. His heart had been shattered, and somehow everyone else had lost their way also.

He waited a moment.

'I believe I will retire,' Quinton said to nobody in particular.

Pleased murmurs answered him, but they were distracted. He felt as if he were in someone else's dream. The perfect little scene was in front of him, only it wasn't. The emotional conflagration had already started, but he couldn't stop it—a conflagration that destroyed all good sense.

For a moment he stared from one person to the next, wondering how much wine had been imbibed before he'd returned. But he saw no empty glasses.

He strode to the door.

He was a physician, but undoing the lovemaking was beyond his powers, and it had felt…like nothing had ever felt before.

Indescribable.

The only concern had been the lingering knowledge that he was likely upending his home life, but he'd not been able to help himself.

He exited, but left the door open just a crack, holding his hand on the brass knob, debating whether he should go back and ask them again what had caused the debris in the floor and why the candlesticks were on the pedestal.

'I don't think I would be good at providing an alibi for Quinton,' Susanna said, her voice carrying through the wood.

'Oh, no you wouldn't,' Nettie said. 'I must give you some advice on that.'

'I will certainly listen,' Susanna added.

'I think you should talk with him about it. He should know.' He heard Celeste's French accent.

'No,' Susanna answered. 'There's nothing to talk about. It is not his concern. We are the family he chose. I can't risk him thinking that I caused this.'

He heard the heavy pause.

'Agreed?' she asked.

Mumbles of agreement.

'I might possibly tell him when the time is right. Thankfully, I don't need an alibi. Alibi. That word is probably Latin. Mostly everything started out as Latin.'

She swore then. In Latin. 'And what does that word mean, Mr Marvin?'

His eyes widened. *That was what Marvin was teaching her?*

'It is not something you should repeat, my lady.'

'Well, I am sure it is suitable for the situation we just faced. Thank you.'

Susanna knew Latin profanities.

'This would have been so much easier on us all if Mother hadn't suggested Quinton was a murderer,' Susanna muttered.

Quinton froze, and he almost tripped over his own feet. His mother-in-law had said that?

'Do not blame yourself,' Marvin said. 'He's a physician. I'm sure it couldn't have been his first accusation.'

'And I was so touched that you were willing to keep the murder a secret. True friends we are.'

'It was nothing.' Celeste's accent. 'You would do the same for us.'

Yes. Susanna did have a family. And they were close. That was indeed compassionate of them to treat her secret as their own, and he was going to move to his brother's home just as soon as he soon as found out what was going on under his own roof.

No wonder Nettie had seemed nervous.

She probably feared for her life. Whether from him or the others, he wasn't sure.

He stopped. He couldn't blame her for not telling him what was going on if she thought him a murderer.

Susanna finally had people around her that she could be comfortable with.

Devil take it, she also had his ring on her finger and she'd tied him to her somehow.

Love. *Amare.* Perhaps it was a true word. Heart *tor-*

mentis. Tormentum? Didn't matter. It was torture no matter how you said it.

He turned back and peered around the door.

'Lady Amesbury, could we talk in my sitting room?'

Her eyes took in her companions. 'Of course. I, um, would like nothing better.'

Chapter Twenty-Two

Quinton went to his sitting room and placed himself at his desk, considering his options. Women, in his experience, were not always known for their honesty.

Susanna walked into the room and he watched her. Her arms seemed to be in her way, and her eyes were a bit too wide.

'You requested to talk with me, husband?'

'Yes. I did.' His lips went up at the sides, but he knew it was far from a smile. He rested his hands on the desk.

She peered in the other direction.

'Ah,' he said. 'It appears this has been an eventful day for you.'

'Oh?' Voice questioning. A lift of the eyebrows. Tension in the arm. She shrugged. 'A minor disturbance only.'

She waved her hand about, and then she pulled it to her chest and covered her fist. Her lips stopped moving for a second, which was good because they'd been forming words but she'd said nothing.

He tapped the desk. 'Susanna. Is there something you should tell me? About a murder?'

She put her hands behind her back, eyes wide. She blinked three times rapidly, and then she let out her breath. 'Yes.' She nodded. 'I thought perhaps you had more of a past than I even realised.'

'I am not proud of my past, nor am I ashamed of it. It is what it is.'

She held out her palms, fingers splayed as if she were pushing up a curtain in front of her face. 'Let's just start over. Today is day one of our—'

He snorted.

'Oh, please Quinton. Do relax.' Her face saddened. 'I am sorry for the grief that you have suffered. We both have had our crosses to bear. I would not live through mine again for the world and I would not want you to either. I was so pleased that you didn't kill Walton's father. It's not that I like him, but I could not bear thinking you'd committed murder for me.' She sighed. 'Well, it would have been for my parents. Let's be honest.'

He pointed to his chest, voice rising out of his control.

'You thought I'd killed someone?'

She sniffed. 'Well, I had imagined that you'd been like an avenging knight. You are a protective man. You do like to help so many people.'

He held up two fingers and tapped his chest. 'Helping and murder are two different things.'

She frowned. 'Well. Be that way. I thought you had a fit of rage, or misplaced conscience, and you had avenged our family. It was touching. Not nice. But touching, perhaps.'

She leaned forward, chin down, eyes up and sparkling. 'I must say, after I discovered Mr Walton was actually alive, I thought it chivalrous that you might have killed him.'

'I have never killed anyone. I have worked extremely hard not to kill anyone. I'm a physician. We don't want to kill people.' He raised both hands, palms up.

She raised her chin. 'You took us in, Nettie and me, and my family and Celeste and Mr Marvin. You gave us all a home. Of course, we would feel a little obligated to give you an alibi.'

'But I don't need an alibi.' He waved an arm in frustration. 'And I took everyone in because it was right for me. Simple enough.'

She clasped his hand. 'I will tell everyone that you were only doing what was right for you. They will be so touched.'

She took in a deep breath. 'I understand that I should stop letting my experiences from my first marriage have any part in my life now.' She touched her fingertip to her bottom lip. 'You may be the opposite of Walton in every way. I had not comprehended that before. It does you a disservice not to accept that, and our home.'

He paused. 'I want to be known for my own faults, not others'.' He spoke softly, but the conversation wasn't over.

'I did swear everyone to secrecy, but perhaps that was the wrong thing to do. We should all tell the truth, even when we don't want to. Especially when we don't want to.'

She surveyed him. 'I know that windows were open.' She tucked her chin down. 'Do you think the neighbours heard?'

'Unlikely, seeing as we have no neighbours close enough,' he answered, realising he was adrift in the conversation. He fell into his physician's manner. He leaned forward, his fingers interlaced. 'Tell me...'

What was going on in his life? His quiet, well-ordered family had disappeared somewhere because he had held Susanna close to his heart—close to his soul.

She blew out a breath and it was as if the air had pushed her backwards. 'I understand supremely that you want a well-ordered, unemotional family life, and everyone under this roof has agreed that we will provide you with that very thing. Even though most of us agree that emotions are to be experienced. But we all want your happiness. Particularly me. So we have agreed not to have emotions.'

'Our feelings are difficult to control.' He spoke out of habit as he mentally listened again to what she had just said.

'You don't have to tell me that,' she muttered. 'I really shouldn't have thrown the vase at him, and I really am not sure about leaving the candlesticks there.' She crossed her arms. 'He is not to enter this house again, but I think he might be afraid to do so now.'

Quinton could feel his heartbeats one after the other, in rapid succession—beating in his forehead, overpowering his reserve.

He planted both palms flat on the desk and jumped to his feet. 'Who was here?'

She took a step to the door. 'I thought that's what we were talking about. The vase being broken and all—my late husband's father.'

'Mr Walton was here while I was gone?' His throat choked. 'He has been in my house, and he broke a vase?'

'No. I broke the vase, throwing it at him.' She raised her shoulders. 'But Mr Marvin and Celeste and Nettie and I were all ready to fight him. I suppose we scared him away. He wanted funds, but I don't have any. And we are all going to economise. It never occurred to me you were sacrificing for us all until that beast pointed out how poor you are.'

She held up her hand. 'This is my jewellery and I am not parting with it. And it was unforgiveable for him to knock Nettie aside. She could have been hurt.'

He unclamped his teeth and softened his speech, using all the power in his body to speak in a moderate tone. 'He touched Nettie?' He leaned forward. 'Tell me every last detail.'

She did.

After he listened, he didn't say anything but got up and strode to the door.

She jumped between him and the door, her back against the wood, stopping him with both palms against his chest. 'Quinton,' she shouted. 'Quinton. Quinton. No.'

'I'm just going to talk with him, and explain that he is not welcome here.'

'No.' She grappled with his sleeve. 'You must calm down. You must. You can't kill him now, not after I found out you didn't kill him before. It isn't chivalry now. It is true murder.'

'I'm perfectly calm,' he said. He was just going to give the man some friendly advice. That was all. And if the man started something, Quinton could finish it.

'Quinton,' she whispered. 'We must talk. Remember, you rescue people. And Christopher will need you. We must not make a big deal of it to Christopher. It is his grandfather.'

'He's not going to be there.'

'Please, Quinton. You have all you ever wanted. He has nothing. Leave it be.' She stayed against the door. 'We are your family, not his.'

He put his hands on her shoulders, and instantly, the feelings inside him cleared enough so that he could see her face.

'He's not coming here again while I'm gone.'

'Quinton.' Susanna threw herself into him, putting her arms around him and hanging on. 'We must talk. You can't kill him now. A trial might be unfortunate.

And we are family. You and I and everyone who lives in the house.'

'We will talk.' He touched her shoulders, but his wife stuck like glue. 'As soon as I return.'

'When you calm down, I will go with you—and—and we should collect Christopher on the way and take him too. And we should discuss how we plan to go on. Everyone here lo… Everyone here is fond of you, or would be if we had emotions. Perhaps not Celeste and Mr Marvin so much, but they are growing fond of each other. And we all want the best for you. We do. You rescue people and we want to rescue you.'

'I don't need to be rescued.'

'Yes. You do. You don't know how to be truly fond of people. You care for them, and you save them from their problems, but you feel emotions are bad. And they're not. Not always. Not the ones I have for you.'

'Emotions are used to control others.'

'Not always, Quinton. Sometimes emotions cause us to want to make others happy.'

'What makes you think that?'

'There is no other reason for us to keep the secret of that evil man being here than because we didn't want to upset you. We want to have the perfect household for you, and if that means that we are not to show emotions, then we won't. Or I won't. Or I will try really, really hard to be emotionless.'

She took in a breath. 'But I like you, Quinton. I just like you so abundantly. Because you have done so much. From the beginning you worked hard, and the more you received the harder you worked. And it is not for yourself. It is always for others. I have told everyone that and they all agree. We do want what is best for you.'

Quinton said nothing, and she reached for him, holding him close. She could feel the tremors through his clothing. 'I am fond of you. And I like you. It is not that other thing that you hate. It is just intense liking.'

He stopped trying to dislodge her, and his arms encircled her. His anger eased so that he could at least feel her against him.

Quinton held her, and she soothed him with her presence.

'We've all changed,' Susanna said. 'We're creating a world that is as perfect as we can make it. But we're not perfect. Our past isn't either.'

'I didn't change,' he said, moving from her. 'Oh, no, I did not. I had my brother to care for, and I did. I needed to provide. If I had avoided my responsibilities, then we could say I had changed. I had a lot of catching up to do to be on the same level as the others I studied with. I never deserted my brother or my auntie—I just could not take them with me.'

'I believe you. But do you believe yourself?'

He nodded. 'I do. I regret terribly that I couldn't be with them when I left to go to university. I made the best of it. And I try not to think of it, but sometimes I cannot help it. But Christopher's grandfather did the unacceptable.'

'I know he is terrible. If he wasn't, he would have contacted me differently. He would not have pushed past Nettie. What if, when Christopher is a little older, Mr Walton starts following him as he leaves? What if his grandfather tells him all sorts of tales about me? It's best that Christopher meets Mr Walton, and it's best that we are there when he does. We do need to protect Christopher from the truth hurting him. We need to make it easy for him to ask us about Mr Walton. No secrets.'

Quinton gave a nod.

She edged closer. 'Promise not to show your anger to Christopher. It could make him think there is a problem with his heritage. Let's have them meet now, and you can *gently* tell Mr Walton that he'd best keep his distance from our home. If he managed for this long, surely he can do so for another five, ten or twenty.'

'Let's get it over with, then.'

She let out a breath. 'I want that part of my life to be behind me. I want to forget the past. And I want you with me when I do so.'

'It is. You can't. I am.'

She put her arms around his waist and put her head against his chest. 'You are a dear, dear friend. You can just forget we are married if you wish and just be my very closest friend. With no other friends as close as I am, I will be happy for you to be my close friend.'

'We *are* married. I *am* your husband.'

She hugged him more tightly. 'And I am your wife.' She stepped back and met his eyes.

'I—' Then she considered her words. She didn't dare tell him she loved him. It would be almost cruel to him. Plus, he'd not reacted well the first time.

'I am just fond of you,' she said again, and a sigh of happiness rushed past her lips. 'Just fond. That's how I feel. Fond. It is truly wonderful to be fond of you and to be your wife.'

'That's how you feel?' he asked.

'Yes. It's a new experience for me.'

'I don't know what I feel,' he said. 'I've never felt it before.'

'You're probably growing fonder of me since we've married, but you're not used to the marriage feelings.' She waved a hand. 'Mere marriage fondness.'

'I suppose.'

'Just accept it. Don't question it. And if is a surprise for you, imagine what a tremendous surprise it is to me.'

'You did not feel this before for Walton?'

'No. I just had that indigestion of the brain. But you have cured me completely. Now I have only happiness. And you. But I wish Christopher's grandfather had stayed away. I wanted to take the secret of Christopher's grandfather to my grave,' she said.

'Take jewellery instead. Its value goes up in the afterlife. But not that ring. It's worth as much as it will ever be.'

'It's priceless to me,' she said, rubbing away the rust on her skin.

She clasped at his waistcoat, and he hugged her and hugged her and just rested with her in his arms.

'Do you think it could be a mistake for Christopher to meet the man?' she asked, stepping back.

'Life is tough. He's tougher. And it's better for him to learn to deal with it now. I would rather him be protected as well. But life is not that way, not for anyone. Just think how innocent and unprepared for real life you really were.'

He took her chin, brushed his lips against hers, and whispered. 'Please let your mother know that I have never killed anyone.'

Chapter Twenty-Three

After they collected Christopher, he asked Quinton, 'Why are we going out again?'

'I want an ice at Gunter's and your mother and I wanted you to see the man who was—was your other grandfather.'

'Will he let me have a bird?'

'No,' Susanna answered. 'And if you ask me again, you will not be allowed to go see the woman with the broken nose with Amesbury.'

'That's mean.' Christopher folded his arms across his chest.

Quinton folded his arms too. 'Will you let me have a bird, Susanna?'

'No.'

'I don't think you're mean.' Quinton uncrossed his arms.

She reached up and touched his hair. 'Good. You may go and see the lady with the broken nose.'

'I just hope she doesn't shout again.'

Christopher uncrossed his arms. 'Can I go with him?'

'Yes, since you're also being good,' she said. 'And you must continue it while we visit your grandfather.'

* * *

The coach stopped in front of Mr Walton's nephew's house. Quinton stepped out and guided Susanna from the steps. Christopher took his time, studying the points that topped the gate. Susanna took Christopher's hand.

The door opened and Quinton stepped inside.

The butler took their names.

When Mr Walton arrived, Susanna noticed that his cravat, a twisted scrap of cloth, appeared to be the same one he'd worn when she was married to his son.

'This is your other grandfather, Christopher,' Susanna said.

'What are you doing here?' Walton said, his voice low. 'Leave. All of you. If I wanted any part of you, you ruined it when you told me to leave your house today.'

He stared at Christopher. 'It is not my fault I have not seen you before. It is the fault of your mother. She doesn't let me visit. I came to see you today and she told me to leave.'

'Because you were rude. But we have brought Christopher here for you to meet.'

He sneered at Christopher. 'Just remember. Your mother is a selfish woman who only cares about herself.'

Christopher looked at his grandfather and made the disparaging fluttering noise with his lips that his mother usually reprimanded him for. 'My mother isn't selfish. She dances with me and plays soldiers and sits in the corner with me.'

She clasped his hand. 'Come along, Christopher. We must go.'

Christopher ran to the door, but hesitated, glancing back as he stood in the opening and listened.

'Please request an appointment through me if you ever

wish to see Christopher again,' Quinton said firmly. 'And you'd best keep your distance from my wife.'

The man swore at him. 'I don't want any part of you, or her, or that brat. He can't be my grandchild anyway. She's lying to you.'

Susanna stepped forward and grabbed Quinton's arm, keeping him from moving towards Mr Walton.

'I would never step foot on my property again if I were you,' Quinton said through clenched teeth.

'Truth be told,' the man said, 'she never cared for my son. He was just someone she used.'

'A woman like Susanna didn't have to use someone like him.' Quinton stepped closer. 'He sweet-talked her because she was innocent. She could have taken one look at any of the men at the soirées and they would have rushed to her. Should you ever talk to my wife or my son again without my presence, you will pay dearly for it.'

'You don't scare me.' His voice wavered at the end.

'I don't intend to scare you. I intend to tell you the truth.' Quinton's voice was a guttural growl now. The man jumped back.

'Don't forget,' Quinton said, 'because if I come here again, I'm not bringing my family to protect you. I'm a physician, remember. I know the most painful ways to make someone pay.' He paused. He smiled evilly. 'And I know a thousand and one poisons.' He held up his fist and inspected his fingernails. 'Have a good day, Walton.'

Quinton nodded to Susanna and she left, scooping Christopher along.

The carriage was silent except for the wheels and a horse neighing as it pulled away.

'I don't want him for a grandfather,' Christopher said, bouncing into the seat. 'I have a grandfather.' He counted on his fingers. 'I already have a grandfather, a grand-

mother, a Celeste, an Aunt Janette and Aunt Esme, and
Mr Marvin and Nettie. And Amesbury and Mother, and
that is so many.' He inspected Quinton. 'What poisons
do you know?'

'I would tell him to take a footbath. That causes toes
to shrivel awfully.' He paused. 'I'd make sure his toes
were really, really shrivelled.'

Christopher held out his little boot and waved it in
the air. ''Bury, I think you should send that mean man a
whole bunch of water and shrivel all his toes.'

'I might,' he said, and chuckled. 'I daresay it would
make him nervous.'

'This is all for you to forget, Christopher,' Susanna
said hastily. 'Amesbury likes a calm, quiet life around
him.'

Quinton crossed his arms. 'Oh, yes. Well ordered.'

'My soldiers are good,' Christopher said. 'They follow orders. And they don't jump on the bed.'

Susanna glanced at him.

'Well, one did. And he had to sit in the corner.'

'Are there any questions you have for your mother?'
Quinton asked Christopher.

'Can I have a bird?' Little eyes turned to her.

She shook her head ruefully.

'Will you help me catch one, Amesbury? I made a bird
trap. I saw a bird with a bug in its mouth, flying, and I
put bread in the trap so I could catch it.'

'It was probably taking care of little ones. If the food
was only for itself, it would have eaten it right after it
caught it.'

Christopher studied Amesbury with wide eyes. 'Drive
faster.' He turned and shouted out of the window behind him.

'What's wrong?' she asked Christopher.

'I have to get my bird trap and make sure nothing is in it. I might have caught a bird, and then it can't take care of its babies. I have to save things. Just like 'Bury.'

'Don't worry,' Quinton said. 'When we get home, if there is a bird in the trap, you can set it free.'

'I will. I'll play with the soldiers now.' Christopher turned to his mother. 'Did you bring them?'

She opened the ties of her reticule and pulled out two military men, and a small card caught in one of the soldier's legs fluttered out.

Quinton saw it, and his vision locked on Susanna's. He retrieved the worn calling card before she could touch it.

'I might like a pet mouse instead of a bird,' Christopher said, chattering away. 'Can I have a mouse?'

'We will see about getting you a pet.' She didn't move.

Amesbury studied the card. Susanna had used a pencil to trace over the letters of his name.

'The one from that day at your mother's when I proposed?' he asked her.

'Yes.' Her cheeks reddened.

He held the card, and with the other hand, reached into his pocket and took out a fresh one and gave it to her. He tucked the old one into his pocket, touched over the pocket where he'd placed it and smiled at her.

She placed the newer one inside her reticule, pulling the bag closed. 'Thank you.'

Then she reached out and hugged Christopher close to her, and he stilled.

'Amesbury, Mother is squeezing me. She needs medicine.' Christopher spoke over her arm.

Quinton watched. 'Kissing the tip of her nose is the best medicine for her.'

Susanna released her son. Christopher used the moment to escape and pecked a kiss on his mother's nose.

He giggled, and Susanna hugged him again, and then Christopher started talking, and her whole attention appeared to be on her son.

But she reached out to Quinton, and he held her hand.

Chapter Twenty-Four

When they arrived at the estate, Quinton studied his surroundings. They were simply another family returning from an outing.

Then he watched her disappear into the house, and he sensed how he would feel if she exited his life. The sinking, empty feeling that had slowly been leaving him returned. He followed her.

He knew by the brief halt of her steps the second she realised he'd not continued on with them.

She waited and peered down at him.

And her walk back down the stairway could only be called a slow whirl of determination.

When she stood one step above him, she put her hands on his shoulders. He reached out, not touching her waist but ready to catch her if she stumbled.

'I'm fond of you,' she said. 'We all are, because of you. Because it's impossible not to be. But even if it were possible not to be, I would still be fond of you. I don't like that other word either.'

Then she leaned and put a kiss on his nose and strolled back up the stairway.

All he cared about was Susanna. She'd traced the letters of his name.

He took the stairs two at a time.

At the top of the stairway, she entered Christopher's room, but he opened the door to her sitting room and went inside. He touched his pocket. The written invitation. His folded calling card that she'd saved.

A maid had everything straightened and it was merely a room, except in the corner where a desk sat. The maid hadn't touched that. It wasn't like any woman's room he'd ever seen.

He walked over and saw the slate, discoloured from chalk. Three books, all ones that had been read to Christopher, lay nearby. She had copied the words *mouse, cat and rat*, and written *Chris* and *Quinton*.

Several books were stacked on the floor, one on mathematics.

He had given the tutor leave to buy all the books his family wished to have and directed his man of affairs to settle the charges.

Something sticking out from under one of the children's books caught his eye. He recognised it. A cravat. His. One that he'd used as a bandage and left with Nettie. It had been cleaned and folded, but was terribly stained.

His gaze wandered to the doorway to her bedroom, knowing that if he stepped inside he'd likely smell the perfume she used. He'd dreamed of that scent.

The door opened and she walked in, cheeks flushed—sunshine in human form. She twirled around.

Eight hooks. She had eight hooks on the back of her gown.

'Christopher is telling Marvin and Celeste about how

'Bury protected us from the bad man and how his 'Bury can do anything.'

'I wish,' Quinton said, 'I wish.'

From his first awareness of women, he'd liked femininity, but he'd not had the finances nor the time to afford a wife.

Quinton had retreated into a world of studies. The world of medicine. He'd wanted to know all there was about medicine and how to treat people and how to make the world safe for everyone.

His past was always reappearing in his present, no matter how much he wanted to detach himself from it.

And when he wanted to tell Susanna how much he cared for her, he seemed he couldn't say it, because it was a word that belonged to the past. The word he'd heard so often when he was young—the meaningless one that had been used to try to control him.

He couldn't imagine Christopher growing up in the stews. He couldn't understand how his own mother hadn't had more funds for something better, but then she'd usually stayed somewhere other than her home. And when she was with them, she was usually too foxed to make sense.

Life had been better without her, and possibly safer for all of them. He realised he'd not noticed much difference in their life after she'd left. In truth, they'd muddled along as well as before. Sometimes better.

She'd left him to others to raise, and resented his presence. And felt nothing for him or Eldon—her children.

Christopher would never live that life. No matter what happened, he'd never have to sell bread on a street corner.

He studied Susanna and reached out and held her hand.

'I can't tell you. Aloud. The words won't come,' he said.

'It doesn't matter.'

He stopped, studied her, and asked the question he wanted answered. 'Do you want to be with the man from the stews, or is it the Earl's heir you see?'

'It is a combination of both. That is who I wed.'

'You wed me because of the life I could give you.'

'The life you could give my son and my parents. The butler. I was fine with the life I had. I sometimes missed the soirées and finery, but Christopher was my life. Even with all that my family had lost, I think they would all agree my son was worth it.'

She paused. 'I was afraid I would lose Celeste. The servants who stayed were either not being paid or being paid little of their true wages. And yet they remained. I had my son. I was truly happy, and only worried for my family.'

She brushed at his hair, more a touch than a correction.

She'd lived in society from birth, and he'd been born in the stews. He'd never understood her feeling lost, but knew she did.

Just like he did at that moment.

His brain told him that he could control his feelings, his needs and his desires. But his body laughed at him.

He just couldn't seem to control his fascination for her. He kept wanting to look at her.

It hadn't seemed to matter so much when he'd first met her. But then he'd heard she was widowed and had wanted to court her, but he'd been a physician and she'd been a member of society.

A woman named Susanna.

He had to think about the future. About wanting her. About stepping forward from his past.

Now he felt the same way he'd felt when Eldon was sick and he'd not known what to do.

He was overwhelmed by the family in front of him

and not sure where he was going to fit in with a wife and child and home that seemed to bounce out of his control and do as it wished.

He knew the direction he had to take.

He wished to be with Susanna. He wanted it more than he'd known possible. She created the world he wanted just in her smile. Her eyes.

No one had ever kissed his nose before. No one.

'I miss you when I am not with you,' he said gruffly.

'I know you will eventually show up here.' She smiled. 'You always go where you are needed. And this is where you are needed most in the whole world.'

He pulled a ladder-back chair in front of her and sat in it. 'I want you to know.' He summoned his strength to the forefront. 'I'm fond of you with all my heart.'

'I know you are,' she said, smiling. 'And you are my fondest husband.'

Six strands of hair were wisping down from her bun. Two arms. One slender neck. He'd not known counting could entertain him so. And a rather nice feminine form was hidden somewhere under there with all the entrancing parts.

He had married her with only a second's hesitation, but it had been the best decision of his life.

'I know where you will always be at the end of the day. Helping others. Or at home. Unless you are upset with me, and then you will be at your aunt's house or your brother's.' She whispered, 'Nettie and Cook make sure the carriage driver always has a treat, and I asked them to find out your habits from him.'

'I didn't realise that,' Quinton said.

'I have helped you become even closer to your family in this home,' she said. 'At least, that is how I look at it. But I hope you will take me next time you go out because I would like to meet your brother.'

He moved nearer, able to sniff the delicate scent of the soap that she used to wash her hair. He was fairly certain it was the same soap he used, only his smelled like…soap. Hers had a wafting, curling scent that sweetened the air. Or perhaps it was the perfume.

'I can't seem to stop trying to fix things. Or people,' he confessed.

'Why should you?'

He reached out and touched the puff of her sleeve, letting his hand rest on her shoulder. Such a tiny arm.

'You don't mind that I don't tell you those other words?' he asked.

'Oh, heavens no. That is nothing compared to fondness,' she said. 'I would choose fondness any day over the other words.' She darted forward and put a kiss on his lips. 'It is the best feeling in the world to be fond of you. And I know you are fond of me too.'

She grabbed the cuffs of his coat sleeves. 'You remembered me, from when we first met. And you wanted a home for us. All of us. So, that tells me all I need to know. You are a rock, Quinton Langford. You are golden. You are fire hardened.' She stepped away and twirled in a circle. 'You are my husband, and you are priceless.' She strolled over and touched the cravat he'd found, lifting it and holding it high. Then she held it out. 'It is the finest fabric, and what did you use it for? To bandage someone, and then you told Nettie to get rid of it because it would remind you of the man's suffering every time you saw it.'

She held it to her heart. 'It reminds me of my husband's kindness. Of him doing things that are difficult because he wants to help others.

She put it back on the table, straightening it so carefully. 'And it reminds me of your strength. Every time I see it.' She stood and gazed at it. 'I know how you read medical texts almost every day. I know how you are the best physician in London, and I don't think, "Poor London." I think, "Fortunate me. He is my husband."'

She blew out a breath that disturbed the wisp of hair at her temple. 'And why do you think you married me?'

'Well…' He lowered his chin, and his gaze remained on her. 'I wasn't wed. I remembered what a good mother you were to all those dolls. You even scolded one for getting jam on her dress.' He gave a long pause, eyes not blinking.

'So, the next thing I knew, I was at your house, and you were bounding down the stairs and I thought, "My house has more stairs than any I've ever seen. I bet she would make a good wife,." So, I proposed.'

'That's preposterous. You are jesting.' She studied him.

'Not entirely. But I also thought that marriage to you would be like having a bread oven in a house. Reliable. I hated that I had to depend on that oven so much, but when I saw my brother he explained to me that he saw it as warmth. Security. And I will never enjoy having bread on my plate, but I went to the kitchen and looked at Cook's oven, and the room smelled nice, and this time it reminded me of the happiness on Eldon's face. I like happiness on faces. Especially yours.'

He watched her, bringing the same temptations of touching her ever so close. But he still didn't reach out.

She leaned towards him, his mouth almost touching hers, and he breathed in her essence.

'I just don't like that you felt you had to rescue me,' she said sadly.

He took Susanna's hand.

'I believe I've helped a lot of people, and I've only proposed marriage once. That must mean something.'

He stood and lifted the top rung of the chair and put it in place.

The warmth of her body touched him. 'Susanna, the first time I saw you, you were the only woman I seriously considered having in my home. Before I had considered…well, if she is the last woman on earth, then I might marry her. I saw you again and decided marriage could be an option in my life—a journey I could tolerate… Might even like, and I do. Our journey.'

He didn't so much as kiss her but moved his lips across hers as he said *like*. Shivers of heat flared in his body.

She put her hand flat on his chest, but didn't leave her fingers still. 'But I want to hear it again, Quinton. I want to hear you say how much you care for me.'

'I am not comfortable with saying that.'

'I'm not talking about that one word.' Her nose appeared to have smelled something unpleasant, but then she smiled. 'The one you are comfortable with.'

He smiled. 'Fond?'

'Yes.'

'I am so very fond of you Susanna. So very, very fond.' He pulled her close, holding her, feeling his heart pounding with emotion. 'I am fond of you. More than I will ever feel for anyone else. No matter what happens. No matter what life brings. You're stuck with me,' he said, 'and I'm so pleased I saw you and we rediscovered each other.'

'Well, that is so good to hear, and… You know, I'm not sure if I like this room, though. There is a lovely unused area right next to yours. Would you be upset if I moved into it?'

'It adjoins my sitting room.'

'I know.'

'If that's what you wish.'

'Yes. I want a true marriage. With all the extras. A husband. I've become so fond of you.'

'I'm truly fond of you as well.'

He sat and reached out and pulled her close and kissed her nose.

The past lingered in his memory. He'd not left it behind, and he never would. But it had become a part of him, and it helped him have empathy for all his patients.

Medicine was lodged into him just as strongly as his wife and son were. A man must do as he should.

Epilogue

He wore the new waistcoat, and she'd noticed he'd not touched the pocket once.

Quinton took the infant from her mother and held the bundle close to Christopher. Marian had her fist in her mouth.

'I really wanted her to be bigger,' Christopher said, peering at Marian. 'About my size. And not so sleepy. She won't laugh when I pull faces at her. All she wants to do is sleep.' He sighed. 'How long until she can play soldiers?'

'Let's just say a few months. We need to take her to the sitting room to introduce her to your Aunt Esme and Aunt Janette.'

Christopher stared at the baby. 'They will be so disappointed that I didn't get a baby brother.'

'They will adjust.'

Christopher left, running. 'When she wakes up, I will tell Marian we can only have pet birds that stay in trees, and I will show her not to jump on the bed,' he called behind him. Then his steps slowed and he called out again. 'And not to run in the house.' He turned back. 'And not to shout,' he called out, before marching out the door.

'I'm not shouting, I'm talking loud.' They heard from beyond the wood.

Quinton helped Susanna up with his free hand.

Susanna stood beside Quinton and gently lifted Marian into her arms. 'You forget too easily Quinton Langford. We must share.'

'Susanna, you may call me a knight, but you are the sunshine in our lives.'

'I know a good thing when I see it. Sometimes it just takes me a while to open my eyes.'

'Just in case I've not mentioned it this morning, I am fond of you, my dear, but in truth, my feelings for you run deeper than words can ever touch.'

He put an arm around Susanna, hugging her, patting her, and then letting his fingers brush the bundle she held, amazed that his heart could contain all the joy he felt.

He laughed, and again patted her. 'When she is old enough, we will let our daughter spell her name however she wishes—Marian or Marianne, or the version Celeste prefers with the French emphasis, or the two words that Mr Marvin thinks will be best. She can decide later. I will take part in no more discussions on that. There are enough people in this house concerned with spelling.'

She raised her glance to the ceiling, then let it linger. Quinton kissed the tip of her nose.

'Kissing my nose does not work for everything.'

'You're right. I prefer kissing you all over...'

He kissed her nose again and held her close. 'It works for most things, though, when I am close to you.'

And then he looked around him one more time. He had a wife, a son and a daughter, a brother and an aunt, and his in-laws were like parents to him, but not like any parents he'd ever known.

He'd received more than he could have ever dreamed of. He had the family he would have wished for, had he known it existed.

He would never want to live through the past again, but he'd survived it and thrived despite it. Because if he'd not known of the harshness of life, he would never have appreciated what he had around him now.

'I'm so grateful that you chose to be a physician and save lives. I have made some little garments to give to the children at Auntie's.' She studied him. 'I would hope to visit your aunt again soon.' She paused. 'Those children could use things I make more than anyone I know. I am so pleased you still watch over people.'

Quinton squinted, noticing the garments she'd knitted during her confinement. 'I cannot take credit for it. I didn't choose to be a physician. It chose me. I once released a butterfly stuck in a spider's web, and it flew away without a word—and I decided that the sight of the wings flying away was all I needed, that I am to treat people for the reward of seeing them recover.'

He picked up the garment she held and felt the warmth of the wool. It infused itself into him, and at that moment, he felt the home around him. He glanced at the walls and knew he belonged within them, and that Susanna belonged in his life in a way he'd not believed possible.

The world fell away and he understood completely why he'd needed to be a physician. It wasn't only to heal others; it was to heal himself. He had married Susanna because he'd seen the life her parents had—the life behind the walls of her house—and he'd understood, somewhere deep inside himself that didn't speak but only felt, that having Susanna in his life was the only opportunity he had to grasp that happiness.

It was not about the deal they'd made. It was about the life of gentleness, of bedtime stories that ended on sunshiny moments with children nestled into their covers—moments that ended with mothers tucking them into a cosy nest and smiling over them in a darkness that only reached beyond their eyelids and never into their hearts.

'You give me sunshine,' he said. 'Beyond words. And I mean that.'

Her lips turned up and she grasped his fingertips. 'You are being too complimentary,' she said.

'If you say so.' But he wasn't. He could feel the sunbeams from her heart. 'Everything I went through was worth it to have a home with you at my side.'

He lifted her hand and kissed the sad ring on her finger, and their eyes met. 'It is our first anniversary, and our daughter is a fortnight old today.'

He reached into his waistcoat pocket and pulled out a small, thin gold band. He kissed it, took her hand and tried to put it on her little finger. It didn't fit.

'That's fine,' she said. 'I can keep it anyway.'

'No.' He returned it to his pocket and pulled out another one. He kissed it, and it slipped onto her smallest finger. A perfect fit.

'You carry around various gold rings?' she asked.

'I picked up a few today so I'd get one that fit. I just felt like you needed something a little more precious.'

He pulled out another, but she slipped her hand from his when he tried to put it on her ring finger.

'Absolutely not. This is my wedding ring, and no other could take its place.'

'If you ever change your mind,' he said, 'let me know. I'll be here with another.'

'I know you will always be here, Quinton.'

The deep fondness he felt for his wife infused him with weakness for her and power for the world. He'd never known that fondness could change his life so.

But it did. And it went so much deeper than that other word could ever touch.

* * * * *

If you enjoyed this story, make sure to pick up Liz Tyner's other great reads!

It's Marriage or Ruin
Compromised into Marriage
The Governess's Guide to Marriage
A Cinderella for the Viscount
Tempting a Reformed Rake
A Marquess Too Rakish to Wed

✦ HARLEQUIN
HISTORICAL

Your romantic escape to the past.

Be seduced by the grandeur, drama and sumptuous detail of romances set in long-ago eras!

Six new books available every month!

Get 4 FREE REWARDS!

We'll send you 2 FREE Books plus 2 FREE Mystery Gifts.

FREE Value Over **$20**

Both the **Harlequin® Desire** and **Harlequin Presents®** series feature compelling novels filled with passion, sensuality and intriguing scandals.

Get 4 FREE REWARDS!

We'll send you 2 FREE Books <u>plus</u> 2 FREE Mystery Gifts.

FREE
Value Over
$20

Both the **Romance** and **Suspense** collections feature compelling novels
written by many of today's bestselling authors.

YES! Please send me 2 FREE novels from the Essential Romance or
Essential Suspense Collection and my 2 FREE gifts (gifts are worth about
$10 retail). After receiving them, if I don't wish to receive any more books,
I can return the shipping statement marked "cancel." If I don't cancel, I will
receive 4 brand-new novels every month and be billed just $7.49 each in
the U.S. or $7.74 each in Canada. That's a savings of at least 17% off the
cover price. It's quite a bargain! Shipping and handling is just 50¢ per book
in the U.S. and $1.25 per book in Canada.* I understand that accepting
the 2 free books and gifts places me under no obligation to buy anything. I
can always return a shipment and cancel at any time by calling the number
below. The free books and gifts are mine to keep no matter what I decide.

Choose one: ☐ **Essential Romance**   ☐ **Essential Suspense**
                     (194/394 MDN GRHV)   (191/391 MDN GRHV)

Name (please print)

Address   Apt. #

City   State/Province   Zip/Postal Code

Email: Please check this box ☐ if you would like to receive newsletters and promotional emails from Harlequin Enterprises ULC and its affiliates. You can unsubscribe anytime.

Mail to the **Harlequin Reader Service:**
IN U.S.A.: P.O. Box 1341, Buffalo, NY 14240-8531
IN CANADA: P.O. Box 603, Fort Erie, Ontario L2A 5X3

Want to try 2 free books from another series! Call 1-800-873-8635 or visit www.ReaderService.com.

STRS22R3

HARLEQUIN
PLUS

Try the best multimedia subscription service for romance readers like you!

Read, Watch and Play.

Experience the easiest way to get the romance content you crave.

Start your **FREE TRIAL** at
<u>www.harlequinplus.com/freetrial</u>.